# The Wager

## A Romantic Comedy As Christian Allegory

Mike Brister

ISBN-10: 1541380398
ISBN-13: 978-1541380394

# Contents

# Acknowledgments

Special thanks to Elizabeth, Stacie, Rosemary, and the people of Thoman, Haiti.

---

But God Himself, alive, pulling at the other end of the cord, perhaps approaching at an infinite speed, the hunter, king, husband—that is quite another matter. . . . Supposing we really found Him? We never meant it to come to that! Worse still, supposing He had found us?
**C. S. Lewis, *Miracles***


Jesus just left Chicago and he's bound for New Orleans.
Well now,
Jesus just left Chicago and he's bound for New Orleans.
Yeah, yeah.
Workin' from one end to the other and all points in between.
**ZZ Top, "Jesus Just Left Chicago"**

.

# Chapter One

## Rock Bottom

Three large men, wearing well-worn overalls, faded baseball caps, and muddy work boots, stood in a circle of light among bar stools, listening to a fourth man.

Voice at the bar: "I've told you boys not to come in here without a shirt on. Those overall bibs don't count. I know at least one of y'all can read. You know what the sign says. . . . I'm tellin' y'all he's back there. I know there're three of y'all, but that ain't gonna stop him. I don't want any trouble in my bar."

At that moment, a barstool came out of the darkness and crashed into one of the large men, sending both man and stool to the floor.

Voice in the darkness: "Ladies, there's just two of you now."

Man in overalls: "Alea iacta est."

———————

Matthew Ezra Shepherd sat on a wooden chair in the front room of the old farmhouse. He was leaning forward and looking at the floor with his forearms resting on his knees. His hands with bloody knuckles were open and relaxed. Blood had run from his split lip and the open wound on his forehead, leaving dried blood on the side of his face and on the heart pine floor between his feet. The only source of light in the house was a shadeless lamp, sitting on the floor. The chair and the lamp were the only furniture in the room.

Outside, two vehicles turned onto the circular gravel driveway, their headlights adding to the light of the lamp. One vehicle was a county patrol car and the other a pick-up truck.

Billy Pruitt, the county sheriff and Matt's uncle, walked into the house without knocking and over to Matt without saying a word. Matt did not move.

Billy: "Are you drunk?"

Matt: "No, sir—not yet."

Billy: "Then you can understand what I'm fixin' to tell you?"

Matt: "Yes, sir."

Billy: "Matt, this has got to stop. I couldn't bear it if I had to arrest you for killin' someone. The Sullivan brothers will survive, just barely. No one'll shed a tear over you beatin' the tar out of 'em, but this has got to stop. When they come to, I'm goin' to tell 'em if they press charges, I'll arrest all three of 'em. . . . If one of those ol' boys had died, it would be a game changer. There's not much I could've done for you. You'd be in Parchman Farm before the cotton was knee high."

"Son, this community needs you. They need to know if they send their children off to war and those children come home, those children can have a life."

Matt remained silent and motionless with his head down.

Billy: "What about the families of the ones that didn't come home? You think they don't live out the hopes and dreams they had for their children through you? Matt, the United States Marine Corps may not need you anymore, but we do."

Billy paused and straightened to his full height, looking down at Matt.

Billy: "Son, this is how it will be. First, you'll make it right with Lester. You're gonna get your uncle's old tools and repair Lester's bar. Next, you'll quit drinkin'. I'll put the word out if anyone sells, gives, or conveys alcohol to Matt Shepherd in this county, I'll put 'em in jail. I may not can keep 'em, but they'll at least spend the night. Judge Thompson will back me up on this."

"Next, you are gonna get a dog, some chickens, and maybe even some goats. Don't get any cows, Matt—not if you really wanna stop drinkin'."

"Outside in the truck are Frank Butler and Pastor Mark. You know Frank was a medic in Vietnam. He has an idea of what you are goin' through. God didn't bring you this far just to have you kill someone in a bar fight. They're gonna come in here now. First, Frank is gonna look at that wound on your forehead. Then all of us will get down on our knees and pray for you."

"Tell me now, son—yes or no? Before you answer, know this: if you say no, I'll take you to jail tonight and put you under a suicide watch. Now, will you do what I say?"

Matt: "Yes, sir."

# Chapter Two

# Sarah

A tall, attractive woman held a cell phone to her ear as she stood on the balcony of a home overlooking a beach.

Woman: "I'm sorry, Collin, but this just isn't going to work. We discussed this last night. Nothing has changed. We both need to move on. I'm sorry. . . . No, there is not someone else. We went over this last night. Look, I have someone coming over. . . . It's Lucy. Lucy is coming over here. . . . Let's part as friends."

The woman lowered the phone.

Woman: "Well, cowboy, don't let the screen door hit you on the way out."

---

Sarah Morgan Leigh DuMont, the oldest child of James and Elizabeth DuMont, was sitting alone on a couch in her Malibu Beach home, watching the sunset through floor-to-ceiling windows on the same evening Matt was hearing from his uncle. She was in her late twenties, five feet nine inches tall, with sandy blonde hair. The only sources of light were from the setting sun and one lamp in a far corner of the room. Lucy O'Malley, who was about the same age as Sarah with black hair and a Boston accent, appeared in the doorway.

Sarah: "Hello, Lucy. Just in time for the sunset. Come and sit with me. Is that a bottle of wine you have there?"

Lucy: "Yes, but not just any wine. I finally found a bottle of the cheap wine we drank together in New Haven."

Sarah: "The wine we drank behind the coffee shop?"

Lucy: "Yes."

Sarah: "I told Lorraine to make her famous turkey sandwiches when you arrived. How does that sound?"

Lucy: "Let the feast begin. Lorraine let me in. She's bringing some glasses and a bottle opener."

Sarah: "Sounds like we're set. You did come prepared to spend the night?"

Lucy: "Why?"

Sarah: "If, in a few hours, you are able to drive home, tonight will not have been a success. You know, Lorraine insists she can't find that wine out here. If you ask me, I don't think she even tries. Where did you find it?"

Lucy: "Now, Sarah, I don't want to get her in trouble. I'll give her the address. I have no intentions of getting between you and Lorraine, especially over a cheap bottle of wine. You know, I'm your best friend, but sometimes you can be a little difficult."

Sarah: "I can be very difficult. Tell me about the store."

Lucy: "We have the financials for the second quarter and things look good. The pottery from British Columbia and the fair labor rugs from India are doing well. They were excellent finds by you. Oh, and Ralph has been helping me with the financial statements."

Sarah: "Speaking of Ralph, how is the romance of the good Catholic girl and the observant Jew going?"

Lucy: "Well, Ralph is meeting with a Messianic rabbi and may join a Messianic congregation. He keeps his Jewish customs and adds Jesus. I keep Jesus and add some Jewish customs."

Sarah smiled.

Sarah: "I guess love conquers all, even religion."

Lucy: "What about you? How are you and Craig doing?"

Sarah: "You are a little behind. Craig is old news. The latest was Collin. I ended it with him last night and had to confirm it again this afternoon. I hate it when men are so obtuse. What is so difficult to understand about adios or see you around?"

Lucy: "Are you working your way through the C's?"

Sarah: "Just practicing catch and release. But I do think it may be time to move on to the D's."

Lucy: "Not sure that's how you find love."

Sarah: "I'm not looking for love. I did that once, and we know how that turned out. I thrive on the competition. Besides, since my divorce, I've developed some rules. As you know, my ex cheated on me. If we had divorced for other reasons, fine. But I'm not going through that again. He told me he loved me at the same time he was having an affair with another woman, cheating on me, Sarah DuMont—what an idiot."

Lucy: "Oh, Sarah, you've done this before. Will these rules replace the old ones or just be an add on?"

Sarah: "Lucy, this is how it will be. The first rule is no cowboy."

Lucy: "What do you mean by cowboy?"

Sarah: "You know exactly what I mean by cowboy—a man like my ex. Outwardly, they are these macho guys, but once you scratch the surface, they're just little boys. I don't intend to take on the job their mothers should have finished—so no more cowboy."

Lucy: "Are there more rules?"

Sarah: "As a matter of fact, yes, two more. They need to be successful on their own, without me or my money. My ex was a hot property a few years ago and is now doing local commercials in Phoenix. I had Sam see if he could find him something. I'm not doing any more career counseling. I've learned if a man is needy, that's a flashing red light."

Lucy: "Let me guess the third, no religion."

Sarah: "That's not really fair. I prefer to say he needs to be enlightened and sophisticated. He needs to know what wine to order, how to behave at a production party, and to not frown at me when I say I don't believe in God."

Lucy: "Each to his own, but I'll take a good cowboy any day. In fact, I'm going to make a prediction. I'm going to predict that one day you are head over heels in love with a grade A, certified cowboy."

Sarah: "Don't be silly. That will never happen. By the way, my calendar has cleared, so I'm spending the last week this month with my family in Connecticut. Both my brothers will be there. I know everyone would love to see you."

Lucy: "I appreciate the invitation, but I don't want to leave the store or Ralph. Tell your mother hello for me. I love that woman."

Lorraine, the live-in housekeeper in her late fifties, entered the room carrying a tray of sandwiches with two wine glasses.

Sarah: "Thanks, Lorraine. Just put the tray on the coffee table."

Lucy: "Sarah is giving me her current rules concerning men."

Lorraine: "Sarah, try one of the sandwiches and let me know if it is okay."

Sarah took a full bite of the turkey sandwich.

Lorraine: "Now that her mouth is full of sandwich, Lucy, if she gives you investment advice, take it. Anything else, I'd ignore it. And, Sarah, I have no intentions of running all over town to find you some cheap bottle of wine. That is beneath you and certainly beneath me. I'm going to my room now."

Sarah and Lucy watched Lorraine walk away.

Lucy: "You do know, you hired a housekeeper who is just like your mother?"

Sarah: "Don't be silly. I've never seen my mother make a sandwich."

Lorraine turned, standing in the doorway.

Lorraine: "Lucy, may I talk with you a minute? . . . Over here."

Lucy rose and walked to the door.

Sarah: "What? . . . Are the two of you talking about me?"

Lorraine: "Not everything is about you, Sarah."

Sarah: "What an odd thing to say."

Lorraine spoke to Lucy in just above a whisper.

Lorraine: "I can tell she's in one of her moods. It's the first anniversary of her divorce. No matter what happens tonight, don't let her go out. I don't want to see some rubbish in the tabloids or on the Internet tomorrow about her. She trusts you, Lucy."

Lucy: "I'll make sure she stays in tonight."

Lorraine: "I don't know why she can't find herself a good rabbi like you did. She has more money than a third-world dictator and is beautiful, smart, talented. Look at her. She is guzzling cheap wine and stuffing her face with a turkey sandwich. If you need help, I do have some pepper spray."

Lucy: "Thanks, Lorraine, we may need the spray."

Sarah spoke from across the room.

Sarah: "Lucy, you wanna go out tonight? I bet I can find a Darrell. What do you wanna bet? Or maybe a David, I've always liked the name David."

Lucy: "She already sounds a little tipsy."

Lorraine: "That's not the wine; it's the mood. I'll go get the pepper spray."

# Chapter Three

# The Farm

In the 1700s, Scots-Irish came to America in droves. These were people who had been denied land for generations. In 1320, Pope John XXII decreed that Scotland was an independent country; however, he never specified exactly where on the ground that independence began. The Scots, living on the disputed border with England, would build barns and farm the land only to see the English tear down the barns and claim the land. The Scots would drive the English off, and the process would repeat itself.

The Sots were Protestant, of the Presbyterian variety, and could talk to God directly while standing up. In the early 1600s, in a scheme of James I, they were offered the opportunity to farm someone else's land in Ulster, Ireland. The goal was to have the Protestant Scots breed the Catholic Irish off the island.

Then they came to America in search of land. The danger the migration of the Scots-Irish posed to England was not lost on everyone. In the British Parliament, the sentiment was expressed if we can't control them while they live among us, how can we control them when they live on the other side of the ocean?

They came to America with a Bible in one hand and a rifle in the other, possessing a burning hatred for the English and a desire to own their own land. They would kill Englishmen at the Battle of King's Mountain during the American Revolutionary War, forcing General Cornwallis to retreat from North Carolina. No country in the world could offer them so much: land and the chance to kill Englishmen.

Their descendants would make up the bulk of the soldiers making Pickett's Charge at Gettysburg, in a fit of rage against the proxy English, Yankees. Their children's children would prefer service in the U.S. Marines because the Marines had not fought in the blue of the 1860s.

On arrival in America, they were told to move on—you can't stay here. In Pennsylvania, they would be given land between the peaceful Quakers and the Indians so they could do the fighting and the Quakers could continue their peaceful ways.

They would move into the Appalachian Mountains and across the wilderness South, which malaria, yellow fever, and Indians called home.

The Scots-Irish and the Indians could not have viewed land more differently. To the American Indian, land was not owned, but lived on. To the Scots-Irish, land had better be owned, lived on, and worked. The Indians reminded the Scots-Irish of the absentee landowners in Ireland, who claimed they owned the land but did not work the land.

Being miles away from the Presbyterian Church of Scotland, they soon converted to other Protestant denominations, such as Baptist and Methodist. They brought with them their own brand of music and art of storytelling. Their view of life was, is, and, perhaps, may ever be markedly different from those who migrated from other countries.

---

The farm was in a rural corner of Southwest Mississippi, not far from the Louisiana line near the town of Macon. The original homestead dated back to the early 1800s, becoming the possession of a Shepherd in the 1850s. A descendant of the original Shepherd would live on the land to the present day.

The age of the farm was obvious to any knowledgeable observer. The main buildings were not oriented to the current county road, harkening back to a time when the county had nothing to do with access to the farm.

A gravel drive connected to the county road. On the left of the drive was a stand of hardwood trees and on the right a pasture. Further down the drive, the main structures of the farm came into view on the left.

The first visible structure was the barn. Although it was the furthest from the blacktop, it was massive and the first to be seen. The size of the barn was out of proportion to the farming enterprise. No one knew why such a structure came to exist on this family farm.

The roof was a waving sea of rusting galvanized tin. The sides were weathered pine board with no protection against the elements. Inside were a vaulted ceiling and a partial second story for storage. The whole thing defied logic, but there it sat.

The barn was built on the highest elevation on the farm. At times, when the mist hung close to the ground in early morning, the structure appeared to float in the clouds. Continuing down the drive, the last building to be seen was a house, making it actually the closest to the county road since the woods on the left blocked the view until the last. In front of the house, the drive circled an ancient oak tree.

This was not the first house built on the sight. The current structure, of mostly old growth Cypress, included lumber dating back to the time before a Shepherd owned the property. As originally constructed, the house was one story with four rooms; two fireplaces; a large hall down the middle; two large porches, front and back; heart pine floors; and a gable roof once covered with Cypress shingles and now covered with galvanized tin.

The house was built to be cool, not warm. The ceilings were twelve feet tall; the central hall ran front-to-back to allow for a breeze; the window seals were no higher than a bed to catch a breeze when sleeping; and the kitchen was not in the house.

In time, part of the back porch was enclosed for a bathroom on one side and a kitchen on the other, while retaining the central hall.

Between the house and the woods was a row of five ancient eastern red cedar trees, which were planted following a yellow fever outbreak in New Orleans in 1853. At the time, cedar trees were thought to cleanse the air and were now a heritage of that disease.

In the 1960s, it was decided that the old farmhouse was not a proper house, and a new house was built along the path to the barn. The new house was a three bedroom, two bath home that paid no homage whatsoever to its surroundings. There was no porch, no porch swing, no great hall, no tall ceilings, no heart pine floors, and no tin roof. The house could have been built in any blue-collar neighborhood in the United States.

Farming is a business, and the old farmhouse, under other circumstances, would have been used to store hay or equipment. The size of the old barn made that unnecessary. The family moved out of the farmhouse but maintained the exterior so that the old house was able to stand quietly, waiting for someone's appearance.

# Chapter Four

# The Wager

New Orleans is the most unique city in America. Almost half of Greater New Orleans is below sea level; a condition monitored continuously by the Mississippi River, Lake Pontchartrain, and the Gulf of Mexico. The city is the home to a Southern Baptist theological seminary, a Catholic theological seminary, and countless voodoo priestesses. Residents are buried above the ground with funeral processions that often become joyous marches of jazz and dancing. Restaurants, in otherwise condemned buildings, serve soups of puréed sweet potatoes, peaches, Andouille sausage, and bourbon. On one street, sex has been pedaled for longer than anyone can remember. The next street over, fine antiques and art are pedaled.

Social status is often determined by the connection to the biggest event on the social calendar, Mardi Gras; the effects of which can be seen for months after as beads, thrown from parade floats following shouts of "throw me somethin' mista," hang in the limbs of trees and on power lines. Parades and associated balls for the Carnival season are the responsibility of organizations known as krewes. Membership in the right krewe has its privileges.

Chartres Fontenot owned a store on Magazine Street, which runs parallel to St. Charles Avenue on the side closer to the river. The store specialized in items for the homes in the Uptown and Garden District neighborhoods along St. Charles Avenue.

She was a life-long resident of New Orleans and had survived numerous hurricanes, Mardi Gras parades, and the death of her husband. He did not leave her a pauper, but the store was an important source of income.

She moved effortlessly in New Orleans society, which she knew to be closed and self-contained. Her late husband often said if the rest of America disappeared, the Times-Picayune, the local paper, would not report it for six months, and then it would not be on the front page.

Almost two yeas after his Uncle's intervention, Matt Shepherd came to the store. At first, she assumed he was one of the workmen, helping with some of the store remolding. She knew by his accent that he was not from New Orleans. He introduced himself as Matt Shepherd, part farmer and part carpenter.

He explained that he made furniture from reclaimed lumber and asked if she would be interested in purchasing any pieces for sale in her store. Her immediate response was no. Her store had a reputation for selling high-end items, and she was not interested in local crafts. She was touched by the polite way he thanked her and turned to leave. There was a story here, one worth knowing.

She took two rocking chairs, a kitchen table, and a dresser, all on consignment, and would pay Matt when the items sold. They sold immediately. Soon she was taking everything he made.

The length of time between deliveries varied, depending on what he was making and the demands of the farm. He would call her and let her know when he was ready to bring more furniture.

While Mrs. Fontenot had a healthy curiosity about Matt, he was short on answers. She had never met anyone that could be so polite and so reticent at the same time. He delivered the furniture in a pick-up truck with a Mississippi license plate and a Marine decal in the back window. He always brought a dog with him, Doodle, and someone to help unload, usually Odell. And he was not married. A condition she found intolerable.

A friend of hers noticed Matt making a delivery and asked Mrs. Fontenot about him. She promised to let the friend know when he would be back. Shortly, on the days Matt was to deliver furniture, foot traffic in the store increased. In time, baked goods began to appear. A business opportunity had presented itself. Having Matt deliver before the store opened would restrict access. Ladies would have to go through her since she had the key.

The whole affair was organized around lists. There were twenty names on "The List." They were broken down into four groups of five. You were assigned to a group, and each group took a turn meeting Matt. There was a "Waiting List" of women to get on "The List."

Mrs. Fontenot benefited because the women on the "Waiting List" would try to curry favor with her by shopping in the store or buying her lunch at Delmonico. Matt benefited from the sale of his furniture and the offerings of food.

Early on, she realized this was not about Matt. He had become a proxy for a Mardi Gras krewe—the Krewe of Matt, and these women were competing for Queen of Carnival. She explained this to him, and he seemed pleased with the arrangement. He would continue to politely decline the advances while selling his furniture and taking home food. Clearly, there was a story here.

The list of items transported back to Macon included chocolate chip cookies with pecans, banana pudding, cheesecake with praline sauce, Mississippi mud cake, pecan pie with a chocolate bourbon sauce filling, bread pudding with a bourbon sauce topping, pecan peach cobbler, key lime pie, lemon icebox pie, chocolate pie, and chocolate brownies with pecans, just to name a few. There were also non-dessert items: gumbo, homemade pimento cheese, shrimp and grits of every variety, red beans and rice with Andouille sausage, shrimp and crawfish étouffée, fried chicken, fried catfish, glazed ham, turtle soup, and jambalaya. Some dishes even included alligator.

The business arrangement depended on restricted access and Matt remaining mysterious and aloof. Since she had a long association with a Mardi Gras krewe, she anticipated that some of the ladies might follow him home after a delivery. She informed Matt of her concerns, and he promised to take care of it.

Not long after, Matt reported that Odell spotted two ladies tailing the truck. Matt called his Uncle, who pulled the ladies over at the Macon exit just long enough for the truck, with Matt, Odell, and Doodle aboard, to top a hill out of sight. Uncle Billy received a dozen chocolate chip cookies with pecans for his services.

She also told Matt not to call her using his cell phone. They agreed to use Odell's gas station as the point of contact. Women had obtained that number, but all they could get out of Odell was Matt is not here, and that took some effort.

---

Sarah was in New Orleans filming a pay-for-view television series to be shot totally on location, so she would be there for several months. She and her assistant were making the rounds of a few of the shops on Magazine Street during an afternoon reprieve from filming. With her shop in LA in mind, Sarah was enjoying the diversion. To avoid recognition, she wore running shoes, yoga pants, an athletic top, a baseball cap, and sunglasses with big black rims, stuffing her blonde hair under the cap.

They entered a store and someone approached. Sarah knew immediately that the person recognized her. Sarah had developed a sixth sense for this sort of thing.

Mrs. Fontenot: "Can I help you with anything today? My name is Chartres Fontenot, and this is my store."

Sarah: "These pieces of furniture—"

Mrs. Fontenot: "Yes, those are made locally. Those are the only two in the store right now; they are both sold. LSU's spring game is this weekend, so she is picking them up next week."

Sarah: "You said made locally. Would it be possible for me to meet who made these?"

Mrs. Fontenot: "Well, he is bringing some more in the morning, so if you come back later in the day, you should be able to see more furniture."

Sarah: "To be honest, I'd like to see if he would be willing to make a few items for my store in LA. Could I meet with him when he comes?"

Sarah assumed that this would be a simple matter of talking to a local craftsman about goods for her store, which was something she had done with considerable success in exotic places all over the world.

Mrs. Fontenot: "I'm afraid I can't do that. There will be five women here in the morning to meet Matt at six a.m. sharp, and fifteen more waiting their turn to do the same. I don't have an exclusive contract with him. He calls me from a gas station when he is ready to make a delivery."

Sarah: "Thank you. I'll just look around a little more."

Sarah turned and began walking away.

Mrs. Fontenot: "And besides, you wouldn't be able to get that ol' boy to meet with you anyway."

She stopped, turned, and faced Mrs. Fontenot.

Sarah: "Excuse me?"

Mrs. Fontenot: "I said, I don't think you can get this ol' boy to meet with you."

Sarah: "You don't think I can get this man to meet with me?"

Mrs. Fontenot: "That's what I said. I don't think you can get this man to meet with you."

Sarah: "Meet with me; he won't meet with me?"

Mrs. Fontenot: "That's right; he won't meet with you."

Sarah: "Is he married? Is he gay?"

Mrs. Fontenot: "He's not married, and I don't think he's gay."

Sarah: "And you don't think I can get him to meet with me."

Mrs. Fontenot: "No, I don't"

Sarah: "How old is he?"

Mrs. Fontenot: "About your age."

Sarah: "So you don't think I can get a heterosexual, unmarried man, approximately my age, to meet with me? A date, if you will?"

Mrs. Fontenot: "Not this one, Ms. DuMont, you are very fetching. But the young women of New Orleans are not crawfish bait. They know how to prepare the gumbo, if you know what I mean. If they can't scale that wall, I doubt if you can."

Sarah: "Excuse me, but I'm not sure what . . . *crawfish bait* and *gumbo* have to do with this."

Mrs. Fontenot: "Well then, how about a friendly little wager? You meet with Matt in the morning. If he agrees to a date, then I'll let you have his delivery tomorrow, no charge, and I'll pay to ship it to your store. If he declines your offer, then you buy the most expensive item in this store, that hideous Louis XVI mirror my sister-in-law acquired."

Sarah: "What can you tell me about him?"

Assistant: "Are you sure you want to do this?"

Sarah: "Yes."

Mrs. Fontenot: "His name is Matt Shepherd. He'll be here at six a.m. sharp. By the license plate, we know he is from Mississippi, and by a sticker on the back window, he is a former Marine. He'll bring someone with him to help him unload. The one that usually comes is named Odell. Matt will be wearing a baseball cap for some minor league baseball team. It took us a while to figure that one out. Who knew the Lookouts was a minor league team in Chattanooga? Doodle, his dog, will be with him. You don't see one without the other. That dog is beautiful. I know women that would give their firstborn to have the same hair color as that dog. And importantly, there will be five other women here, all loaded for bear, with some of the finest culinary delights outside of Commander's Palace."

Sarah: "Mrs. Fontenot, I accept your wager."

Mrs. Fontenot: "Just so we are clear, Matt must agree and actually meet with you at the arranged time and place. As they say, we are only counting the butts that are actually in the seats. There won't be any of this creative Hollywood accounting that I hear so much about."

Sarah: "Understood. I'll see you in the morning at six a.m. sharp.

And here is the shipping address for my store. You will need this."

Sarah handed Mrs. Fontenot a card. They shook hands, sealing the arrangement. Once in the car, Sarah gave her assistant instructions.

Sarah: "If New Orleans has a minor league baseball team, get me a hat. If not, then use the closest team to New Orleans. Also, I need a charm bracelet with five or six lockets that can be opened. Have catering fill each locket with cooked bacon. I'll need these by five-thirty in the morning."

Assistant: "Those other women will have food to give him."

Sarah: "I don't need a casserole to bag this cowboy, just some dog food. This woman has no idea who she is dealing with."

The next morning, Willie Roberts drove Sarah to Mrs. Fontenot's store in a luxury German car. She was sitting on the backseat, opposite the driver. A truck crossed Magazine Street just ahead of them. In the back of the truck was furniture and in the cab were two men with a dog. The dog had its head out the passenger window, and the second man sat in the middle.

Well, that must be him. A truckload of cowboy, this shouldn't be a problem or take very long.

Willie: "Ms. DuMont, I'll let you out and find a place to park. Here is a card with my cell phone number. Call that number just before you leave. I may not be able to park near the store. You just call that number, and I'll be right on."

Sarah: "What is your name?"

Willie: "Willie Roberts, ma'am."

Sarah: "I will be in here only a few minutes. I'm due at make-up on location by seven. You have the address?"

Willie: "Yes, ma'am."

Sarah: "If you do anything to make me late for make-up, I'll see to it, Mr. Willie Roberts, that you are fired. Do we understand one another?"

Willie: "Yes, ma'am. You just call the number on the card, and I'll be here to get you."

Sarah exited the car in front of the store wearing a Zephyrs' baseball cap and a charm bracelet loaded with bacon. Mrs. Fontenot was operating the front door.

Mrs. Fontenot: "Good morning, Sarah. Right on time. Matt's truck just pulled up in the back, and he should be inside any minute now. Come—stand with me and wait for him. You will have first crack before the other ladies get their chance. . . . I see you are trying it without food. This should be interesting. The Zephyrs, you don't miss a trick, do you, Ms. DuMont?"

Sarah and Mrs. Fontenot walked to the center of the store. Along the way, they passed a very large, very ugly Louis XVI Chateau mirror. Along a far wall were five belles of New Orleans. All were well-appointed and standing near covered dishes arrayed on a table.

Sarah loved the thrill of competition. This was an opportunity to beat an opponent on their home field. Perhaps she could make them cry like her younger brothers often did when she taunted them after a defeat.

Matt entered, found Mrs. Fontenot, and made the walk over. He was wearing a baseball cap with a capital letter M on the front. Mrs. Fontenot leaned over and whispered in Sarah's ear.

Mrs. Fontenot: "That's the Montgomery Biscuits, Double A minor league team for the Tampa Rays. That thing looking around the M is a biscuit, apparently. A little too precious if you ask me."

Sarah: "Thank you, and I'm impressed."

Mrs. Fontenot: "I know my minor league teams now."

Matt was wearing a white t-shirt with "See Rock City" in red letters across the front. The shirt caught him on the chest then hung lose around his waist. His pants were heavy cotton and khaki colored, with a loop sewn on the outside of the left leg about halfway up the thigh. Sarah had no idea why anyone would want such a loop. Beneath the pants were dark brown boots with laces showing.

As he approached, he removed his cap and smiled. Sarah noticed the teeth. She worked with actors that had paid thousands of dollars to perfect their smiles, and their teeth were not this white. His hair was short all over, more so on the sides than on the top. His face did not have a uniform tan. The forehead was a shade lighter than the lower part of his face. The only time she had seen that was with professional golfers. On a side of the forehead was a scar running from the hairline to just over one eye, disturbing the natural arc of the eyebrow.

In all, he was slightly larger and rougher around the edges than she had imagined.

Then, there was the dog, a Border Collie with small pointed ears. The coat was curly, reddish brown with the white underside beginning at the chin. Even the inside of the legs were white, with each leg having a white sox of a different length. The tail was a mass of reddish brown hair. She immediately detected a bond between the man and his dog.

Mrs. Fontenot: "Matt, I'd like you to meet Sarah DuMont. She is interested in your furniture."

Matt smiled and extended a hand.

Matt: "Nice to meet you, Ms. DuMont. I'm Matt Shepherd, and this is Doodle."

Sarah: "Please call me Sarah. Hello, Doodle."

She shook his hand, immediately noticing the size and roughness. Men in her chosen profession did not have hands like this.

Mrs. Fontenot: "Are you by yourself?"

Matt: "No, ma'am. Odell's outside. He and Doodle had a bet on the number of lovebugs that'd be stuck on the windshield by the time we got here. Odell lost the bet but demanded a recount. I've told him to quit gamblin' with this dog. It won't be long, and she's gonna own his gas station. Odell's hardheaded. I've asked her to explain to me what she is goin' to do with the business. I don't know why she wants the thing. Who wants to buy gas from a dog? I know I don't."

Matt addressed Sarah, with a slight tilt of his head to one side.

Matt: "How about you, Ms. DuMont? Would you wanna buy gas from a dog?"

Sarah: "I'm not sure."

Sarah continued to smile but was unsure about what she just heard. Perhaps it was the accent, and she missed some words along the way. She watched as the dog and owner exchanged a glance. There was a moment of silence while she collected herself.

Sarah: "Rock City, is that some kind of rock-and-roll club around here, like the House of Blues?"

Matt: "No, ma'am. It's a place in Tennessee with rocks. Doodle and I may take a vacation later this year. We thought we'd go see Rock City and Ruby Falls, come home by Memphis, eat at the Rendezvous, and see Graceland. Doodle thinks Elvis is still alive. I thought seein' the grave might give her some closure. Though I'm not sure if they'll let her into the Jungle Room."

"Doodle wants to go to the Peabody Hotel to see the ducks in the lobby. I was born on a Tuesday, but it wasn't last Tuesday. She just wants to chase those ducks. Now, I'm not opposed to spendin' some time in jail for a good cause, but I'm not gonna do it so she can chase ducks. But I might be willin' if it's just one night. I'm not exactly sure what the penalty is for duck chasin'. Mrs. Fontenot, do you know?"

Mrs. Fontenot: "No, Matt, I don't."

Matt: "How about you, Ms. DuMont? Would you be willin' to spend one night in jail so Doodle could chase those ducks?"

Sarah: "I suppose so."

Matt: "Well, that's not a ringin' endorsement. Perhaps I should get another opinion before I commit to a night in a Memphis jail. . . . That sounds like a line from a country song."

"Anyway, once we finally get out of Memphis, we'll drive down Highway 61 and see the Blues Museum in Leland. That's in the Miss'sippi Delta. The Miss'sippi Delta is not the Delta of the Miss'sippi. Are you with me on that, Ms. DuMont?"

Sarah: "I'm not sure."

Matt: "The Miss'sippi Delta is actually an alluvial plan that runs from the lobby of the Commodore Hotel in Memphis down to Vicksburg. The Delta of the Miss'sippi is at the mouth of the Miss'sippi River. The name Miss'sippi Alluvial Plan doesn't exactly roll off the Southern tongue, now does it, Ms. DuMont?"

Sarah: "I guess not."

Matt: "Now, there're two theories about why we call it the Miss'sippi Delta. The first one's to confuse Yankees. The second is that folks from Miss'sippi just don't know any better. While I'm partial to the first, I'm afraid the latter's more likely. Ms. DuMont, do you have an opinion in the matter?"

Sarah: "Mrs. Fontenot, may I use your restroom."

Mrs. Fontenot: "Certainly, dear, it's over there."

Sarah: "Matt, please excuse me just one minute."

Matt: "Certainly, Ms. DuMont."

Sarah sensed that Mrs. Fontenot was enjoying this immensely. Once in the restroom, she attempted to compose herself. Is this man insane or is he doing this on purpose? Like the cowboy, she assumed the latter more likely. The competitive Sarah knew the biggest mistake was to underestimate your opponent. Round one went to the cowboy, but the fight was not over.

Sarah returned to find Mrs. Fontenot standing alone. They made eye contact, and she pointed toward the wall where the five belles and food were located. This was getting out of hand. Sarah had hoped to be on her way to make-up by now. This was not how her advances toward other men had progressed. She approached Matt and his suitors. He spoke to her with a mouth full of brownie.

Matt: "Ladies, I'd like y'all to meet Sarah DuMont. Ms. DuMont, this is, don't tell me now, Vicki, Ashley, Susan, Linda, and Linda. Did I get that right?"

Vicki: "Yes, you did. Ms. DuMont, it is an honor to meet you. I'm a big fan. May I ask you a question? I saw your most recent movie. In the final love scene, how naked were you?"

Sarah: "That wasn't me. It was a body double. My contract doesn't allow nude scenes. Well, it doesn't anymore. Matt, could I talk to you? Please excuse us, ladies. Nice to meet you."

Sarah took Matt's arm and led him back to Mrs. Fontenot.

Matt: "It's none of my business, Ms. DuMont, but if the first thing someone asks you when you meet is how naked were you, you may want to consider another occupation. That's the kind of question you get in Lester's bar on a Saturday night. Would you like a bite of brownie?"

Sarah: "I'll consider it and no."

Matt: "These brownies sure are good—made with pecans and still warm."

He approached her, leaned forward, and held a brownie up for her to inspect as if it were a rare diamond. Sarah opened her mouth, and he moved the brownie near her lips.

Matt: "You sure have pretty eyes, Ms. DuMont. I bet you hear that all the time. And how's that brownie?"

Sarah: "It's good."

Matt: "You have a little brownie on your chin. Let me get that for you."

He brushed the bits of brownie off her chin while she looked into his face.

Sarah: "Matt, I own a store in New Orleans. . . . I mean LA. I own a store in LA."

Matt: "Is it near Foley? Foley is in Lower Alabama and has a mess of stores. Doodle and I go through Foley on our way to the Redneck Riviera. Doodle sure loves the beach."

Sarah: "Los Angeles."

Matt: "I don't think there is a Los Angeles in Alabama. Now, there's a Philadelphia in Miss'sippi and an Albany in Louisiana, but

I don't think there's a Los Angeles in Alabama."

Sarah: "My store is in Los Angeles, California. Matt, I'm asking you, please be quiet just one minute and let me ask you something. We'd like to show some of your furniture in our store. What you make is unique. I'd like to meet with you, say for lunch or dinner, and discuss it further. We like to do a write-up about each craftsman and artist that produce our merchandise."

"The catering service for the production company is excellent. I could have them prepare something, just for us, in the dining room of the house on St. Charles Avenue where I'm staying. How about it Matt?"

Matt: "Don't get me wrong, Ms. DuMont. That's a very temptin' offer, but I'm afraid I'll have to pass. Thank you though."

Sarah: "This would be a real opportunity to show your work. Let me help you?"

There was a moment of silence as Matt paused and smiled.

Matt: "'You know not what you ask,' Matthew 20: 22."

Sarah: "What, are you a preacher now?"

Matt: "I think this is goin' well, don't you, Mrs. Fontenot?"

Sarah paused to make an adjustment in strategy.

Sarah: "This store is important to me. My best friend is my partner in this business. It would mean a great deal to us if we could show your work. You would be helping me."

Matt: "I don't know, Ms. DuMont. I have a pretty full schedule right now, what with my vegetable garden, my beehives, and fishin'. I also promised Lee Arthur I'd help castrate some bull calves. As my ol' daddy would say, I don't have time right now to scratch my behind with both hands."

Sarah stood in stunned silence. No man had ever given her such excuses. She was now desperate and used her best acting skills to hide the fact.

Sarah: "I see that you are a very . . . busy man. I'm only asking for a few minutes of your time so we can meet and discuss a business arrangement. I would not want to interfere with your vegetable garden, your beehives, your fishing, or your activities with Mr. Lee Arthur."

Matt: "Okay, Ms. DuMont, we'll leave it up to Doodle."

Matt looked at his dog who, as usual, was by his right side.

Matt: "Doodle, do you want to meet with this nice lady and talk business?"

At the mention of her name, Doodle's tail began to wag. Sarah was standing directly in front of the man and his dog. She extended her left hand with the charm bracelet toward Doodle. The dog immediately approached and licked Sarah's hand, wrist, and bracelet.

Matt: "Well, it looks like we have a date. However, if you want to know about the furniture and me, you'll need to come to the farm. So if you are serious, let's plan on meetin' at my place. It's not too far from here, just over the Louisiana line in Miss'sippi."

Sarah was so elated by the apparent victory that she would have agreed to most anything.

Sarah: "Sure, what's the address?"

Matt: "It's a rural address, so I'll give you the GPS coordinates. Do you have somethin' I can write on?"

Sarah gave him Willie's card, and Mrs. Fontenot gave him a pen. Sarah took great delight in the shocked look on Mrs. Fontenot's face.

Matt: "If you have any trouble findin' it, just call this number. It's the number of Odell's gas station. At least as of now, it still belongs to Odell. If you call that number and Doodle answers, you'll know Odell has lost the business. When are you free?"

Sarah: "I have this Saturday afternoon free."

Matt: "Good. That won't interfere with Mr. Lee Arthur's plans, so why don't we say around two o'clock?"

Sarah: "I'll see you then."

Sarah took the card and did everything but skip out the store. She had beaten the best New Orleans had to offer, without preparing one dessert or casserole and on her opponent's home field. Sarah called Willie.

Sarah: "You can come get me now and take your time. It is a beautiful morning."

_____

Sarah's beautiful morning was followed by fourteen hours of work. With work completed, she was in her room in the house on St. Charles, sitting up in bed, reviewing scripts, and talking with her assistant.

Sarah: "Tomorrow, call that dreadful woman at that store and buy the mirror."

Assistant: "You're not going to meet with the cowboy?"

Sarah: "No, I got what I wanted. Have the mirror given to the homeless or let orphans play with it. If they don't want it, have it thrown in the river. Call the gas station and give them my regrets. The card is around here somewhere. If a dog answers, hang up— what an idiot."

Assistant: "That reminds me, Lorraine called and Mark left you a gift at the house."

Sarah: "What could a man possible buy for me? What is it?"

Assistant: "A dog."

Sarah: "A dog!"

Assistant: "Actually, a puppy."

Sarah: "What kind of puppy?"

Assistant: "Lorraine said it was the kind that barks, pees and—"

Sarah: "Tell Lorraine to have the puppy put to sleep. . . . No, tell her to board the thing, and then tell Mark where it is. Tell him thanks, but no thanks."

Assistant: "He called today and said if you were free this weekend, he could fly in."

Sarah: "What did you tell him?"

Assistant: "Of course, I told him your plans were uncertain, and I would have to check with you."

Sarah: "What are you eating?"

Assistant: "A brownie. . . . It's good. . . . You want me to get you one? . . . There's a whole plate of them in the kitchen. . . . I'll go get you one if you like. . . . This one was still warm. . . . Would you like a bite? . . . It's made with pecans. . . . I'll be glad to get you one."

# Chapter Five

# A Day In The Country

The car with driver, Willie Roberts, and passenger, Sarah DuMont, turned off the blacktop road onto the Shepherd place around two o'clock. Sarah had a lunch prepared by the catering service to take on the trip and had nibbled on the contents. She gave no thought to the dietary needs of the driver.

As they pulled onto the gravel road, Sarah looked over the top of her designer sunglasses.

Sarah: "Driver, I need to give you some instructions. For all I know, this man is homicidal, but we checked, and he doesn't have a criminal record. I requested that my driver be a big, burly black man, and they gave me you, so pay attention while we are here. In thirty minutes, I want you to find me. Do you have a cell phone?"

Willie: "Yes, ma'am. The company provides me with one."

Sarah: "Good for you. In thirty minutes, come find me. Say that the production company has called, and I'm needed back in New Orleans, immediately. Have you got that?"

Willie: "Yes, ma'am, thirty minutes, production company, New Orleans."

Sarah: "What is your name?"

Willie: "Willie Roberts."

Sarah: "You can let me out some place that doesn't involve cow manure and park over there in the shade. Remember, thirty minutes. Mr. Willie Roberts, if you don't do exactly what I say, I'll see to it that your employer fires you."

Willie: "Yes, ma'am. I understand."

Matt and Doodle were waiting on the front porch. They watched as the back seat passenger was gesturing, talking, and leaning toward the driver. The luxury German car, with the gesturing, talking, and leaning passenger, pulled onto the circular driveway.

Sarah exited the car, and Willie proceeded to the shade.

Sarah: "Hello, Matt. Good to see you again. You have a lovely place here."

Matt: "Hello, Sarah. I believe you know Doodle."

Matt gave Sarah a two-pump handshake then proceeded around her to where Willie was sitting in the parked car.

Matt: "I need to meet this young gentleman in the car."

Sarah: "Matt, I'm on a schedule today."

Matt continued to walk away and gave Sarah a backwards wave.

Matt: "Won't be but a minute."

Matt shook Willie's hand through the open car window. They talked a few moments, and Matt began to laugh along with Willie. Matt slapped the roof of the car, and the laughing intensified. He then bent over with both hands on his knees, still laughing. In one choreographed movement, Willie, Matt, and Doodle looked directly at Sarah. It was not over. Matt would eventually be down on all fours with Doodle looking at Sarah.

Decorum was restored. Willie exited the car with Matt's assistance. He put his arm around Willie as they walked past Sarah toward the house. Matt spoke over his shoulder to her.

Matt: "Willie's gonna sit on the front porch, and I'll get him some sweet tea. With lemon, Willie?"

Willie: "With lemon, much obliged."

They proceeded to the porch. Matt went inside and immediately returned.

Matt: "Here's a cushion for that rocker. We can't leave'em out cause the squirrels chew on'em."

Sarah: "You have squirrels?"

Sarah looked around nervously.

Matt: "Of course, we have squirrels. Let me get Willie his tea, and I'll show you around."

Matt went inside and did not return. Sarah waited. She looked at her watch, no Matt. What is that fool doing? She looked at her watch again. They were leaving in thirty minutes, regardless. She had not moved since Matt shook her hand as if she were standing on the only solid ground in a farm of sinking sand. She surveyed her surroundings and took in the smells of pasture grass, cows, cedar, jasmine, and honeysuckle—all mixed together and intensified by the Mississippi sun.

It was early spring, so not as hot as it would soon become. She had been warned about the heat in New Orleans in the late months of summer and could only imagine what it would be like standing on this spot in August at two o'clock in the afternoon. She pressed her finger to her upper lip to blot tiny beads of sweat while shooing away flies with her other hand. What kind of person lives in such a dreadful place?

She then noticed the curtain move in a front window. Was he watching her? Had he been standing there the whole time? Had he left her standing in the open, under the Mississippi sun, just to see what she would do? She felt a flash of rage as she made a quick stride off the solid rock toward the house. Immediately, Matt opened the screen door.

Matt: "Willie, here's your sweet tea. Now, let me show Ms. DuMont my estate, chickens, and all."

Matt motioned for Sarah to join him, and each headed to the path leading to the barn. Matt stopped and turned toward the farmhouse where Doodle was standing on the porch near Willie. Sarah looked and assumed the dog must be waiting for permission.

Matt: "Doodle, come on, but remember, we agreed I'd do all the talkin'."

Sarah: "Matt, the dog can't talk."

Matt kneeled down as Doodle approached and held her head with his hands.

Matt: "See, Doodle, Sarah agrees with me. You need to let me do the talkin'."

Matt moved his hands to cover Doodle's ears and looked at Sarah.

Matt: "If you let her talk, she just goes on and on."

Sarah: "Matt, . . . never mind."

They walked from the house to the barn with Matt leading the way and Doodle accompanying Sarah. The path led past the week's laundry hanging on the clotheslines.

Sarah: "I see you are a boxer man."

Matt: "When I wear them."

Sarah: "Let's hope today is one of those days."

Matt: "You're safe. It wasn't a full moon last night."

Sarah: "Well, you've just ruined the beauty of a full moon for me."

Matt: "When was the last time you took notice of a full moon?"

Sarah: "You are not going to make this about me. I'm not the one that . . . never mind."

Matt: "I saw you in that movie, the one where you pretend to be from Georgia."

Sarah: "Children pretend. I act. I was acting as if I were from Georgia."

Matt: "Well, your Southern accent said otherwise. I understand you're from Connecticut."

Sarah: "A good actor can play the part, if coached, and yes, I'm from Connecticut. Have you been checking up on me?"

Matt: "You know Connecticut's not a real place. Miss'sippi's a real place. The last movie star we had out here was a complete disaster. Doodle said never again. But apparently, you charmed her."

Sarah: "I had them check up on you. I know you don't have a criminal record."

Matt: "Yet. I don't have a criminal record, yet. The day's not over."

Sarah: "And the last cowboy I knew was also a complete disaster."

Matt had followed his uncle's advice and acquired some laying hens. The path to the barn led past the hen house. He continued up the path and turned to see her looking at the chicken coop inside the chicken yard. During the day, the gate to the chicken yard was open, and the chickens ranged around the house and barn. As evening fell, the chickens would instinctively seek the shelter of the chicken coop. At night, the gate to the chicken yard was closed.

The coop was an impressive structure that resembled one of the antebellum plantation homes that grace Natchez. It had a two-story, wrap-around front porch with classic Greek revival columns, green shutters on windows, and red fireplaces on either side. The chickens entered by way of a plank that led them through the great front door and, apparently, into a massive front hallway with a grand circular stairway with more grand rooms on either side of the hallway; however, the interior was best left to the imagination. A sign beside the chicken coop read, "As God is my witness, I will never be hungry again. I have chickens."

Matt: "Odell and Lee Arthur came over one Saturday morning to help me build a chicken coop. We started drinkin' beer, and four days later, Tara was born. When it was done, Lee Arthur had to spend a night in jail for givin' me beer. We're not sure if the columns are Greek revival or neoclassical. Look at it from the chickens' point of view. We eat their eggs, cook their flesh, and stuff our pillows with their feathers. The least we can do is give them a decent place to ovulate."

Sarah: "Just looking at it makes me want to ovulate."

They exchanged a look and a brief moment of silence.

Matt: "This chicken coop's the second reason why I don't drink anymore."

Sarah: "What's the first?"

Matt: "Let's just say it's a public safety issue. The rooster's name is Rhett. I don't see Scarlett right now, but her days are numbered. She's stopped layin'."

Sarah: "What does that mean?"

Matt: "Winner, winner, chicken dinner."

Sarah: "That's terrible. I'm calling PETA."

Matt: "And tell them what? You know of a bunch of free range, organically fed chickens that live in a mansion."

Sarah: "No, I'm going to tell them I've found one of Colonel Sanders' henchmen."

Matt: "You mean Saint Colonel Sanders, the patron saint of fried chicken. Besides, it's a farm—everything must bear fruit."

Sarah: "Do you have an answer for everything?"

Matt: "No. I don't know what Scarlett saw in Ashley Wilkes."

Sarah: "Some women like sensitive, caring men who don't cut the heads off chickens."

Matt: "Are you tryin' to say Ashley Wilkes, who lived on Twelve Oaks Plantation in the state of Georgia, never ate fried chicken? . . . Well?"

Sarah: "Give me a second."

The man and his dog were looking expectantly at her.

Sarah: "Well if he did, somebody else cut the chicken's head off."

Matt: "That's my point. He wasn't a very manly man. Now the first time I saw Rhett Butler, I thought there's a man that'd cut the head off a chicken."

Sarah: "Maybe, Ashley was a vegetarian like me."

Matt: "In Miss'sippi, a vegetarian is someone who doesn't eat their chitlins boiled."

Sarah: "I forbid you to talk to me for three minutes. I'll let you know when the time is up."

They turned and headed up the path waiting for the moratorium to end. There is a point on the upward path to the barn where much of the active part of the farm can be seen. Matt stopped at that point.

Matt: "May I talk on my own property now?"

Sarah: "Yes, but you are on probation."

As Matt pointed and talked, Sarah shielded her eyes from the rays of the Mississippi sun, which was required even with her sunglasses. She took the opportunity to steal glances at him while feigning interest in the farm. She was an actress.

Matt: "Over there are some beehives. There're my blueberry bushes. I keep a vegetable garden over there, a few pecan trees. You've seen the chicken house. Those cows aren't mine. Lee Arthur rents my pastureland. My uncle won't let me have cows for public safety reasons. Up ahead's the barn where I make the furniture."

Sarah: "Are those flowers in the vegetable garden?"

Matt: "I always grow some Zinnias each year. They can take the Miss'sippi summers, and my mama always had'em around. I tend to this, make furniture durin' the day, and work on the farmhouse at night."

Sarah: "Doesn't sound like that gives you much time to sit and think."

Matt: "Lee Arthur asked me to check on an expectin' cow. We can use the truck, make a quick pass in the pasture, and look for her. What do you say, Sarah?"

Sarah: "I'm on a schedule today. This won't take long will it?"

Matt: "No. I'll drive instead of Doodle. Besides, how many times have you had the chance to ride in a pick-up truck through a pasture lookin' for a cow and calf? If you're ever in a country music video, you could use this experience for your motivation."

Sarah: "That will never happen."

Matt: "As my ol' daddy would say, never say never."

Matt, Sarah, and Doodle walked to the pick-up truck parked by the side of the path. The truck was a blue, four-wheel-drive step-side with a five-speed manual transmission on the floor. Matt had purchased the truck, second hand, from his Uncle Billy. Just the kind of vehicle a real cowboy would own.

He helped her into the truck on the driver's side telling her to slide over. Even though she was tall, his assistance was helpful. Doodle followed, without his help, sitting next to Sarah on the bench seat.

Matt: "First time in a pick-up truck?"

Sarah: "First time without a camera rolling."

When sitting on the truck's bench seat, Sarah noticed that she and Doodle were practically nose-to-nose. As Matt eased the truck to the pasture gate, Doodle was animated, looking at Matt then at Sarah. He stopped the truck.

Matt: "I'll open the gate. Sarah, I hate to ask this, but if we don't let Doodle ride with her head out the window, we'll never hear the end of it. While I get the gate, could y'all trade places?"

Sarah: "Sure. Anything for the dog."

Sarah moved toward the center of the bench seat as Doodle moved across her lap toward the window in one graceful motion with her tail hitting Sarah full in the face. The two looked at each other, eye level, with their noses only inches apart.

Sarah: "Doodle, you did that on purpose. Next time, you can have the window seat first thing. You happy now? Can I do anything else for you?"

Matt: "I see y'all've made the switch. Thanks. She's already mad about not drivin'."

# A Day In The Country

They drove through the gate. Matt stopped the truck and closed the gate. Once back in the truck, the three were off in search of the newest member of the Shepherd farm.

Sarah could hear the sound of twigs from the pecan trees cracking under the truck tires as they slowly drove through the pasture among small groups of cows.

Sarah: "Do these cows not know to get out of the way of a truck?"

Matt: "Once they realize you're in here, they'll get out of the way."

Sarah turned and looked at him. Is there anything this man won't say?

Sarah: "Matt, are you gay?"

Matt: "Not sure where that came from, but, yes, I am gay. I promise, Ms. DuMont, I'll not let my sexual orientation interfere with my ability to do good furniture."

Sarah: "Don't be silly. You're not gay."

Matt: "I can't be gay on my own property if I want to?"

Sarah: "Okay, gay man, name one musical currently on Broadway."

Matt: "Cats."

Sarah: "Nice try, cowboy."

Matt: "You know, I've tried to explain to Doodle that the cats in Cats are not real cats. I think she would listen to you."

Sarah: "I refuse to let you talk me into telling that dog that the cats in Cats are not real cats."

Matt: "Well, they're not, and somebody needs to explain it to her. She won't listen to me."

Sarah: "You're insane, but you're not gay."

Matt: "Then why did you ask?"

Sarah: "What is it with all that Calvin Klein designer underwear?"

Matt: "I'm not allowed?"

Sarah: "No you're not. I'll speak to Calvin and have you blackballed."

Matt: "If you get a chance to talk to Calvin, I could use a little more room. You know, some of us are—"

Sarah: "Don't be silly. Where do you get them anyway?"

Matt: "At the gittin' place."

Sarah: "I don't know about the *gittin'* place, but they don't sell them at Walmart."

Matt: "How do you know what they sell at Walmart? Do you shop there?"

Sarah: "I don't shop. I have people that do all my shopping."

Matt: "Then what were you doin' in Mrs. Fontenot's store? Looked like shoppin' to me."

Sarah: "I'm a buyer. I buy merchandise for my store in LA."

Matt: "Did you buy anything from Mrs. Fontenot?"

Sarah: "No."

Matt: "Then you were shoppin'."

Sarah: "See, you don't know the difference between someone who shops for breakfast cereal, and someone who buys for an LA store."

Matt: "I know this, you said breakfast cereal because you don't know the names of the cereals you eat."

Sarah: "Don't be silly. Of course, I know the names."

Matt: "Okay, name one. The actual name on the box."

Sarah: " . . . Mr. Flakey—"

Matt: "Mr. Flakey's not a real cereal."

Sarah: "Yes it is."

Matt: "I know. We could put your picture on the box, and you could be Mrs. Flakey."

Sarah's expression changed. Her eyes moistened showing the beginnings of a tear, and her bottom lip quivered slightly.

Matt: "Sarah, I'm sorry. I was just teasin'. Please, I'm sorry."

She smiled.

Sarah: "Be careful, cowboy. I can turn a man into a quivering bowl of jell-o in a heartbeat. I come well armed. Understand?"

Matt: "Yes, ma'am. And next week, I'm gonna buy me a box of Mr. Flakey at the Piggly Wiggly. Doodle, make a note of that."

Sarah: "That's better. I recommend the kind with nuts. That would seem appropriate."

Matt: "Doodle, did you get that? Mr. Flakey with nuts."

Matt pointed toward a cow on an adjacent hill.

Matt: "I've been saved by the apparent birth of a calf. Mrs. Flakey, you wait in the truck. That bull's around here somewhere, and he's a Cheerios man. Doodle, you stay in the truck, too. Lee Arthur will have your hide if you don't stop herdin' his cows. You two ladies stay here and talk among yourselves. Let me warn you, Sarah, she'll tell me everything you say about me."

Sarah: "We have much more important things to discuss. Don't flatter yourself, cowboy."

Matt exited the truck, walked about twenty yards away, and knelt down on one knee as he looked in the direction of the new mama cow. Sarah and Doodle waited in the truck as told. Finally, Matt rose, turned, and headed back.

Sarah: "Doodle, I should have said Cheerios. I couldn't think of it. He's made me so angry. The Piggly Wiggly is a real place?"

As quick as a Cotton Mouth Water Moccasin in a Mississippi swamp, Doodle licked Sarah from her chin to her forehead. Sarah covered her face with both hands and fell over onto the driver's side of the bench seat. Apparently in dog sign language, this was a request to please lick her face or any exposed areas around her face. Doodle put her front paws on Sarah and complied with the stated request.

Sarah: "Matt, help me! Please help me! Doodle, get off of me! Stop!"

Matt stood at the driver's door looking through the window.

Matt: "Sarah, please quit abusin' that poor animal. You should be ashamed of yourself. I leave you alone for one minute. I assumed you two could be civil to one another. But it looks like I was wrong."

Matt shook his head slowly.

Matt: "Fightin' over a cowboy. There's plenty of me to go around."

Sarah: "I was just asking her about the *Piggly Wiggly*."

Matt: "Well, she doesn't want to talk about it. Now reach in the glove compartment and get out the binoculars."

Sarah: "All right, but nothing better jump out at me."

Sarah reached for the glove compartment, keeping a wary eye on Doodle.

Matt: "Just get the binoculars and come with me. I recommend you don't say any more about the Piggly Wiggly in front of her."

Climbing onto the bed of the truck, they stood behind the cab. She noticed he had a clean outdoor smell about him. He must have bathed just for her visit.

There was a brief awkward moment as Matt put his hand on her shoulder, leaned in beside her face, and helped her point and adjust the binoculars. He was so close that his voice tickled her ear as he spoke. By force of will, she concentrated on the cow and not the cowboy.

Sarah: "That's so sweet. The calf is nursing for all it's worth."

Matt: "Yes, life goes on, even for cows. I'll call Lee Arthur when we get back to the barn."

Sarah continued to watch the cow and calf for a few more moments.

Sarah: "Thank you for showing me. I'll remember that for a long time."

The two moved to the open tailgate of the truck bed.

Matt: "That cow had a swollen teat, but looks like the calf was nursin' on all of 'em."

Sarah: "I don't think you should talk about that in front of me."

Matt jumped to the ground from the tailgate and motioned for Sarah to bend her knees. He put his arm around her waist, pressed her against his side, and swung her off the tailgate. No man had ever done that before.

Matt: "It's a farm with cows, teats matter."

Sarah: "They matter in my business, too."

He looked at her and smiled.

Matt: "That's funny, Sarah. I guess even a blind hog finds an acorn every now and then."

Sarah: "Well, you know us blind hogs."

Matt: "Don't talk about yourself that way. Let me do it. By the way, Doodle really likes your perfume. She said you smell like a spring day after a rain shower. I told her I'd get her some for Christmas."

Sarah: "I'm glad she likes my perfume, but it is very expensive."

Matt: "That's gonna be a problem. Dogs just don't get the concept of money. She never makes it home with my change."

Matt helped Sarah into the cab of the truck as Doodle seemed pleased to see everyone.

Matt: "We have one more thing to show you, or I should say,

Doodle wants to show you."

Sarah: "Not sure I have time."

Matt: "If you say no, Doodle is gonna lick your face until you say yes."

Sarah looked at Doodle and was convinced the expression on her face said please say no.

Sarah: "Okay, just one more thing."

Matt: "Doodle's beside herself to show you this. We have been doin' some extra practice just for you."

Sarah: "Well then, let's see it."

Matt drove to a large lake shared with Lee Arthur. On Matt's side of the lake was a long dock that extended out into the water. Matt eased the truck next to the dock. When he opened his door, Doodle was the first out of the truck. With everyone out, Matt reached behind the seat and retrieved a cylinder dog toy.

Sarah: "She's apparently excited. What is she about to do?"

Matt: "You're in Miss'sippi. She's not about to do anything. I can tell you what she is fixin' to do."

Sarah: "What is she . . . *fixin'* . . . to do?

Matt: "All of this is her doin'. One afternoon, she watched a show on TV about dogs competin' by jumpin' off a dock. They have competitions for distance and height. First, we had to remodel our old dock to meet the competition specs, forty feet long and eight feet wide. She's been workin' with me and Odell and teachin' us how to toss the toy to help her get the height and distance."

Sarah: "This I have to see."

Matt: "You're gonna do more than see. I'll do the first toss, then it'll be all you and Doodle."

They walked to the dock. On the shore end was a white circle with "Dodle" painted in the center with black paint.

Matt: "We let Doodle paint this. She can't spell. She gets in the circle. Whoever's tossin' the toy stands at the other end. She stays in that circle until you say go. As she comes runnin' past, you toss the toy just ahead of her in an upward motion to get her to follow it up. The dog can get some air."

Sarah: "Wow, let's get started."

Matt: "One more thing, while it's not part of the competition, it's fun to toss the toy just right so that she can snatch it out of the air just as she starts her descent. She can't do many of these. As you can imagine, this is a tirin' exercise. Once she gets fatigued, it throws the timin' off. So we practice a little most every day."

Matt motioned to Doodle who obeyed the command and stood in the white circle. He went to the water end of the dock and gave Doodle the command to go. Doodle sprinted down the dock, and as she approached the end, Matt tossed the toy in an arch in front of her. Doodle took flight defying the forces of gravity in pursuit of the toy. Eventually, gravity won, and both toy and dog splashed into the water.

Doodle retrieved the toy and headed in a dog paddle to the dock. Matt had built stairs down into the water so that Doodle could go from swimming to standing on the dock in a few strides.

Sarah: "That is amazing. Look at her. You can tell she just loves to do this."

Matt: "Don't get too close. She'll get you wet when she shakes the water off. She really enjoys gettin' me soaked. Your turn, here's the toy. Doodle, go get in your circle."

Doodle and Sarah did as instructed. Sarah gave the command and watched as a ball of energy, covered in wet, reddish brown hair, exploded past her. Her first attempt at the toss went array. Doodle sailed over the toy and gave it a glance as she achieved a higher trajectory. On splash down, Matt reminded Doodle to retrieve the toy.

Matt: "Not bad, Sarah, for your first attempt. Try it again and give it a little more air."

Once again, Doodle raced down the dock. This time Sarah's toss over shot the mark. Doodle's head was still chasing the toy as the rest of her descended to earth.

Matt: "Sarah, you are gettin' the range. I think the third time will be the charm."

Sarah: "I don't know, Matt, but this is fun. I've never done anything like this before."

Matt: "Sarah, there are many, many, many things I've done that you haven't."

Sarah: "There is one less now."

Call it beginner's luck or credit Sarah's competitive nature, but on her third attempt, the toss was perfect. There is a moment in the ascent and descent when the dog seems suspended in space. At that very moment of floating, the toy and Doodle's mouth were inches apart. They started as two but landed in the water as one. Sarah squealed with excitement.

Sarah: "Did you see that? It was like a ballet. It was beautiful. Again, again, let's do it again."

Matt: "Ain't you somethin'. Sarah DuMont, you just won't do. I tell you what."

Once on the dock, Doodle made a beeline to Sarah. Ignoring Matt's advice, she received a Doodle shower then hugged the source of the shower.

Matt: "I make Doodle ride in the back when she's this wet. You may have to join her."

Sarah: "I don't care. Doodle and I can sit in the back and say terrible things about the cowboy driving the truck. That may be even more fun."

Doodle made a total of ten jumps with Sarah tossing the toy. She was three out of ten on perfect tosses. With Doodle thoroughly soaked and her tongue hanging out, the three made their way to the truck. Sarah brought up the rear watching the man and his dog.

Matt: "You know, Sarah, that's about the most fun a person can have with their clothes on."

Sarah laughed. He was a cowboy, but he could make her laugh and do it so easily.

Sarah: "You may be right about that, Matt. You just may be right."

With Doodle in the back, Matt started the truck and headed to the barn. He turned and looked at his dog in the bed of the truck.

Matt: "Look at her, Sarah. She's give out. I think she's asleep. She's been so excited about your visit. She doesn't have enough female company, and the cows don't count. She won't talk to an animal that eats grass all day."

Sarah: "Do the women around here fall for this little . . . act of yours?"

Matt: "What are you talkin' about?"

Sarah: "This Southern fried, baseball cap, pick-up truck, my dog's my best friend act you have going on. Just curious."

Matt: "Yes, they do. That's why I live alone in an old farmhouse with a dog."

Sarah: "The dog is part of your problem."

Matt: "So, you're sayin' if I get rid of the dog, I'd have all these women friends?"

Sarah: "Yes, maybe."

Matt: "Uh-huh. . . . I'll just keep the dog."

Sarah: "You do realize that the way you talk about her is ridiculous?"

Matt: "You know determinin' what's ridiculous is in the eye of the beholder. Have you ever seen Picasso's *Bather Opening a Cabin*? The paintin' is ridiculous. He wanted to call it Cow Eating Grass but his manager said sex sells, so they put bather in the title."

Sarah: "Art is subjective. He painted that to elicit a response from the viewer."

Matt: "Maybe, I'm a performin' artist, and Doodle's my canvas. I've certainly gotten a response from you."

Sarah: "This is exactly what I'm talking about. I make a perfectly reasonable observation about your behavior, and you twist it around, by means of Picasso, to make it about me."

Matt: "Of course it's about you. I can tell by the packagin'. If someone painted you as a bather, it couldn't be confused with a cow eatin' grass. If you were the model for Picasso, then he'd clearly be suspect, not me."

Sarah: "Matt, that is sweet. Okay, you can say whatever you want about Doodle as long as you pay me a compliment first. Deal?"

Matt: "Deal."

Sarah: "Let's practice."

Matt: "What do you mean?"

Sarah: "Practice, you know practice. Pay me a compliment and say whatever you want about Doodle. Didn't you play sports in high school? Practice."

She sat up straight and pulled back her hair, displaying the profile of her face.

Sarah: "What do you think?"

Matt: "What do I think about what . . . your ears?"

Sarah: "My profile, my bone structure."

Sarah traced her profile starting at her hairline down to her chin using the side of her finger.

Matt: "I give you this, you're clean."

Sarah: "What? Clean! That's not a compliment. Ugly people can be clean."

Matt: "Well, if they are, then I think it is incumbent on the rest of us to let them know."

# A Day In The Country

Sarah: "The rest of us, what group do you think you're in?"

Matt: "I've always assumed that if the world were divided into the ugly and the not ugly, I'd be in the latter. But I guess you're tellin' me, I need to rethink this?"

Sarah: "What about my eyes? You said something about my eyes in the store."

She turned toward Matt with her eyes wide open.

Matt: "I don't know, Sarah. I'm not really gettin' anything. Must've been the lights in Mrs. Fontenot's store."

Sarah: "How about this?"

She took off her shoes and athletic socks, putting her feet on the dash.

Matt: "Wiggle your toes."

She complied.

Matt: "Still not gettin' anything."

Sarah: "You're not very good at this, are you? I'm not sure what else I can do."

Matt: "You know sometimes, us ugly people don't really appreciate beauty in the not ugly people."

Sarah: "That's what I'm doing. Giving one of the ugly people some practice."

Matt: "I appreciate it. . . . Wait, I'm gettin' something."

Sarah: "Finally."

Matt: "Humility, you got humility written all over you."

Sarah: "Well, I try. In my profession, you meet some of the most vain people. They are insufferable bores. Why, just the other day —"

Matt: "Is that Willie up there wavin' his arms?"

She sat up straight and began putting on her socks and shoes.

Sarah: "I'll take care of the gate. I think I can do that. You park the truck, and I'll see what Willie wants."

Sarah worked the gate and Matt, with Doodle still asleep in the back, drove the truck into the barn. Sarah walked over to Willie.

Sarah: "What, in heaven's name, do you want?"

Willie: "You told me to find you after thirty minutes and to say they needed you back in New Orleans. It has been longer than thirty minutes, but I couldn't find you."

Sarah: "Plans have changed. You go sit on that porch and leave me alone. You better not give me any more trouble, or I'll have you fired."

Willie: "Yes, ma'am, Ms. Sarah."

Matt and Doodle were standing in the door of the barn, watching the exchange between Sarah and Willie. As Willie headed to the farmhouse, Matt cupped his hands around his mouth and yelled to him.

Matt: "Willie, there's banana puddin' in the refrigerator. Help yourself."

Willie waved acknowledgement. On the walk to the barn, Sarah regretted sending Willie packing, but she wasn't ready to leave yet.

Matt: "Doodle, go show Willie where the bowls and spoons are."

Doodle headed to the farmhouse in pursuit of Willie as if she completely understood what Matt said. Sarah watched as the dog went past on a mission from her owner. She thought this cowboy eventually wears you down until you enter an alternative reality, his reality. She was determined not to go there.

Matt called Lee Arthur and told him about the cow and calf.

Sarah: "Mrs. Fontenot said you called from a gas station, but you apparently have a cell phone."

Matt: "I don't think you know what you're talkin' about. You're in way over your head."

They entered the cavernous barn, and the air temperature fell ten degrees. On one side, Matt parked his truck and his John Deere tractor with its distinctive green color. That side had implements that attached to the tractor and various tools, oil cans, and gas cans needed for farming. On the other side was his woodworking shop. A concrete floor had been poured to provide a level base for all the various equipment used for making furniture. Lights had been added in the work area since barns, by nature, can be dark places.

Sarah: "Wow, the equivalent of St. Peter's Basilica for the family farm. Have you ever been in St. Peter's?"

Matt: "No, I've never been to France."

Sarah stared at him. A small grin came on his face.

Matt: "You know, a man can derive a great deal of satisfaction from pressin' your buttons."

Sarah: "My buttons are real, and they are spectacular."

Matt: "Yes, I saw them briefly in a movie."

Sarah: "My buttons and your underwear, I guess according to Mississippi law, we have to get married now."

Matt: "Only if we're also first cousins."

Sarah: "Oh, are those the tool things you use to make the furniture?"

They walked to the area that functioned as his workshop.

Matt: "Yes, and over there's the reclaimed lumber I use."

They moved to the racks that held the lumber. She noticed the lumber smelled of earth and oil.

Matt: "I've always liked the name Sarah. I suppose, you're either named for the Sarah in the Old Testament or for the lady that makes the pound cakes."

Sarah: "It's an old family name. What about you?"

Matt: "My mama named me Matthew after one of the twelve disciples."

Sarah: "You look more like a Mark to me."

Matt: "Mark was not one of the twelve."

Sarah: "Yes, he was, Matthew, Mark, Luke, John."

Matt: "No, he wasn't."

Sarah: "He wrote one of those books."

Matt: "Not everyone who wrote a book was a disciple, and not every disciple wrote anything that we know of."

Sarah: "Are you saying that Jesus picked disciples that couldn't read or write?"

Matt: "Jesus didn't care if you could read or write."

Sarah: "Now you are saying that Jesus doesn't care about education. Does the Pope know? I mean, they have this money tied up in Catholic schools, and according to you, Jesus doesn't care about education. Somebody needs to tell the Jesuits. I'll get my father to call the Pope and tell him."

Matt: "Is your father Catholic?"

Sarah: "Don't be silly. He is an investment banker. Catholics can't talk to the Pope."

By now, the two were sitting in rockers Matt had made and kept in the barn.

Sarah: "Since you like talking about religion, how about that other religion down here?"

Matt: "What are you talkin' about?"

Sarah: "College football."

Matt: "Sarah, you're in way over your head now."

Sarah: "Why are you people down here so crazy about college football? I don't get it. I enjoy a good game, but this is ridiculous."

Matt: "You have lived a sheltered life. My people are from Miss'sippi. Like most of the South, my people's people are Scots-Irish. The three pillars of Scots-Irish culture are liquor, allegiance to a clan, and violence. The three pillars of college football are liquor, allegiance to a team, and violence. It's a match made in heaven."

"Where are your people's people from?"

Sarah: "They were French Huguenots on my father's side. They came to America in the 1700s."

Matt: "Well, there's your problem. This is why you don't know anything about the game. The French can't play football. The helmet messes up their hair."

Sarah: "What about Canadian Football? Canada is French."

Matt: "I'm really disappointed in you, Sarah. Everyone knows Canadian Football is a myth like the Loch Ness Monster. People talk about it every now and then. Sometimes, they even show you a picture. But it's just a myth."

Sarah: "It is beautiful in here."

Like the turning of the leaves in New England, there was a three-week period in the year when the inside of the old barn was bathed in golden rays of light at evening. The conditions were perfect. The massive vault of the old ceiling, the numerous places for the light to enter, and the color of the ancient tin roof and the weathered wood made it quite a sight.

This was not a widely known phenomenon. If a barn was new or small or faced in the wrong direction, then the beauty may have gone unknown.

Matt: "This time of year, Doodle and I will sit down here till dark. I'm sure she'll be back soon. She hates to miss this."

As if on cue, Doodle appeared at the barn door having completed her mission.

Sarah: "I said that the barn reminded me of St. Peter's. But now I think St. Peter's would remind me of this barn. Do you and

51

Doodle sit alone?"

Matt: "Sometimes some of the chickens will be down here. Chickens don't have the ability to appreciate aesthetic beauty."

Sarah: "Why is that?"

Matt: "Doodle and I think it's because their heads are too small. Also, their eyes are on the sides of their heads. We tell them to look up, and they just see side to side. Doodle loses her patience with them."

Sarah: "I'm not a patient person. I lost my patience today with a man at the rest stop while driving up here with Willie."

Matt: "I'd love to hear about it."

Sarah: "We had crossed the Mississippi line, and Willie tells me he has to use the restroom. Being the benevolent person I am, I let him relieve himself at the Mississippi rest stop. Anyway, I get out of the car just to stretch my legs. Two men are looking at the car. One says, 'That's a mighty fine automobile.' The other says, 'I tell you what.' And I listen, and they don't say anything else. They just stand there. I get a little closer expecting to hear the what. But there is no what. Finally, I just can't take it anymore, and I walk over. As polite as I know how, I say, excuse me, but I couldn't help but over hear. You said, I tell you what, and then you didn't say anything. May I ask what the what is?"

"Do you know what he said to me? He said, 'What?' Well, that did it. He and I started to get into it pretty good. Willie grabbed my arm just before I—"

Matt: "Jerked a knot in him."

Sarah: "Yes, jerked a knot in him. . . . Is that what you and Willie were laughing about when we first got here?"

Matt: "Sarah, you know Willie told me not to tell."

There was a moment of silence as they rocked and took in God's handiwork as it filtered through the roof of the old barn.

Matt: "I'll tell you a secret that only Doodle knows. The lumber I use for the furniture is reclaimed from old schools, churches, stores, even the floor of boxcars. Now, that lumber was around certain sounds, for some almost a hundred years. The wood absorbed those sounds. You know dogs have enhanced hearin'. Oh, by the way, be careful. Doodle also reads lips. Anyway, Doodle told me that this time of year, when the barn looks like this, you can hear those sounds comin' out of the wood. If you listen very carefully, you can hear the sound of children playin', an old hymn, or a train. Try it, Sarah. Look up. See all the light and colors. Now listen. Do you hear the children playin'? Do you hear a choir singin' 'Amazing Grace'? Off in the distance, do you hear a train whistle?"

She put her head against the rocker and looked up. They sat in silence.

Sarah: "I do hear it."

Matt: "That's the reason when I make a piece of furniture, I don't mix the wood. I want it to have the same sound. I always put on the furniture where it came from. I don't think whoever buys it will take the time to listen, but if they have a dog, he'll hear it."

Sarah: "Will you make some furniture for our store?"

Matt: "You sound drunk."

Sarah: "I know. It happens to me sometimes."

Matt: "Why? You're not drinkin'."

Sarah: "I won't tell you."

Matt: "Well, if my uncle sees you, it'll be a night in jail. I had some issues. My uncle, the local sheriff, said he would put anybody in jail that sold or gave me liquor."

Sarah: "Is that what happened to your friend?"

Matt: "Yes."

Sarah: "But, Matt, I don't want to go to jail."

Matt: "Be a man, Sarah. It's just one night."

There was a reflective silence while Sarah considered her options and other questions.

Sarah: "Why do you live here, alone?"

Matt: "It does get lonely, sometimes, what with the banality of post-feminist society. But I have family and friends. There's always somethin' to do. The chickens are hilariously stupid and entertainin'. I have peace here. Someone once said, 'Peace I leave with you; my peace I give you.' Mine is here."

Sarah: "Do you have any idea what the banality of post-feminist society means?"

Matt: "No, not a clue, but Odell does. Let me ask you somethin'. What are you doin' here? What are you lookin' for?"

Sarah: "I want you to make furniture for our store."

Matt: "You want me to believe a wealthy actress has driven here from New Orleans on her time off, so I will make a few pieces of furniture for her."

Sarah: "Well then, why don't I just leave?"

Matt: "I have another idea. Why don't you and Willie stay for supper?"

Sarah: " . . . Will Scarlett be joining us?"

Matt: "No, not tonight."

Sarah: "Okay, . . . but I still don't want to go to jail."

Matt: "If my Uncle comes over, we'll hide you out by the compost pile. You should be safe there."

She immediately regretted agreeing to stay. The regrets were piling up. She could only assume that some strange force had taken over her body. She said yes, when she meant no. She stayed, when she meant to leave.

They continued to rock and absorb the beauty of the old barn.

Matt: "Sarah, one of your shoes is untied."

Matt rose from the rocker, walked over in front of her, kneeled down, and began to tie her shoe. Doodle walked over to observe and give the shoe strings a sniff as if this activity involved her. Sarah thought of herself as a queen with her attendants fussing over her every need.

Matt: "Let me know how tight you want it."

Sarah: "That's perfect, Matt."

Matt: "Once, I got one shoe much tighter than the other. I just walked in circles."

He reached over and rubbed Doodle's head.

Matt: "Doodle thought it was so funny. It was noon before I figured out what was causin' it."

Matt rose and looked down at Sarah in the rocker.

Matt: "Sarah, if you find yourself goin' in circles, check your shoestrings. You may just have one shoe too tight. To go anywhere, you need your shoestrings to be perfect."

Sarah: "I'll remember that, Matt. I'll remember that."

Matt: "We need to go back to the farmhouse so I can start supper."

The three left the barn with all its beauty and headed down the path. Matt was leading the parade with Doodle on his heals and Sarah bringing up the rear, once again observing the man and his dog. She spoke to Matt from the back of the parade.

Sarah: "Matt, how did you get that scar on your forehead?"

Matt: "We had a visiting preacher one Sunday, and he was going a little long. I went to sleep, fell out of the pew, and hit my head."

Sarah: "That's a lie."

The parade stopped as Matt and Doodle turned to look at Sarah. She returned the look. After a momentary standoff, the parade resumed.

Matt: "I walked into a limb on one of my pecan trees."

Sarah: "No."

Matt: "I fell off the roof of the barn."

Sarah: "No."

Matt: "I slipped on a bar of soap in the shower."

Sarah: "No."

Matt: "My tractor ran over me."

Sarah: "No."

Matt: "I tripped over Doodle gettin' out of the bed."

Sarah: "No."

Matt: "I fell off a bar stool in Lester's."

Sarah: "No."

Matt: "Lee Arthur's bull—"

Sarah: "No."

Matt: "Not to change the subject, you all right back there? You're not walkin' in circles, are you?"

Sarah: "I'm fine, Matt. I guess you are not going to tell me, are you?"

Matt: "Excuse me just a minute, Sarah. I need to deal with this dog. Doodle, you can't make the biscuits. No one wants dog hair in their biscuits, as funny as you may think that would be. You can peal some of the potatoes and help make the tea. Did you get the lemons?"

There was a moment of silence.

Matt: "Doodle, I take it by you your silence that you didn't. I told you that if you couldn't get everything on the list, I wasn't gonna let you go to the Piggly Wiggly by yourself anymore. . . . Don't you growl at me."

Matt squared off at Doodle as if he were guarding her in

basketball. Doodle spread her front legs and lowered her head with her ears back.

Matt: "This is why you didn't want to talk about the Piggly Wiggly, isn't it? You knew you were gonna get in trouble."

The stalemate was broken when Doodle raced for the farmhouse with Matt in pursuit.

Sarah was left standing in front of the chicken yard. Matt was right, you really couldn't tell where the chickens were looking. She did not want to visit the farm, but she did. She did not want to ride in the truck, but she did. She did not want to stay all afternoon, but she did. She did not want to stay for supper, but she was. She resumed her walk to the farmhouse. The cowboy was going to pay for this. She was just the woman to make him, or at least she once was, right now not so much.

Sarah arrived in the kitchen in time to hear Matt talking to Willie.

Matt: "Willie, y'all are stayin' for supper."

Willie: "Great, I never turn down a free meal."

Matt: "Good. Willie, I need you to do somethin' for me. Get in the car, go back to the main road, turn left, and drive about three miles. On the left you will see a gas station. Right behind the station is an old shack. Park behind the station and go in the shack. There should be someone in there."

Sarah: "Wait, are you sending him to buy drugs?"

Matt: "No, I'm sendin' him to get some pulled pork. Willie, tell them you want enough pork for two grown men and one emotionally stunted woman and to put it on my tab. If they question you, just say, tell Odell Matt says hey. You shouldn't have any problems after that."

Willie: "Anything else?"

Matt: "No. I've got the rest covered. We're havin' pulled pork; roasted new potatoes; butter beans, seasoned with parts of a pig that are illegal to eat in some states; buttermilk biscuits, for which I am known; copious amounts of sweet tea; and banana puddin' for dessert. Food prepared with love for the heart, the body, and the soul."

Willie: "That does sound good."

Sarah: "Well, Willie, the cowboy talks a big game. We'll see if he can deliver."

Sarah sat down at the kitchen table. In the middle was a vase full of Zinnias and on one end a Bible. What kind of single man kept a Bible and a vase of flowers on his kitchen table?

Sarah: "So you keep your Bible on the kitchen table."

Matt: "Yep. Where do you keep yours?"

Sarah: "I don't believe in God."

Matt: "Well, I'm pretty sure, He believes in you."

Sarah: "Do you read it everyday?"

Matt: "What?"

Sarah: "Your Bible. That book in the leather cover that has Matthew Ezra Shepherd in gold letters on it and is sitting right there. Do you read it everyday?"

Matt: "Yes. I usually get up around five-thirty, put the coffee on, and read the divinely inspired word of God before I go out and feed chickens."

Sarah: "Even when you were drinking?"

Matt: "Even when I was drinkin'. That's what the thing's about, redemption for sinners."

Sarah: "Are you a sinner?"

Matt: "This is a trustworthy sayin' and worthy of full acceptance. Jesus Christ came into the world to save sinners of whom I am the worst,' but enough about me."

With Matt focused on his cooking, Sarah was focused on Matt. She had done benefits with the New York Fire Department where firemen prepared a meal for celebrities. He reminded her of the way the firemen moved about a kitchen.

Matt: "You call me a cowboy. I don't wear cowboy boots or a cowboy hat. I don't drink anymore so I don't have cows, and I don't have a horse."

Sarah: "So sinner is fine, but you draw the line at cowboy. You don't like it when I call you cowboy, so cowboy it is."

Matt paused in his food preparation and looked at Sarah. What followed was Sarah's first attempt at her Matt voice. She was a professional actress.

Sarah: "[Matt voice] You know a girl can derive a lot of satisfaction from pressin' your buttons."

Sarah knew she could wield her tongue as efficiently as a surgeon wields a scalpel. The concern of a true surgeon was the health and welfare of the patient. That was not her concern. Matt was a different kind of patient. He was either numb on the inside or had a very high threshold for pain. Clearly, more surgery was required.

Sarah: "Matt, tell me why everyone down here is so polite. It's always, yes ma'am, no ma'am, let me help you, bless your heart, how's your mama. Makes me want to puke."

Matt: "We all have guns. When your neighbors are armed to the teeth, you learn to be polite."

Sarah: "It makes sense now."

Matt: "Speakin' of polite, do you want somethin' to drink while we wait on Willie and the pulled pork?"

Sarah: "I'd like a scotch on the rocks, but I don't think I'm going to get it."

Matt: "If there was scotch in this house, then somebody would've spent a night in jail. I do have refreshments that don't involve incarceration. We have water, milk, orange juice, sweet tea, with lemon and without. I can even fix you a pot of coffee with chicory."

Sarah: "I'll take a sweet tea with lemon. And someday you will have to explain to me about this whole sweet tea thing."

Matt: "Sweet tea is the house wine of the South. Nothin' offends a Southerner more than to be served tea and told they have to stir little packages of sugar. It's uncivilized, vulgar, and rude."

"Besides, havin' someone sweeten the tea for everyone gives us all a chance to practice Christian charity. If they don't do it to suit, you drink it anyway and are polite about it. Demandin' your tea a certain way is contrary to the Gospel. Any more questions?"

Sarah: "And to think, I didn't have to show my passport to come here today."

Sarah rose from the kitchen chair, took the tea, and walked into the front parlor. Along one wall was a bookshelf that she assumed Matt had made. The number of books and the variety of subjects surprised her. One appeared to be a college textbook, *Applied Statics and Strength of Materials*. How dreadful.

Sarah: "What kind of books do you like to read?"

Matt spoke to Sarah from the kitchen as he continued preparing supper.

Matt: "Mostly history. I read anything I can get my hands on about Stonewall Jackson. His campaign in the Shenandoah Valley was somethin', always outnumbered and always underestimated. The Union Generals didn't know whether to scratch their watches or wind their butts. Once he—"

Sarah: "That's nice, Matt. Anything else?"

Matt: "Well, I don't read fiction. Why read about it if it didn't happen? That's what I always say."

At the moment he was proclaiming the shortcomings of fiction, she was looking at a complete collection of the works of William Faulkner and Eudora Welty.

Sarah: "Well, what's all this Faulkner and Welty doing in here?"

Matt: "That's not fiction."

# A Day In The Country

Sarah: "Pardon me."

Matt: "That's the truth."

Sarah: "But it didn't happen."

Matt: "I think I see your problem. Suppose Faulkner lived his whole life in Connecticut. I agree this is a trick question because he probably would have committed suicide before he could write anything. But assumin' he didn't kill himself, would he have written *The Sound and The Fury*, . . . Sarah?"

Sarah: "I'm not participating, so it doesn't count."

Matt: "No, he wouldn't have. Which means somethin' happened in Miss'sippi to cause him to write; therefore, somethin' happened which means it's not fiction. It's the truth. If you don't agree with me, ask Doodle. She's in there."

Sarah: "Don't be silly."

Matt: "Okay, let's have a contest. You start namin' all the famous authors from Connecticut, and I'll name the ones from Miss'sippi. Whoever shuts up first, loses."

Sarah: "That's not fair. You talk too slow. You can make Faulkner an eight-syllable word. Good thing the North won the Battle of Gettysburg. If the South won, Jefferson Davis would still be giving the Gettysburg Address. I bet he talked even slower than you if that's possible."

As Sarah walked around the parlor, she saw framed photographs in various means of display. Doodle followed her as if the dog instinctively knew this woman may have food—she once smelled of bacon.

Sarah: "Let's play the picture game. I'll get a picture, bring it into the kitchen, and you will tell me all about it. But first, I'll try to guess who it is and the story."

Matt: "Why in the world would a sane man want to play that game with you?"

Sarah: "There are no sane men in a post-feminist society. I would have thought Odell had explained that."

Sarah returned from the parlor with her first selection. Doodle did likewise, only without a picture.

Sarah: "Mother and father standing in front of a house that I don't recognize."

Matt: "Yes, my mother was a Pruitt. Her younger brother's the Sheriff. She died of cancer when I was fifteen. My father was the farmer, and his brother was the carpenter. My family built that house in the picture. I grew up in that house. My father died in a farming accident my sophomore year of college. Lightening struck the house, and it burned to the ground. That house sat about where Tara, the chicken coop's, located."

Sarah: "See, you are good at this, all that from one picture. Sorry about your parents. Mine are very much still with us."

Sarah returned with a picture of a much younger Matt standing next to a slightly older girl.

Sarah: "Picture of you and an older sister. Considering the religious rituals of your tribe, I'd say the two of you are dressed for church. Since you go to church every Sunday, what makes this one special enough for a picture? I know, it's an Easter Sunday. Wait, considering your considerable charm, it could be you are dressed for a dance, and your sister is the only one that would go with you. Which one is it?"

Matt: "Both. My sister's name is Ruth. She's married to John Anderson. He's an emergency room doc at the hospital. They have two daughters. My sister's very protective of me. With a strange car in front of the house, I figured she'd make me a chocolate pie as an excuse to come over here and meet the stranger. In all honesty, Sarah, the only reason I agreed for y'all to come up here today was so I could get a chocolate pie out of the deal."

Sarah: "All that information and honesty from just one picture. And just think, cowboy, the game has only started."

Sarah returned to the parlor and retrieved another picture with Doodle as her shadow.

# A Day In The Country

Sarah: "I'd say girlfriend holding your hand in a park."

Matt: "That's Olivia Nelson. We were engaged. She's a Smith now. Married a banker and lives in Texas. They have two kids. The park's the Grove at Ole Miss. We had just gotten engaged when that picture was taken."

Olivia was a brunette with big dark eyes and a big smile.

Sarah: "What happened?"

Matt: "Nine-eleven, I don't blame her. The whole war on terror was too much reality for her. She was a sweet girl and a fine person. I lost a fiancée. Some of my friends lost a limb or a life. Don't see the point of poor me. She broke the news to me in a letter durin' my last tour. She asked me to forgive her for not havin' the courage to tell me in person."

Sarah had sympathy for Olivia. This cowboy was a load. But why would he display her picture? All pictures of her ex have been disposed of by LA County Public Works. The cowboy must have closure issues.

Sarah: "If it helps, I have an ex. I've been on that expressway. Let me go get another picture so we can put Olivia Smith behind us."

Sarah and Doodle made another pilgrimage to the parlor.

Sarah: "Let's see. A picture of you and your little soldier friends standing in front of a Humvee with your little guns. Everyone is smiling, and I think I see vapors of testosterone in the air."

Matt: "Those aren't soldiers. They are Marines. That picture was taken just before the Second Battle of Fallujah. And yes, I'm a testosterone donor. Some men got it. Some men need it. All you get is one more picture. After that I need you to do somethin' for me."

Sarah: "Fine, one more picture."

There were several pictures of smiling groups of Marines. Matt was in some and not in others. But one picture was different. It was a picture of a single Marine. He had a big smile on his face as if that was the norm and not the exception. He was younger than most of the others. She returned with that picture. By instinct, she thought better of guessing the circumstances surrounding the young Marine.

Sarah: "What's the story behind this one?"

Matt's hands were covered in flour. He stopped pinching off biscuit dough and looked straight into her eyes.

Matt: "Sarah, the game's over. Take the picture and put it back in the parlor, exactly as you found it. It's not your fault. I should have said somethin' when the game started. Please, for once in your life, just do as someone asks."

Sarah did two things she very seldom did, if ever. She did as she was told without saying a word.

Matt: "Sarah, are we friends?"

She knew what had just happened. The picture incident had just given him a competitive advantage, and he had taken it.

Sarah: "I don't have friends. But since you are making me supper, I'll make an exception in your case, a temporary exception. So, yes we are . . . temporary friends."

Matt: "Even in a post-feminist society, a simple yes would have been fine. Friends do things for one another and help each other out, right?"

Sarah loathed the answer.

Sarah: "Yes, temporarily."

Matt: "Good. I'm glad we both see it that way, temporarily. Looks like rain. My clothes are still out on the line, and I'm busy with your supper. It would be a great help to me if you would get my clothes in before the rain starts. The basket is on the back porch. Doodle should be able to answer any of your questions. Tomorrow is Sunday. I could go to church commando, but the deacons have asked me not to do that anymore."

Sarah: "Would you like me to iron anything?"

Matt: "Maybe next time. However, it would be great if you could fold my stuff. Are you familiar with the Navy way of foldin' clothes?"

Sarah: "No, but I'm familiar with the Sarah way. The help does it."

She headed to the back porch to get the basket with Doodle. As she approached the clothesline, the wind began to pick-up with dark clouds moving in. She had a feeling of foreboding as she stood on the farm's higher elevation and looked at the sky. Somehow, storms in the city could come and go almost without being noticed, not so out here.

Just as Matt had said, she saw the chickens were congregating inside the wire at Tara. They may be hilariously stupid, but even they seemed to sense something was coming. She wondered which one was poor Scarlett.

Sarah: "Run, Scarlett, run. Make a break for it."

None of the chickens responded. The wind made gathering the clothes more difficult. As she reached for one boxer short, the one next to it would hit her in the face. Good thing they were in Nowhere, Mississippi. If someone had a picture of Sarah DuMont wrestling a Marine's underwear in the wind, it would be all over the tabloids. How would she explain it to Lorraine? Lucy would be insufferable. Bringing in his laundry was not exactly making him pay for the dinner invitation. Doodle sat near by and watched the laundry retrieval.

Sarah: "You are the smartest dog in the world, but you can't help me with the cowboy's clothes. I ask you Doodle, which one of us is the dumb animal? I'm standing out here talking to chickens and a dog. Yet, somehow it seems like a reasonable thing to do. I hate that cowboy."

Sarah removed a t-shirt from the line and held it in her hands. Concealed from view by the waving laundry, she pressed the shirt to her face. Mingled with the smell of fresh laundry was the scent of the cowboy. The scent made her blush. How dare him! She again pressed the shirt to her face and inhaled deeply.

Willie returned from his pork mission just in time to see Sarah doing her clothesline dance. When the wind blew, Sarah would momentarily disappear behind a curtain of white, blue, and plaid.

Willie entered the farmhouse with the pulled pork safely tucked away in two plastic grocery bags, one with a Styrofoam plate with a lid that contained the pork and the other full of little plastic containers of barbecue sauce, some sweet and some hot.

Willie: "Looks like a storm's comin'. Man, it smells good in here. I could smell the biscuits on the front porch. How'd you get that woman to bring in your laundry? I didn't think she knew how a clothes pen worked."

Matt: "She doesn't. She's gonna talk the clothes into the basket. Those clothes don't stand a chance."

Willie: "Preach it, brother. Sorry I took so long. The place was filled with folk. Somehow, they all knew I had been at your house all afternoon. They asked me a bunch of questions. But I didn't tell them anything. I'm not supposed to talk about the folk I drive around. They didn't get anything out of me."

Matt: "Willie, I can tell you are a man of discretion. Besides, if you were tellin' them about Sarah, you'd still be there."

Willie: "I aught to write me a book, but I'm scared of her."

Matt: "Me too, Willie."

Matt set the table, and then the two men stood at the kitchen window watching Sarah returning to the house with the basket. Doodle was following, and Sarah appeared to be talking to herself.

Matt: "Willie, when you got up this mornin', did you ever think you'd be watchin' Sarah Dumont bringin' in the laundry for a broke down Marine while she's talkin' to herself?"

Willie: "No, but it's about the funniest thing I ever saw."

Matt: "That's kinda ironic considering neither one of us is laughin'."

Willie: "Uh-huh. . . . I wonder what she's sayin'."

Matt: "By the expression on Doodle's face, it ain't good."

A Day In The Country

Willie: "My uncle had a dog like that once."

Matt: "I suspect Doodle's learnin' some new words."

Willie: "I bet that woman could make a sailor blush."

Matt: "Uh-huh."

Just as Sarah reached the back porch, the rain began to fall.

Matt: "Much obliged, Sarah. Leave the basket in the pantry. Supper is ready. You can wash your hands at the kitchen sink."

Through the window at the sink, Sarah watched the distant flashes of lightening and the dark clouds moving in, covering an orange sky. She vividly recalled the clean, fresh smell of the laundry; the cool, damp wind on her face; and the fertile smell of the approaching rain. Even now, the warmth of the kitchen, the aroma of the food, and the sound of the rain on the tin roof were intense. Had the approaching storm heightened her senses? Had Matt put something in her sweet tea? Was this life on a farm? Regardless, it was surprising and wonderful.

Matt: "Sarah. . . . Sarah."

Sarah: "Yes, sorry, I was thinking about work."

Matt: "You sit here in the place of honor. Willie, you sit there, and I'll sit over here by the sink. All the food is on the table, family style, so just help yourself."

Sarah noticed as Doodle quietly took her place on her bed in the corner of the kitchen, in the knowledge that Matt would feed her in her turn.

The bowls with butter beans and roasted new potatoes, the platter with the pulled pork, and the basket of buttermilk biscuits were all passed around the table. Even Sarah cooperated.

Before she could take her first bite, she saw Matt reach out a hand to Willie and her. Willie seemed to immediately understand and took Matt's hand, extending a hand to Sarah. At that moment, both men looked at her. Apparently, down here you hold hands before you eat. Sarah took hold of each, completing the circle. Matt and

Willie closed their eyes and bowed their heads. Sarah's head tilted forward ever so slightly, but her eyes remained open. She did not want to appear too religious. After all, she was an atheist.

Matt: "Dear Heavenly Father, thank you for this food we are about to eat. May it nourish our bodies for your purposes. We thank you for friends and simple pleasures. We ask for travelin' mercies for Sarah and Willie as they return home later tonight. We ask these things in the name of Jesus. Amen."

Willie: "Amen. I got both the sweet sauce and the hot sauce for the pork. The lady said the hot sauce was really hot today, so be careful which one you use. I tell you what. You get a little of this sweet sauce on the biscuit, and it makes a meal all by itself. My wife can't make biscuits. Bless her heart. She tries, and I eat'm, but they're barely fit to eat. But these biscuits are fine."

Matt: "Some folks roll'm out and cut the dough. I never roll mine. Just pinch'm off. I'll write down what I do for your wife."

Willie: "Much obliged. She does need help with her biscuits."

Sarah watched Matt and Willie for a moment. What was it about men and food?

Matt: "Sorry I don't have any sliced, fresh tomatoes on the table. Just not time for them yet. I usually have a bumper crop of Better Boy tomatoes each year. I think it's the fertilizer I use. I have all that sawdust from the barn, so I compost it with chicken manure I get from chicken houses. You can't sling a dead cat by the tail around here without hittin' a chicken house."

A noise came from Sarah's side of the table. Willie was pointing to his own nose.

Willie: "Ms. Sarah, you have a little sweet tea comin' out your nose."

Sarah took her paper towel and wiped her upper lip.

Sarah: "You know western civilization has given us the plays and sonnets of William Shakespeare, Dante's *Divine Comedy*, Milton's *Paradise Lost,* and Austen's *Pride and Prejudice*. And with one phrase, you managed to have all those individuals turn over in their graves.

Well done, Matt. Well done."

Matt: "William Shakespeare wrote the King James Bible."

Sarah: "He did not!"

Matt: "Willie, back me up on this."

Willie: "I thought King James wrote it."

Matt: "So if I quote the King James Version of the Bible, I'm quotin' Shakespeare. 'Thy word is a lamp unto my feet and a light unto my path.' Your turn, Sarah. Quote some Shakespeare for Willie and me."

Sarah: "Oh, cowboy, thou art an ass."

Willie: "I don't think there were cowboys in Shakespeare's day."

Matt: "Willie's right. You lose. Now where was I, oh yea, chicken manure."

Willie: "Now that chicken manure is good stuff. It grew hair on my bald uncle's head."

Sarah: "Willie, now you know that's not true, and if you say it again, I'll insist that your employer fire you."

Matt: "I don't know, Sarah. Science doesn't have an answer for everything. They can't explain how a hummin' bird flies, how glass is formed, or why women need so many shoes. Willie may be on to somethin' with this natural remedy for baldness."

The rain continued during the meal, at times very hard. The sound of the rain on the tin roof was very comforting. The old farmhouse was saying things are bad out here, but you are safe inside. The sound of the rain, the smell of the food, and the security of the old farmhouse all caused Sarah to momentarily forget her regrets.

Willie: "Laugh at me if you want. But the man grew a full head of hair, divorced my aunt, and married a woman ten years younger."

Matt: "Wait a minute. I'm gettin' an idea."

Sarah: "Is it painful?"

Matt: "We could put chicken manure in some fancy bottles, and you could sell it in your store in La-La Land. Call it Willie and Matt's Hair Restorative. Put words like organic, homeopathic, glutton free, no GAO, and all natural on the label. I even have a slogan. Buy Willie and Matt's Hair Restorative; it's *willie* good."

Sarah: "I think I see where you are going with this. We could put your pictures on the label. I know I would pay good money for a bottle filled with chicken manure that had your picture on it."

Matt: "That a girl. Open your mind to new ideas."

For a few minutes the conversation waned as the eating and rain intensified. Sarah was glad for the relief from the conversation, amused by the eating, and grateful for the protection from the rain.

She let her eyes wonder around the kitchen. As she continued to eat, she thought about the men who had cooked for her many times before. But it seemed to always be some kind of fish, usually salmon, cooked in the most modern of kitchens. The food, the kitchen, and the men were nothing like this. She felt like an archeologist given a chance to dine with the last surviving Neanderthals. She wondered how she could work that into the conversation as she chased the last of the butter beans on her plate with the last bite of biscuit.

Matt: "Sarah, look at you. That plate is so clean, I won't have to wash it."

Sarah: "Don't tease me about my eating. Why are you smiling?"

Willie: "Ms. Sarah, you have some barbecue sauce in the corner."

Willie gestured to the corner of his mouth. Sarah used her paper towel and looked at Willie. He motioned to the other side of his face.

Willie: "It's on the other side, too."

Matt: "I scream; Sarah screams; we all scream for Matt's butter beans. And it looks like she even screams for Odell's pulled pork. I'll take the clean plate as a commentary on my cookin'."

Sarah: "As much as it pains me to say this, it was good."

Matt: "And you a vegetarian."

Sarah: "I'm beginning to believe vegetarians are just people who haven't tried pull pork yet, or your butter beans, for that matter."

Willie: "You mind if I take one of the biscuits home? I'd like to show that to my wife."

Matt: "Sure, Willie, now, who's ready for dessert? You know what we say down here, save your fork—the best is yet to come."

Sarah: "Yes, I'll have just a little. Might as well experience everything, but just a little. People actually care what I look like, you two not so much. Matt, I need to borrow your rest room."

Matt: "Sure, it's across the hall at the back of the house."

# Chapter Six

# Going Commando

Sarah was leaving the bathroom when her eyes focused on the medicine cabinet. She wondered what super drug for sexually transmitted diseases she might find in there. Certainly a lady could be forgiven for an honest curiosity. She opened the cabinet and saw only one prescription bottle for Zoloft. The date on the label indicated that the prescription had been filled years ago and was still mostly full. So that was it; he was bi-polar and off his meds.

As she closed the medicine cabinet, there was a loud clap of thunder followed by darkness. She was startled by the complete absence of light in the room. There was no light around the door; no tiny, blue glowing lights as seemed to populate all the rooms in her Malibu home; no streetlight through the bathroom window; no light of any kind.

Matt: "Everyone give me a minute. Let me get my flashlight. This happens out here sometimes durin' a storm."

Sarah: "Hurry, Matt. It's really dark in here."

Matt held his small LED flashlight, casting a narrow blue beam, and rescued Sarah from the bathroom. The rain was coming down even harder with occasional lightening and thunder.

Sarah: "Does it rain like this down here very often?"

Matt: "Often enough."

She followed behind Matt as they made their way through the dark house to the kitchen, finding Willie standing by the kitchen table.

Matt: "Y'all get your sweet teas and puddin', and let's go into the parlor. I've got a story I can tell you while we wait on this storm to pass. Once it passes, you can get in the road back to New Orleans."

Willie: "Ms. Sarah, I really do think we should let this pass. These old country roads are challengin' in the dark, even without all this rain."

Sarah: "Fine, but when the storm lets up, we need to go."

Willie and Sarah sat in two of Matt's rockers. Sarah took her shoes off, putting her feet on a small stool. Both had a glass of sweet tea, and Willie was still eating banana pudding. Matt lite an old hurricane lamp, giving a faint glow to the whole proceedings, and sat down in a straight back chair, with a woven cane bottom, opposite his two guests with Doodle nearby. Sarah noticed a blood stain on the floor at his feet, or perhaps, it was something else. The light was dim.

As Matt started his story, there was a bright flash of lightening followed by a clap of thunder, which made the farmhouse shudder from the pains of glass in the windows down to the heart pine floors. Sarah could even feel the vibration in her feet perched on the stool.

Matt gave a dramatic pause and began his story in a calm, practiced tone.

Matt: "Shadrach Shepherd was known to everyone as Shade. He loved Caroline McKnight, the daughter of the local minister. But Caroline McKnight loved Phillip Langston, the son of a wealthy planter from Natchez. Shade's love for Caroline only grew over time and was not dimmed by the marriage of Caroline and Phillip."

"Once, after the marriage, Caroline's father came to Shade, told him Phillip had been missin' for several weeks, and asked Shade to find him. Phillip was a man of low character, and Shade knew exactly where he was. He saddled two horses, rode one, and led the other."

"He found Phillip, passed out and broke in a brothel in New Orleans. He paid for a hotel room and after several days had Phillip sober and clean. Shade then took him back to Caroline."

"Phillip was a hot head. When the Civil War broke out, he volunteered immediately. Caroline came to this very house, stood in that hall, and told Shade that Phillip's temperament was goin' to get him killed. Shade told her that he'd volunteer along with Phillip and look after him. He promised Caroline that Phillip would come home to her."

"Both were excellent horseman and found themselves ridin' with Turner Ashby, in the 7th Virginia Calvary under Stonewall Jackson in the Shenandoah Valley. These were hard men who could live in the saddle."

"In 1862, they were in search of a Union Army. Jackson needed them to make contact with that army, attackin' them with the purpose of slowin' their movement while he unleashed his fury on another Union Army that had fallen into his trap."

"Turner's men had been ridin' hard for several days when they first made contact with the rear of the lumberin' Union Army, at about three o'clock in the afternoon. Ashby could be as rash as Phillip, and he ordered an immediate attack. The fightin' only gained fury over time as the Union Army began to send men and cannon to the rear. At about five o'clock, the Union artillery began to boom from a nearby hill overlookin' the fight."

The timing of the weather could not have been more perfect for the telling of the story. As the battle in the story intensified, so did the weather.

Matt: "The Union cannons would roar!"

Matt slapped his hands together, and both Willie and Sarah jumped as thunder shock the old house.  Sarah had traveled all over the world with the experiences to go along with such travel, but she had never sat in the dark in an ancient farmhouse with her shoes off, listening to a gothic tale with all of nature seeming to participate.

Matt: "Ashby knew that if his men could just hang on until nightfall, then Jackson would have what he needed. Ashby's men could ride off in the cover of darkness. The Union Army would take two days to resume their movement, and by then, it would be too late. Mercifully for the Confederates, darkness finally came with the battle a stalemate."

"Shade had survived and lay in the tall grass waitin' for the orders to ride off in the darkness. That's when he heard a moan comin' from the battlefield followed by Caroline, Caroline. He knew it was Phillip."

"Shade, with water and bandages, crawled on his belly lookin' for Phillip. When he finally found him, he saw that Phillip had a terrible leg wound. He used the bandages, as best he knew how, and gave Phillip the water. Phillip was wounded too badly to drag back to safety, so Shade stayed with him that night, knowin' that by daylight the Confederate Cavalry would be gone."

"They were both taken prisoner the next mornin' and sent to a camp on Belle Isle in the James River. Surgeons immediately removed Phillip's left leg and promptly forgot about him. Conditions in the camp were dreadful. Shade nursed Phillip daily, givin' him a major potion of Shade's own meager rations. As time went own, Shade grew weaker, and Phillip grew stronger. Finally, Shade died from a camp fever, and his body was thrown into a mass grave. Three days later, Phillip was paroled home, spendin' the rest of the war on what was left of his father's plantation."

"Two years after the war, Phillip was killed in a card game in New Orleans. Then Caroline said publicly she had married the wrong man. A headstone was prepared for Shade at her request and placed in the church cemetery even though Shade wasn't buried there. She would visit the grave everyday for the rest of her life. When she died, she was buried next to Shade's gravestone, having never remarried or born any children."

Matt lowered his voice to barely above a whisper. Both Willie and Sarah leaned forward to hear him.

Matt: "On nights like this, when the thunder rolls like that Union cannon, some have seen Shade in the hallway of this house lookin' for Caroline at the last place he ever saw her alive."

There was silence. The rain and lightning had begun to subside. The only light was the faint glow from the hurricane lamp. Just beyond the glow was total darkness. After a dramatic pause, Matt spoke in his normal voice.

Matt: "Looks like the storm's passin'."

Both Willie and Sarah jumped.

Matt: "Sometimes when the lights go out like this, it trips the main breaker. Let me go check and see if we can get the lights back on."

Willie and Sarah sat silently and could see the beam of Matt's LED light from the back of the house as he went to check on the breaker.

At the edge of the darkness, Sarah saw a figure pass quickly by the door that lead from the parlor to the hallway. It was only for a moment and was barely visible.

Sarah: "Willie, did you see that! At the doorway in the hall, did you see that?"

Willie: "Yes I did!"

Sarah: "Matt, we saw a man in an old cap with a beard pass by the doorway."

Matt replied from the back of the house.

Matt: "What? I can't hear you."

At that moment, the lights came on. Matt returned to the parlor, walking through the kitchen. Both Sarah and Willie were pointing at the parlor door that lead to the great hallway.

Sarah: "Right there in the doorway, just for a moment, we saw a man with a cap and a gray beard. It was just for a moment."

Matt: "Let me see."

Matt walked across the parlor to the doorway, wearing a Civil War forage cap, a gray beard, and an old gray coat.

Willie: "I knew it was you all along, but it still scared me pretty good."

Sarah: "That's a mean thing to do. . . . But it was fun."

As he walked across the parlor, Sarah tossed her shoes at him.

Matt: "I had to do it twice for Ruth's two girls and some of their friends one night."

Sarah: "So you like scaring little girls?"

Matt: "Who doesn't? But what I really like is scarin' big ones."

Sarah: "Then put my shoes back on. You already know how I like them."

Willie: "You need us to help with the dishes?"

Matt: "Willie, Doodle and I will clean up. Y'all need to get in the road."

Willie: "Let me use the restroom, and we'll get Ms. DuMont back to St. Charles Avenue."

Sarah: "I need to call Lucy, my partner, and I can't get a signal."

Matt: "Sometimes that happens. The rain has stopped. Just go to the path and walk to the barn. You should get a signal. A light comes on at the barn about this time. Stay on the path and walk toward the light. It's mostly gravel so the path won't be muddy."

Sarah: "Tell Willie we'll leave as soon as I make this phone call."

Matt: "Let this be your first Sunday School lesson. Use the lamp, stay on the path, and walk toward the light."

Matt held up the flashlight for her. As she took hold of the light, Matt tightened his grip, tilted his head slightly, and raised his eyebrows.

Sarah: "Use the lamp, stay on the path, and walk to the light."

Sarah started to say something else, and Matt put his finger across her lips.

Matt: "Down here, we don't say ugly things about our Sunday School teacher."

Sarah: "I was going to say thank you, but not now."

Matt: "One more thing, when you go by Tara, please close the gate to the chicken yard."

Sarah did as Matt instructed. She stayed on the path closing the gate to the chicken yard, a day and night of many firsts for her. She headed to the barn, and as he said, she had a signal. Standing next to the large barn under the light, she called Lucy.

Sarah: "Lucy, it's Sarah. I've talked with our cowboy. He's agreed to ship us some furniture. . . . Well, I actually won a wager, and you should be getting the equivalent of a pick-up truckload in the next couple of weeks. . . . A woman bet me that this cowboy wouldn't give me the time of day. . . . I'm Sarah DuMont. What do you think? I've got to go. Headed back to New Orleans. I'll call you again as soon as my schedule allows."

She turned and headed down the path. It was cloudy, so there were no moon or stars visible. The only lights were at the barn and the farmhouse. She was walking deep in thought about the production schedule for next week and began to mock Matt.

Sarah: "Use the lamp, stay on the path, walk to the light—what an idiot."

Suddenly, out of the corner of her eye, she thought she saw Shade. She looked, no Shade.

Sarah: "Matt, this is not funny."

She looked toward the house and could see Matt silhouetted in the parlor window. As she looked to the path in front of her, the beam from the flashlight was reflected in the eyes of three raccoons, six fluorescent orbs of pure evil. Sarah ran and not toward the house or barn.

Willie and Matt were sitting in the parlor, discussing Saints football and waiting for Sarah.

Matt: "Sarah should be back by now. I hope she stayed on the path."

Willie: "Do you hear that? Sounds like a cat in heat."

Matt: "I don't have a cat, but I do hear somethin'."

Doodle, who had been lying at Matt's feet, stood, walked to the front door, and stuck her nose up to the door frame.

Willie: "I think it's comin' from the front porch. Matt, you have a gun?"

Matt: "Yes, but I also have neighbors, and Sarah's out there, well neighbors anyway."

Willie watched as Matt walked to the front door, switched on the porch light, and opened the door. He stood there, motionless.

Matt: "Oh, it's just Sarah."

He closed the door, switched off the porch light, and returned to his chair. Willie sat on the edge of his chair and watched Matt expectantly.

Sarah: "Matt Shepherd, you come out here right now and help me. I need you, Matt."

Matt stood and headed to the door a second time.

Matt: "Willie, prepare yourself. You ain't seen anything like this before."

He turned on the porch light again, and the two walked out to look at Sarah. Matt circled her at a safe distance, inspecting her as if she were a milk cow at auction.

Willie: "What have you done?"

Sarah: "I fell into a mud pile."

Willie sniffed the aura around her.

Willie: "I don't think that's mud."

Matt: "Looks like you failed Sunday School and found the compost pile. You are a walkin' sermon illustration. But I'm guessin' that's not what you intended. Where's my flashlight? You didn't lose it, did ya?"

Sarah: "No, Matt, I still have it."

Sarah was covered in chicken manure from the hair above her forehead to the toes of her athletic shoes and all the expensive real estate between. The manure had a remarkable adhesive quality.

Sarah: "It even got in my mouth. Will it kill me?"

Matt: "Perhaps. But more than likely you'll just crow at sunrise. The only thing I know to do is take her to the side of the house and hose her off."

Matt gingerly took the flashlight from her.

Matt: "Willie, you operate the hose, and I'll shine the flashlight on her."

The three went to the side of the house. Matt gave Willie the hose and turned on the water.

Sarah: "Oh, Willie, the water is cold!"

Willie: "I'm sorry, Ms. Sarah. Nothin' I can do about that."

Matt: "Man up, Sarah. It's in her hair and ears. Sarah, how did you get it in your ears?"

Sarah: "I don't know."

Matt: "You finally have what you wanted. The spotlight is on you. You're the center of attention."

Sarah: "How can you say that? I didn't do this on purpose. Sometimes you can be so mean to me."

Matt: "Sometimes chickens can be so mean to you. I didn't have anything to do with this."

Matt directed the light as Willie directed the hose.

Matt: "Sarah, raise your arms up above your head so Willie can get under there. Did you try to swim in it?"

Sarah: "Please don't make fun of me."

Willie: "Bless your heart, Ms. Sarah."

Matt: "If Willie and I had a camera right now, we'd never have to work another day in our lives. We'd be millionaires, Sarah DuMont with chicken manure all over her."

Matt laughed, and Sarah smiled, revealing white teeth peeking through black chicken manure.

Sarah: "I guess it is funny, not pleasant, but funny."

Matt: "We'll do the best we can for you with the hose. Then you take off what clothes you can subject to the rules of modesty, go to my bathroom, strip down, and get a shower. I'll get you somethin' to put your wet clothes in and find you somethin' to wear. One thing about it, the grass around your feet aught to be lovely this summer."

This was the second time today that Sarah did not say anything and did as she was told. She removed her shoes, athletic socks, sport jacket, and top while leaving her athletic bra and yoga paints. She went in the house to the bathroom, stripped, and entered the shower. Matt found the plastic bags Willie had been given to bring home the pork and sauce.

Matt: "Willie, I don't have any clothes that would fit that woman."

They both could hear the shower running.

Willie: "Don't look at me."

Matt: "I'll give Idella a call. They're about the same size, and she's near by. My sister lives in town, and that's thirty minutes away."

The water had stopped in the shower. They could hear Sarah shout from the back of the house.

Sarah: "Matt, have you found me some clothes? . . . Oh by the way, I really like what you've done with the bathroom. I like the way it matches the kitchen, the tile, and fixtures."

Matt: "Thanks. Doodle wanted me to use another tile in there. But you can't follow her decorating advice; she's color blind."

Matt dialed Lee Arthur's number and walked to the bathroom, standing outside the closed door.

Matt: "Sarah, I'm callin' someone now. Lee Arthur, this is Matt."

Sarah: "Why do you get to talk in the house, and I had to go to the barn?"

Matt: "Hush, woman! No, I'm not talkin' to you, Lee Arthur. I've a naked movie star in my bathroom, and I've got to get this woman some clothes so she'll leave. Let me talk to Idella."

Matt covered the phone with his hand.

Matt: "Sarah, Lee Arthur's tellin' Idella that it's me, and that I have a naked movie star in my bathroom. Just want to keep you apprised of the situation."

Sarah: "Thank you, Matt. I wouldn't want you to miss the opportunity of a good laugh at my expense."

Matt: "Hey, Idella. . . . Oh she's fine. . . . Yes, and both the children are doin' well. The oldest one's doin' a solo with the choir. . . . She does have a lovely voice. How's your mama? . . . Well, glad to hear that. . . . Yes, I will continue to pray for her."

Sarah: "Matt, please get me some clothes."

Matt: "Idella, I've a temporary friend about your size that ran and jumped in the manure pile. . . . You would think. Well, she's a Yankee. . . . Sarah, Idella says bless your heart. We just need some clothes to get her back to New Orleans. Nothin' fancy at all. She lives a very simple life. . . . That aught to do the trick. . . . No, she won't need any underwear. Thanks, Idella. I'll leave the porch light on."

Sarah: "Matt, did you get me some clothes?"

Matt: "Yes, I did."

Sarah: "Thank you."

Matt: "Don't thank me. Thank Idella. She and Lee Arthur should be here soon."

Willie and Matt went to the kitchen table, sat down, and started on additional helpings of banana pudding. Doodle went to her bed in the corner.

Willie: "I feel guilty eatin' all your banana puddin'."

Matt: "Trust me, Willie. There's plenty more where that came from."

Sarah: "Matt—"

Matt: "Sarah, if you insist on talkin', Willie and I will need to move into the hallway so we can hear you."

Matt stood and gathered his banana pudding and kitchen chair.

Matt: "Come on, Willie. This could be real entertainin'."

They moved to the hallway near the bathroom door and resumed eating their pudding.

Matt: "Okay, we want to hear this. You may need to holler."

Sarah: "Why did you tell her that I ran and jumped in the manure pile? That's not how it happened. She is going to think I'm an idiot."

Matt: "Idella's a fine Christian woman. She's not gonna judge you over this."

Matt winked at Willie.

Sarah: "There were big squirrels in the path. They were wearing masks. That's what made me run into the mud pile."

Matt: "They weren't squirrels. They were raccoons."

Sarah: "I hate squirrels. They have those beady little eyes, those sharp little teeth. You never know which way they are going to go. You try to run away from them, and first thing you know, they are running at you, then away from you, then with you. I hate them."

Matt: "And that wasn't mud. It was chicken manure. You know, Sarah, Jesus used mud to heal the eyes of a blind man. Maybe he needs somethin' a little more potent for you."

Sarah: "I don't think Jesus had anything to do with this."

Matt: "The Lord works in mysterious ways, certainly a lesson in stayin' on the narrow way."

Sarah: "That Sunday School thing again, well, I'm glad both of you were here to help me."

Matt: "You sound pleasant. Do you have liquor in there?"

Sarah: "No, I wish I did."

Matt: "What, have liquor or sound pleasant?"

Sarah: "Both."

Matt: "Talkin' to us while naked has made you much more pleasant, Sarah. Why don't I build you a box with wheels on it? You could get naked, get in the box, and your staff could roll you into all those fancy parties you go to. You could talk to everyone through the door. You'd be pleasant and not have to get drunk."

Sarah: "Matt, that's mean, . . . but funny. Oh, I know! My father's country club has an annual costume ball to raise money for poor kids, obese kids, hungry kids, mean kids. I forget which. Anyway, I could go as an outhouse. Matt, you could push me around. But you'd need a costume, too."

Matt: "I could go as a corn cob. Would the outhouse have a wood or porcelain seat?"

Sarah: "I would think porcelain. Willie, what do you think?"

Willie looked at Matt and spoke through a mouth full of banana pudding.

Willie: "I think you two are crazy. Y'all can talk longer about nothin'—"

Matt: "He says porcelain."

Sarah: "I'm going to open the door a little so I can hear better. But this is not a peep show."

Matt: "Your virginity is safe in this house."

Sarah: "Matt, . . . I'm not a virgin."

Matt: "Well, that's all water under the bridge now. You know what the Apostle Paul says, 'Forgetting those things which are behind me, I press on to take hold of that for which Christ Jesus first took hold of me.'"

Sarah: "Is that from the Bible?"

Matt: "Yes."

Sarah: "I don't think you are supposed to talk about the Bible, or God, when you're naked."

Matt: "God made you. He knows what you look like naked."

Willie: "That doesn't mean he wants to see it. I agree with Ms. Sarah. You ought to have your clothes on when you talk about God. The angels aren't naked."

Matt: "You two are both wrong. Haven't y'all seen all that naked religious art in Europe? Y'all's theology would come as a surprise to Michelangelo. Besides, the Bible says David, pretty much, danced naked before God."

Sarah: "I had a friend named David that did that once."

Matt: "What, dance naked before God?"

Sarah: "No, just dance naked."

Willie: "Then why don't we ever go to church naked? Explain that to me."

Matt: "Y'all are proving my point. We wear clothes to church because of people like you and Sarah. You care, but God doesn't."

Sarah: "I don't go to church, naked or otherwise."

Matt: "See, Willie, Sarah doesn't have a say in this cause she's a heathen."

Sarah: "Are you sure there is no liquor in this house?"

Matt: "None. I've quit."

Sarah: "Because you are a boozer, I can't have a drink when I need one. Matt, ... I'm sorry. I didn't mean that. I think what you are doing is real brave. I just wish you were starting tomorrow. What kind of clothes is your lady friend bringing me?"

Matt: "Her name is Idella, and you are gonna be nice to her. Practice it with me, thank . . . you . . . Idella. She played basketball in high school, and she's bringing you some old gym clothes."

Sarah: "Oh, Matt, I don't want to wear someone's old gym clothes."

Matt: "The real question is why Idella would let you have any of her clothes. Besides, you are in no position to complain. Exactly what position are you in?"

Sarah: "I'm sitting on the toilet. I put the top down."

Matt: "I know your mama would be proud."

Sarah: " . . . You are not going to tell her, are you?"

Matt: "Only if I ever get the chance."

Headlights from a pick-up truck signaled the arrival of the anticipated clothes.

Matt: "Your clothes are here. Just think, Sarah, you came to Miss'sippi this mornin' all prim, proper, and rich. You're leavin' tonight in borrowed clothes with no underwear. If you stay much longer, I'll be forced to shoot you to put you out of your misery. . . . I don't even think you are a practicin' vegetarian anymore."

Sarah thought, this man can cook, keep house, carry on a conversation, and is easy on the eyes. If Mrs. Fontenot's friends knew all this, he would need an armed escort to get out of New Orleans. Something must be wrong. He is either gay, or there are old girlfriends buried all over this farm. Glad Willie is here. Without him, I would be dead by now. None of this is my concern. Lucy will deal with him on the business end, and Mrs. Fontenot's pals can deal with the mass murderer. I will be Sarah Morgan Leigh DuMont very soon; just as soon as I am no longer naked in a mass murderer's bathroom. Though, it is a nice bathroom.

Idella and Lee Arthur made their way into the house.

Matt: "I really appreciate y'all doin' this. Idella, Lee Arthur, this is Willie Roberts."

Greetings were exchanged.

Idella: "Am I gonna get the chance to meet this person?"

Matt: "That depends on you. If you can keep a secret and not tell my sister, then the answer's yes, otherwise no. This naked woman in my bathroom doesn't need my sister's attention. She just needs some clothes."

Idella: "Ruth won't hear it from me. Now, who is it?"

Matt: "Sarah DuMont."

Idella: "You are kiddin'?"

Matt: "Willie can verify."

Willie: "I guess since you're bringin' her clothes, I can verify. That's Sarah DuMont back there."

Lee Arthur: "I don't know the woman."

Idella: "That blonde headed woman in the movie we saw the other night that you kept goin' on and on about."

Lee Arthur: "Excuse me while I sit down."

Matt: "Idella, she's in the bathroom. Just go on back. But Ruth doesn't hear it from you. I'm countin' on you. Knowin' Ruth, she'll know soon enough."

Idella proceeded to the back of the house and paused at the closed door of the bathroom, giving the door a soft knock.

Idella: "Ms. DuMont, I have you some clothes."

Sarah cracked the door and extended a hand. Since there were only a sweat top and gym shorts, dressing did not take long. Sarah opened the door and was relieved to finally have clothes, even old gym clothes.

Sarah: "You must be Idella. I'm Sarah. Thank you so much for doing this."

Idella: "You are very welcome."

Sarah: "Well, how do I look?"

Idella: "I declare, Ms. DuMont, you could stop a Mardi Gras parade wearin' those old clothes."

Sarah: "You are just being kind. Thank you."

As Sarah moved from the bathroom, Idella gently took hold of her hand.

Idella: "Ms. DuMont, your relationship with Matt is none of my business."

Sarah: "Matt and I just have a business relationship. We will sell some of his furniture in our store."

Idella did not let go of Sarah's hand.

Idella: "Matt's very special to the folks around here. He's mostly grown man with a little boy thrown in. The grown man part had to do some hard things. The little boy in him is havin' trouble with some of those things. We look out for him. I just want you to know how special he is to us, and how much we care for him."

Idella let go of Sarah's hand, turned, and walked to the parlor without further comment. Sarah watched her walk away.

Willie led the way to the car, carrying Sarah's new luggage, two plastic bags full of designer clothes with some material amount of chicken manure. These would definitely go in the trunk of the car. Sarah met Lee Arthur, but he was unable to speak.

Matt and Doodle stood on the front porch. Sarah was facing him with her back to Willie. Her hair was toweled dried, and all her make-up was gone. She wore an old gray sweat top with "MACON ANTHERS BALLETTES" emblazoned in royal blue across the front. The "P" was missing, and ballettes was no longer a politically correct name for a girls' basketball team. Below the sweat top was a pair of royal blue gym shorts that came to her knees. On her feet were lime green flip-flops.

They shook hands.

Sarah: "Thanks for showing a girl a good time."

Matt: "Come back to see us anytime. We'll be here."

Matt handed Sarah a paper bag.

Matt: "Inside are two jars of my honey. One's for you and the other for Willie. Make sure he gets one."

Sarah saluted.

Sarah: "Yes, sir."

She turned and headed to the car almost reaching the first step off the porch.

Matt: "Sarah DuMont, I have to say, you are one pretty woman."

She made no acknowledgement. She used her best acting skills to convince him that she had not heard what he said.

She flip-flopped around to the passenger side of the car and put her hand on the handle of the back door. Moving to the front door, she opened the door and sat next to Willie.

Sarah: "Take me to St. Charles Avenue, Willie."

Willie: "Yes, ma'am."

Matt and Doodle remained on the front porch. Nothing was said in the car until the man and his dog were out of sight, under the apparent assumption that if Matt could see you, he could hear you. She also knew Doodle read lips.

Willie: "I sure do like your boyfriend."

Sarah: "He's not my boyfriend."

Willie: "And the man knows his way around a kitchen."

Sarah: "That I agree with."

Just south of Hammond, Louisiana, Interstate 55 elevates above the ground to carry vehicles quickly over the Manchac Swamp, which borders New Orleans. The highway remains elevated until inside one of the levees protecting the city that care forgot. The luxury German car, containing Willie and Sarah, produced a faint monotone beat as the tires crossed joints for each span of the elevated roadway.

The clouds had dissipated, and the full moon spread a pale blue light over the swamp. Sarah could have used this light a few hours ago. She laid her head against the headrest and closed her eyes. Traveling commando into New Orleans, another first, must be what Matt meant when he prayed for traveling mercies. All of this because her assistant was eating a brownie. A smile appeared on those famous lips as she fell asleep.

# Chapter Seven

# Poultry

Sarah slept in Sunday morning and had a light production schedule Sunday afternoon on the reshoot of some scenes in which she had a minor role. She was needed bright and early, however, Monday morning.

The twelve episode pay-for-view television series involved a wealthy South Louisiana family that owned property south of Baton Rouge. They had property in New Orleans and surrounding areas. The crown jewel of the property was a Creole plantation home in St. James Parish.

The story was originally written for a family in the Northeast, but it had been revised due to the romance, flavor, and tax credits of shooting it on location in Louisiana. Sarah could attest to some of that local flavor.

Sarah's character was the wife of a family member who had hired two local brothers to kill her. The attempt had gone awry, and the brothers determined that the wife was worth more to them alive than dead.

The scene they were filming today took place in an abandoned shack in a swamp infested by alligators and snakes. Sarah's character was being held hostage. She was in make-up at six a.m. that morning. Through the art of make-up, Sarah's left eye was swollen shut, her right cheek was bruised, and her lower bottom lip was split on one side.

She had no speaking part in this scene, and as initially conceived, she was to be gagged with duct tape. There were to be several close-ups of her face. The producer knew that he was paying a premium for those lips and did not want them covered. The director assembled his brain trust to see if an accommodation could be made. The Hollywood reasoning went as follows: the shack was isolated, in fact, so isolated that the brothers didn't need to gag her because who could hear her if she scream; therefore, gagging her would not be consistent with the storyline.

Sarah knew Matt would have been on the side of gagging her, but he had no say so in the matter.

As the scene opened, Sarah was siting on a wooden bench in the shack. Her feet were bound at the ankles by duct tape, and similarly, her arms were bound behind her. Brother number one, the criminal mastermind, was waiting with Sarah for the return of brother number two.

Brother#2 entered the shack.

Brother#1: "Did you get it?"

Brother#2: "No, he never showed. The money wasn't there."

Brother#1: "Did you look around?"

Brother#2: "Of course, I did. But I couldn't very well walk around the dock asking people if they'd seen our extortion money."

Brother#1: "Don't get smart."

Brother#2: "One of us needs to."

Brother#1: "How about that wifey? Your loving husband hopes we will kill you for a few bucks. He won't even spring for a decent murder."

There was a pause in the action to allow for a close-up of Sarah's face and to give the audience the idea that the brothers were thinking. There had been a slight rewrite in the script. It only affected the speaking parts. Since Sarah had no speaking part, no one thought it necessary to give her a copy of the rewrite. Besides, what possible impact could the name of the antebellum mansion have on the scene?

Brother#1: "We need to convince hubby that we are serious. Go get your cousin. Tell him we have a job for him. We'll burn Tara to the ground!"

The laugh started low in Sarah's stomach. As it moved upward, it increased in force until her body began to convulse. When it finally burst forth, it carried noise and spittle with it. Sarah rolled over on the bench. She rolled onto the floor. She rolled around on the floor.

Sarah: "Oh, the poultry! The poultry. Poor Scarlett."

Tears and spittle were marring hours of careful make-up work. A miraculous healing was taking place, like in those New Testament stories in Matt's Bible. Her eye, her lip, and her cheek were being healed. It was truly a miracle. The only problem, this was not a Bible epic.

Everyone was so mesmerized by what they saw, someone had to remind the director to say cut.

After some consultation and a call to the producer, it was concluded that the shack was actually near a Walmart, and Sarah needed to be gagged. For take two, gray duct tape covered those lips. She had the cowboy to blame for this.

# Chapter Eight

# Ruth

Sarah's workday had begun at six a.m., had included the Tara incident, and had finally ended at six p.m. as she approached the side door of the rented mansion on St. Charles. All she had on her mind were to take a shower, eat in the room, run some lines for tomorrow, and sleep. Everyone had to enter the mansion through this side door. She had noticed the young, handsome security guard before. Today he seemed especially glad to see her. Before she could offer a greeting, the guard spoke.

Guard: "Your boyfriend's sister is waitin' inside to see you."

Sarah: "Excuse me?"

Guard: "She's been here since two o'clock. She's the nicest lady. She brought me a chocolate pie. She's the nicest lady."

Sarah: "Help me out; I only met her once. Remind me her name again."

Guard: "Her name is on the sign-in sheet. It's Ruth Anderson."

Sarah: "Of course, Ruth. Thank you."

Sarah could only assume that Matt had sent her, but why? The cowboy that just keeps on giving. Perhaps this was some Southern thing akin to boiled okra or fried pickles. There was nothing to do now but meet Ruth. Having her forcibly removed was not an option, yet.

Sarah walked into the mansion. A concierge smiled at her, pointing to the front room. She positioned herself so that she could see

Ruth without being seen. Yes, that was the girl in the picture, only older. Ruth sat ramrod straight on the edge of the chair. The only reasonable assumption, based on her posture, was that she had sat there for four hours without moving.

Sarah: "You must be Ruth Anderson. I'm so happy to meet you. Can I have them bring you anything?"

Sarah thought the nicer that she was to Ruth the more the cowboy looks like a jerk when they compare notes.

Ruth: "Yes, ma'am, I'm Ruth. Thank you very much for seein' me, and no I don't need anything. Thank you."

Ruth sat down, and Sarah sat in a chair directly facing Ruth. Their knees were only a few feet apart. Apparently, Ruth had arranged the chairs.

Sarah: "What can I do for you?"

Ruth: "Before we get started, Ms. DuMont, I must say that you are even prettier in person. I'm sure my brother was just speechless when you visited with him."

Sarah: "Thank you, and your brother was delightful."

Sarah knew then that Ruth Anderson was a woman of substance. Ruth knew full well that her brother was never speechless.

Ruth: "Let me preface what I need to say. I know you're a very busy person. And I would never do anything that would inconvenience you or make you feel uncomfortable in any way. My brother doesn't know I'm here. In fact, he's said nothin' to me about you."

Sarah: "You can appreciate that someone in my business goes to considerable effort to keep what she does private. Not that I wouldn't have invited you here myself if we had met, but how did you know it was me, and how did you get in here?"

Ruth: "Fair questions. If a strange car pulls into my brother's driveway, Odell gets the license plate number and gives it to my Uncle Billy. He is the local sheriff, so he has access to a considerable amount of information. We traced the car to the car service, but they wouldn't give us a name. But the driver bought pulled pork from Odell's Barbecue. Odell wasn't there, but his cousin, Francis, was. Francis heard the driver say his name was Willie. Fortunately for us, that is his actual first name and not a nickname. So then we had a first name and an employer. So Uncle Billy was able to track down an address and a phone number. Are you still with me, Ms. DuMont?"

Sarah: "Yes, and please call me Sarah."

Ruth: "Yes, ma'am. I called Mr. Roberts, Willie. He couldn't have been nicer. When I told him I was Matt's sister, he just went on and on. He didn't tell us your complete name, but he did let the Sarah part slip that you were stayin' here on St. Charles and that his second cousin was a security guard here. So here we are."

Sarah: "And the chocolate pie?"

Ruth: "Just a little insurance against the unexpected. Ms. DuMont, I don't know why a person, such as yourself, would want to visit my brother on that old farm. But if you have a moment, there are some things you need to know about him."

Sarah: "I admire your tenacity on the part of your brother. If you have something you think I should hear, then by all means tell me."

Sarah would pay money for information on the cowboy. Now she was getting it for free.

Ruth: "My brother graduated from Ole Miss with a civil engineerin' degree, a lovely fiancée, and a commission in the Marines. He did multiple tours of duty in Iraq and Afghanistan. He fought in the Second Battle of Fallujah. He came home after his discharge with two Purple Hearts, no fiancée, and Post Traumatic Stress Disorder."

Sarah: "Is he violent?"

Ruth: "Yes, but not in the way you may think. My brother is a protector. I doubt he would defend himself in a fight. He was no good at football because he just couldn't bring himself to run into anybody. But let someone hurt or attack someone he thinks can't defend themselves, and he can get violent."

"He hit rock bottom about two years ago. He was drinkin' and gettin' into bar fights. We thought he might commit suicide. Ms. DuMont, I just don't think I could go on if my brother did that to himself."

Ruth's bottom lip began to quiver, and she took a moment to compose herself.

Sarah: "Ruth, are you all right? Can I get you anything?"

Ruth: "No, ma'am. Thank you. I need to keep goin'. One night he was in Lester's bar drinkin'. Matt was back in a booth, and Odell was at the bar, keepin' an eye on him."

Sandra: "I hear the name Odell come up often."

Ruth: "Matt and Odell have been friends forever. Odell stutters. He has his whole life. Matt says if you are goin' to have a conversation with Odell, you better bring your lunch because it will take all day. Matt's always looked out for him. Matt would tell Odell that Moses stuttered and look how God used him."

"The three Sullivan brothers came into the bar that night. Ms. DuMont, they are big, rough men that haul pulpwood for a livin'. Whenever my Uncle has to arrest one of 'em, he always brings an extra deputy. They've made fun of Odell, unmercifully, ever since they were little boys. Lester saw immediately what was goin' to happen. He called my Uncle Billy, but by the time he got there, it was over. Lester had to pull a shotgun on Matt to keep him from killin' 'em. Mrs. DuMont, he beat those boys like a rented mule. That's how he got that scar on his forehead. Odell drove Matt home. All my Uncle found was Lester's bar torn up and those three large men on the floor, unconscious and bleedin'."

"Ms. DuMont, are you all right? Can I get them to bring you anything?"

Sarah: "No, I'm fine. Please continue."

Ruth: "My husband patched them up. He said Matt was just plain lucky one of those boys didn't die. They threatened to bring charges, but some business men in town paid their medical bills, and my Uncle said he'd charge them, too."

"Well, all things work together for good for them that love the Lord. God answered prayer and turned that bar fight into a blessin'. My Uncle, Pastor Mark, and another man, a veteran, had a come to Jesus meetin' with Matt that night. Matt doesn't know I know this, but my Uncle said, at one point, Matt cried like a little boy."

"Matt quit drinkin'; at least he did after they built that chicken coop. He got a dog. He tells people that Doodle is a service dog. He even has some official lookin' papers to prove it. But I know Matt found that dog, or that dog found Matt. That dog knew where she was; Matt was the one lost. He got someone at the VA to make up those papers. He uses those papers so he can take the dog into restaurants and the Piggly Wiggly."

"Matt also fixed up Lester's bar. That's what got him interested in makin' furniture and restorin' the farmhouse. What he did in Lester's was the talk of the town. Well, none of the ladies in the church could see it. They can't be seen in Lester's bar. I'm the president of the WMU."

Sarah: "Excuse me, but what is the WMU?"

Ruth: "That stands for the Women's Missionary Union. Just about all Southern Baptist churches have'em. We try to educate and encourage the church members about missions. Anyway, since I'm the president and since Jesus ate with sinners, we decided that we'd have a WMU meeting in Lester's bar. We'd keep Lester from selling liquor for about two hours, and the ladies of the church could see what Matt had done in the bar."

"Each lady normally brings a little somethin' for our refreshments. Well, it turns out, Lester makes a wonderful pound cake. It all went over so well that we now meet once a quarter at Lester's, all because of Matt."

"Also, the Sullivan brothers leave Odell alone now. I don't think you could put a gun to one of their heads and get them to say an unkind word about Odell. At least not as long as Matthew Shepherd walks this earth."

Sarah smiled.

Sarah: "I bet not. I'd hate for Matthew Shepherd to get after me."

Ruth: "Oh, Ms. DuMont, that would never happen. The safest place on this earth is standin' next to my brother."

Sarah: "Unless you are a Sullivan."

Ruth: "Ms. DuMont, you do have a quick wit."

Sarah: "What can you tell me about his PTSD?"

Ruth: "Matt explained it to me this way. He said in combat he never felt fear, anger, or rage. He didn't have time. He was too busy keepin' his Marines alive. But all those feelin's were there and just got stored up. He said your body could process this over time, like the way a person's body cleanses the blood. But sometimes more emotions get out than can be processed. Then you have all the emotions of combat while you're lyin' in bed or readin' a book. You'll do anything to make it stop."

"When he first got home, he got help from the VA in Jackson, but he stopped goin'. He sees the VA as a zero sum game. If he is gettin' help, then someone who may need it more is not. He participated in some group counselin' before he stopped. Apparently, they had them write down some of their experiences. I have a copy of one Matt did. He doesn't know I have it."

Sarah: "How did you get it?"

Ruth: "A chocolate pie."

Sarah: "Excuse me?"

Ruth: "When Matt is eatin' a slice of chocolate pie, the house could burn down around him, and he wouldn't know it. I baked a pie, took it to him, cut him a slice then went through all the stuff in his room. I know that may sound awful, but that was back when we thought Matt might hurt himself."

Sarah: "I see now that our highly trained, young security guard was out matched. You Southern women come well-armed."

Ruth: "Thank you, I think. Anyway, I've made a copy for you. I'd like you to read it. It is written in his own hand. He has wonderful handwritin'."

Ruth handed Sarah a white business envelope that contained Matt's composition, which Ruth had retrieved from her purse. The snap of the purse clasp gave a dramatic note to the transaction.

Ruth: "Please, either read it or destroy it. Matt deserves that much."

Sarah: "Yes, I agree."

Sarah paused. She wanted Ruth to understand that Matt really did deserve that much.

Sarah: "When I visited Matt, I found Zoloft. I researched it and found it was given for depression and can be used for PTSD. So this all makes sense now."

Ruth: "Matt won't take pills of any kind. How did you find it?"

Sarah: "Banana pudding."

Ruth: "That works, too."

Sarah: "Does this mean I qualify as a Southern woman?"

Ruth smiled a faint smile.

Ruth: "Well, we'll have to see."

Sarah could see that obtaining entrance to Juilliard School of Drama might be easier than obtaining entrance into this Southern sorority.

Ruth: "Matt needs structure and routine in his life. As he improves, he can do more and experience more, but it needs to be done in small steps. In a few months, our church is sendin' a mission team to Thoman, Haiti. It is mostly a medical mission. My husband and two doctors from the Medical Center are goin' along with nurses. Matt is goin' to build furniture for the clinic, school, and church. He will work with young men from the village to teach them carpenter skills. He can't take Doodle. He will be in a third world country again, and the terrain around Thoman looks like parts of Afghanistan and Iraq. The medical clinic, where they will be stayin', has a wall, armed guards, and guard towers. Matt's workin' very hard to be ready for this trip. This is very important to him. Ms. Dumont, please keep all this in mind if you see my brother in the future."

Sarah could tell Ruth was done.

They rose to say good-bye. Sarah extended her hand. Ruth moved past the hand and gave Sarah a substantial hug, speaking into her ear.

Ruth: "Sarah, I know you have a good heart, and you won't do anything to hurt my brother. God bless you for takin' the time to talk to me."

Ruth turned and left the room, never looking back at Sarah. She had said her peace and the rest was in her god's hands.

# Chapter Nine

# Fallujah

That night Sarah was sitting in bed, having showered and eaten supper in her room. She had removed her contacts and was wearing her designer, black reading classes. On the nightstand were the jar of honey from Matt and the white envelope from Ruth.

The label on the jar read, "Honey From the Shepard Family Farm Macon, Mississippi." Sarah had not opened the jar but liked the way the honey glowed from the light of the bedside lamp. The contents of the envelope were unread.

Sarah was trying to ignore the envelope and not think about it. She would run some lines, glance at the envelope that wasn't really there, and look at her feet. She always thought that her feet might be her best feature.

She thought that perhaps she could be a foot model. Or was it feet model. And Matt didn't even give her a compliment on her feet. Humility. What an idiot.

She had done a scene in a movie where she wore a short skirt and sat in a chair while reaching with her toes to pick up some keys. The keys were for the handcuffs holding her. The whole point was to show her feet and legs and have the camera shoot up her skirt. She looked down toward the end of the bed and wiggled her toes. She ran some more lines.

She wondered if she could use her feet and toes like in the movie to get Matt's story out of the envelope. She wouldn't use her hands. It would be like soccer. But they don't play soccer in Louisiana, do they? She knew they played football in Louisiana. But Matt was no good at football.

All of a sudden, she knew exactly what was going on. This was a setup. Ruth was in on it. Matt didn't know, bull! Aunt Soodie tells Odell, who tells Uncle Billy, who knows everything. What did they think? Am I stupid? I bet that envelope contained a piece of paper that said, "Gotcha!" I'm no fool. If I open that envelope, someone is going to jump out with a camera, and Sarah Morgan Leigh DuMont would be the victim of a prank.

There was only one way to settle this. She opened and read the contents of the envelope.

> We had been in combat almost continuously for three days. It had been against dead-enders and was house-to-house. My men were spent. I needed to get them off the line for a few hours to rest, eat, and reload. Exhaustion leads to mistakes, which leads to dead Marines.

> But they were Marines, and I knew their blood was up. They didn't want to leave the line, but they would follow orders.

> CO agreed and they gave me the coordinates of a safe house. The pull back was done in good order. These men were professionals.

> When we reached the safe house, we took inventory and had a missing Marine.

> Andrew (Andy) Perkins was from Rural, Kansas, which was both a proper name and a description. He was the youngest, only nineteen. Andy was always smiling, the harder the training, the bigger the smile. He was always more concerned about others than himself. He was a joy to lead. He did as told with a smile and an ooh-ra! Andy was my brother.

> No one remembered seeing Andy during the pull back. I told the men I'd go look for him, but under no circumstances was anyone else to go

looking for Andy or me. This was a direct order. I told them not to worry; we'd both come back.

I found Andy in an empty house sitting up, leaning against a wall, his rifle in his lap. Both the chamber and clip in the rifle were empty. Andy was dead. I had failed him. Insurgent voices were approaching, the number unknown. I dragged Andy's body to the side of the room behind some bundles and covered us both with a rug. The rug was vermin infested and smelled of urine.

I needed time to formulate a plan. I would not leave him. Insurgents were mutilating the bodies of any dead U.S. soldiers they could find. They took his life, but they would not get his dead body. Soon the room filled with fighters. This room was to be their camp for the night. The rug was so filthy that none of them used it for bedding, saving us from discovery.

We lay under the rug for about three hours. Eventually, I heard snoring and knew it was now or never. I rose, leaving my weapon behind, and put Andy on my back by draping his arms over my shoulders—his chest was against my back. I dropped a grenade and headed to the door. I only had seconds to make it out. The room was wall-to-wall insurgents. For most of the time, I was walking on sleeping men.

We made it to the door, but the limited light outside illuminated our silhouette. Two shots were fired, both entering Andy's body. The dead Marine was protecting the live Marine. We turned to the left as we exited. The grenade went off and shrapnel caught me in my left calf and through my boot into my heel.

After a few strides, an insurgent jumped on Andy's back and reached his arms around to my neck. We were able to get him on the ground. Andy was between us doing what he could.

I knew this was the insurgent that had killed Andy. I just knew it. After Jesus and my mother, Andy was the purest light I had ever seen. You don't kill Andy. My war had become personal.

So, I did what Andy could not do. I choked that man with my bare hands. I squeezed so hard and so fast that I heard his neck crack in three places: one for the Father, one for the Son, and one for the Holy Spirit. We shared a look in that moment before he went to his god, and I called to mine.

Andy and I moved on in the darkness. At one point, I know I heard him say, 'Thank you Matt.' We made it because God loved Andy and had compassion on me, a sinner.

I received a Purple Heart for my wounds in retrieving Andy. You should not get a medal for bringing your Marines home dead.

Months after my discharge, I drove to Rural, Kansas and gave Andy's parents my Purple Heart. I told them Andy had saved my life, but I didn't tell them the last time was with his lifeless body. They didn't want to keep it, but it wasn't leaving Kansas with me. In the end, they kept it for my benefit.

Outside of Rural, Kansas, I stopped at a roadside rest area and found an abandoned puppy eating out of a turned over garbage can. That dog came home with me.

Matt Shepherd

Sarah removed her glasses, turned off the bedside lamp, reached for the jar of honey, and pressed it close to herself. She rolled to a fetal position on the bed with tears running across her face.

# Chapter Ten

# Beautiful Lake Maurepas

St. Charles Avenue runs from downtown New Orleans to the Mississippi River levee. Along the way are universities, Catholic schools, protestant churches, Jewish synagogues, a hospital, a gated community, a zoo, a park, restaurants, mansions, and neglected houses. The trolley cars on St. Charles are the iconic image of New Orleans.

The grand avenue begins in town as a one way, two-lane road with lanes that compete with streetcar lines and pass the Statue of Robert E. Lee in Lee Circle. It becomes a two way, four-lane boulevard as it moves upriver and eventually terminates in the shadow of the Mississippi River levee at the River Road, the backdoor way into New Orleans.

The trolley cars, pedestrians, one way side streets, and stop lights hidden by the low limbs of live oak trees can all make turning left off St. Charles Avenue a challenge for the novice. Residents can do it with their eyes closed and often do.

Sarah contacted Matt, and they agreed to meet at a restaurant, Middendorf's, located on beautiful Lake Maurepas in the middle of the Manchac Swamp.

Willie made the left turn off St. Charles and saw Sarah waiting. She was standing on the sidewalk with the security guard and holding a shopping bag. She opened the back door, tossed in the package, opened the front door, and sat opposite Willie.

Sarah: "You're late."

Willie: "Now, Ms. Sarah, you know I'm not late."

Sarah: "And stop calling me Ms. Sarah. Unlike the yahoos around here, I'm enlightened. Idella's clothes are in the bag. I also had my assistant get her something to say thank you; something she could wear to church. What would the women at Matt's church wear on a Sunday morning?"

Willie: "Oh, Lee Arthur and Idella don't go to Matt's church. They go to the black church on the blacktop, just before you turn into Matt's place. We drove right passed it. Didn't you see that black church?"

Sarah: "I remember seeing a church and thinking, my gosh, they are everywhere. But how did you know it was a black church?"

Willie: "It had a gravel parkin' lot. You see, white folk don't go to black churches, and black folk don't go to white churches."

Sarah: "Well, the truth comes out. And why not?"

Willie: "White women don't cook on Sunday."

Sarah looked at Willie, squinting at him through her designer sunglasses.

Sarah: "What?"

Willie: "The white women don't cook on Sunday. They start church early so they can get to the restaurants before the other white folk. Black women cook so the church starts much later to give them time to cook before church starts. If white folk went to black churches, and black folk went to white churches, then somebody's men folk would starve on Sunday."

Sarah: "You know, Willie, from the outside, people down here just look like a bunch of inbred yahoos. Then you come down here and get to know them. Break bread with them. Understand their aspirations and dreams, and you realize they are a bunch of inbred yahoos."

Willie: "Oh, Ms. Sarah, you just won't do."

Sarah: "And by the way, when we get back, I'm having you fired. You told Ruth Anderson everything about me but my bra size."

Willie: "I know. You could know that woman was pickin' your pocket, and there ain't nothin' you could do about it. She beats all I've ever seen."

Sarah: "Preach it, brother. She picked me clean yesterday afternoon. You know she's president of the WMU. I'm surprised there's a sinner left in this country. We sent the wrong Shepherd to fight the war on terror. If we had sent her to Iraq with some of her chocolate pies, we'd know exactly where those WMD were."

Willie: "And those Muslims would be singin' 'What a Friend We Have in Jesus.'"

Sarah: "Amen to that."

There was silence in the car as Willie focused on his driving, and Sarah was thinking about Fallujah. They were crossing the Bonnet Carre' Spillway on Interstate 10 when she spoke again.

Sarah: "Willie, do you think I'm a good person?"

Willie: "Oh, yes, ma'am."

Sarah: "Name one good thing I've done."

There was a lull in the conversation.

Willie: "Well, you sit up here with me and talk to me like I'm a real person. I understand that our clients are busy and important folk. I don't mind if they look past me, but it's nice when they don't."

Sarah: "You know I do this because of Matt. If it weren't for him, I'd be on my third driver by now, and I wouldn't know your name."

The last comment hung in the cooled air of the car for a few moments.

Sarah: "Go faster. I think I'd take an overdose of sleeping pills if that cowboy got to the restaurant before me."

They eventually crossed the overpass at Lake Maurepas, exited Interstate 55, turned onto the frontage road, and headed south a few yards to the restaurant. Sarah searched the parking lot and did not see Matt's truck. Good for Willie.

Sarah: "Willie, I need to talk to Matt alone. If he sees you sitting in the car, he won't come in the restaurant. Here is some money. Go in, sit at the opposite side of the restaurant, and have a meal on me."

Willie: "Ms. Sarah, a hundred dollars is way too much to pay for one meal in here."

Sarah: "Use the money left to take your wife out. Speaking of your wife, Matt will want to know if she made his biscuits."

Willie: "Yes. They were much better, but not as good as his."

Sarah and Willie entered the restaurant. Willie was seated on one side and Sarah the other. Sarah positioned herself so she could see the front door. A waitress came over, and Sarah ordered two sweet teas with lemon. She smiled as she looked at the glasses of sweet tea.

Shortly, Matt and Doodle arrived. She wanted to see the whole drama of the manager confronting Matt about his dog, Matt fumbling around for fraudulent papers, a heated discussion, and Matt standing outside looking through the window at Sarah. Instead, a waitress patted Doodle on the head. The manager shook Matt's hand and pointed in Sarah's direction. Obviously, Matt had been here before.

He approached the table with a big smile. She had forgotten how white his teeth were. She was sure he used bleach as a mouthwash.

Matt: "Hey, Sarah. Is that Willie over there? Why isn't he eatin' with us? I'll go get him."

He stopped, reversing his direction. Doodle did the same.

Sarah: "Matt, Matt, please just come back and sit down. Willie is fine."

Matt: "But I need to ask him if his wife made the biscuits."

Sarah: "Yes and two hours later you would remember that I was sitting over here. She made the biscuits. They were much better, but not as good as yours."

Matt: "The perfect outcome. I see you ordered sweet tea. What if I wanted a beer? My uncle has no jurisdiction here."

Sarah: "Do you think that would stop him from arresting me?"

Matt: "No."

Sarah: "Okay, this is your restaurant. What's good?"

Matt: "They are known for their thin cut, fried catfish. I've never understood how they can cut catfish that thin. I bet the fella that does it, doesn't have ten fingers. Anyway, comes with fries, hush puppies, and some slaw."

Sarah: "Matt, you must be some kind of savant. You've found a Louisiana restaurant whose specialty is something fried. What are the chances?"

Matt: "Somethin' cut very thin and then fried. Sarah, you are sittin' in the midst of people capable of a culinary art form that would make a French chef weep."

Sarah: "Well, the last time I was with you, I enjoyed a mouthful of chicken manure. At this point, the only way is up. I'm in. This whole vegetarian thing is out the window when you are around. Even the butter beans you fixed were a meat group."

Matt: "I don't remember seeing any uneaten butter beans on your plate. In fact, there wasn't any uneaten anything. At one point, Willie and I feared for our lives."

Sarah: "I asked you not to tease me about my eating."

He ordered two thin catfish dinners, one small and one large.

Sarah: "Matt, I need you to do me a big favor tonight and not be Matt. I need you to listen and not neuter me with all that Southern charm."

Matt: "You want me to put my light under a bushel. Got it."

Sarah: "About the day we first met, Mrs. Fontenot and I made a friendly wager. She bet me that I couldn't get you to meet with me. Call it a date. If she won, then I had to buy some mirror. If I won then—"

Matt: "You got that day's load of my work for free, shipped to your store. . . . I knew about the wager. Mrs. Fontenot told me the day before."

Sarah: "That woman—"

Matt: "Now, Sarah, no reason to stop actin' like a lady."

Sarah: "Then why did you take the date?"

Matt: "Well, my sister was after me to expand my horizons. And you were just so cute wearin' the Zephyr cap. None of the other women had ever done that. And you look like fun. And, if you remember, I left it up to Doodle."

Sarah: "Well I have a confession to make about—"

Matt: "The bacon. Doodle told me. It wasn't until we got to Ponchatoula that I realized it was in the lockets on the charm bracelet."

Sarah: "Doodle told you about the bacon but not where it was hidden."

Matt: "Yea. She thought that was so funny."

Matt looked at Doodle in disgust.

Sarah: "What about Mrs. Fontenot? I'm sure she was a little upset."

Matt: "About that, I felt bad, so I bought the mirror, gave her my furniture, and paid the cost of shippin' it to your store. She got what she wanted."

Sarah: "You don't have that kind of money."

Matt: "We worked out a payment plan."

Sarah: "Matt, what did you do with that mirror?"

Matt: "It's too big for the farmhouse, so it hangs in the barn, just a little reminder of you second only to the compost pile. Oh, by the way, the chickens send their apology. They feel partly responsible."

Sarah: "Tell the chickens that is very gracious of them. A Louis XVI mirror hangs in your barn?"

Matt: "Well, the chickens made it very clear that thing wasn't goin' in the coop, and Odell didn't want it either. He said it didn't fit the décor of the barbecue shack. Took him a while to say décor. He's pretty particular about that shack."

Sarah: "That mirror is so ugly. Matt, you shouldn't have done all this. I don't know what to say. But I do have more."

The catfish arrived. Matt looked at Sarah.

Sarah: "Matt, tell me you are not going to make me pray in this restaurant in front of these people."

Matt: "'Be joyful always, pray continuously, give thanks in all circumstances for this is God's will for you in Christ Jesus.' What do you think?"

Sarah: "Oh, Matt, tell me what to do."

Matt: "Just take both my hands in yours, bow your head, and, this time, close your eyes. I'll do the rest."

Sarah did as he said, and he began speaking in a low, private tone.

Matt: "Lord, thank you for today, thank you for Willie, thank you for Sarah, and thank you for your gift of grace. Amen."

She had to admit; the man could sure say a sweet prayer. The first man she had ever known that could.

Matt: "You had more you wanted to tell me."

Sarah: "Matt, your sister came to see me."

He sat his fork down, looking at her.

Sarah: "I know about Lester's, about Odell and the Sullivan bothers. I finally know how you got that scar."

Matt: "That's just common knowledge in Macon. Then you also know things have been gettin' better."

Sarah: "Yes. Matt, what you've done with the farmhouse and the furniture is impressive. I know about the trip to Haiti, and I want to help. I'm going to my parents in Connecticut for a week. The whole family will be there. This will give you a chance to try on something new, without Doodle or Odell. If you can handle this, Haiti will be a snap."

Matt: "I don't know, Sarah. We haven't known one another very long, and I come with a lot of movin' parts. Bein' up there with strange people, people who don't know me. I don't know. You know, I have Doodle and Odell around and that farmhouse. I don't know."

Sarah: "I know about the PTSD."

Matt: "Gee, Sarah. I don't know. Your family and all. I don't know."

Sarah: "I know about Andy and where Doodle came from."

Matt's demeanor and tone changed.

Matt: "How do you know about that? How could you know about that?"

Sarah: "Your sister. She has the story you wrote about Andy. About how you saved him."

Matt: "I didn't save him! This is not right. This is not right. You and her have no right to do this."

Matt became visibly agitated. Nearby restaurant patrons glanced toward their table.

Sarah: "I know that I don't understand."

Matt now stood abruptly, causing the chair he had been sitting in to fall over, and Doodle to stand alert at his heel.

Matt: "I know you don't understand, Sarah. You're rich. You're from Connecticut. It's not even a state. Miss'sippi's a state. Connecticut's a suburb. You live in LA, for heaven's sake. You work in a business of pretend where men act brave because somebody shoots a blank pistol at'm.''

Sarah's eyes were moving from side to side, but she was not seeing. The manager started toward the table but stopped. Willie was now standing near the manager.

Matt: "Let someone shoot a real gun at you a few times, and you'll learn how to pray. Sleep in sand in a country where you are fightin' for people that hate your guts, and you'll read your Bible. And while sittin' in that sand, get a letter from the only girl you ever loved tellin' you she just can't wait any longer. That she's marryin' a rich guy from Texas. And you fight in that sand so that the rich guy can be safe when he sleeps with her. And all that time, have a group of Marines dependent on you to keep'em alive. Do all those things, Sarah DuMont, and maybe you will understand.''

The tone in his voice, as he said her name, hurt her deeply.

Matt: "I know what you think. Give the cowboy a trip to Connecticut, and he'll be right as rain when it's over. A little Sarah time and Haiti will be a snap. What if it's not a snap? What if it doesn't work out? How many trips to Connecticut do I get? How much Sarah time do I get then? There are people in this with me for the duration. Are you telling me you want to be one of them? I don't think so.''

He turned around and every eye in the restaurant was on him. There was no sound, whatsoever, not even from the kitchen. Matt waved his arm in a wide motion.

Matt: "And some of you in here don't deserve to live in the same country with my Marines.''

Matt and Doodle headed to the door. Halfway across the floor, they both stopped. He stood motionless for what seemed an eternity, then turned and addressed the room.

Matt: "I apologize for my behavior here tonight. My actions do not bring credit to the Corps that I love. I hope you can find it in your hearts to forgive me.''

He walked back to the table where Sarah was sitting. As he approached the table, a man in the corner of the restaurant stood and began to clap. Soon others joined him. Sarah was looking down and did not raise her head.

Matt: "Sarah, I'm very sorry. Can you forgive me?"

She shook her head yes without raising her eyes.

Matt: "It would be an honor to meet your family. Am I still invited?"

This response took longer. When Sarah finally said yes, the clapping in the room became louder. Matt turned to leave, took a few steps, stopped, and turned to face her.

Matt: "Sarah, I give you my word that I will not embarrass you or your family."

He turned and headed out the restaurant. Willie stepped in front of him, blocking his exit, and placed his hand on Matt's shoulder.

Willie: "I'll get her home safe. You take that dog and go straight home. Don't stop at any bars. You be safe. Don't mess up. It may not look like it, but she needs you."

Matt turned to look at Sarah.

As Willie approached the table, Sarah spoke first with her head still down.

Sarah: "Willie, is he gone?"

Willie: "Yes."

Sarah raised her head.

Sarah: "I was just trying to help. We've got to call his sister and Uncle Billy and Odell and Idella. They need to know and look out for him. He's alone in that truck driving home. I don't care what he says, that dog can't talk to him. I was just trying to help. Willie, you don't know. He had to do terrible things."

Willie put his arm around Sarah.

Willie: "Give me your phone. Do you have the sister's number?"

Sarah: "Yes. No, Willie, I don't have it. She said she called you. Was that on the company cell?"

Willie: "Yes. Give me just a second."

Willie retrieved his phone, searched through recent calls, and dialed Ruth.

Sarah: "Ruth, this is Sarah. Ruth, I made a terrible mistake. Matt and I were at Middendorf's. He got upset about something I said and left. I'm worried about him. . . . No. I told him we knew about Andy. Ruth, he got so mad at me. . . . Thank you, but I should have known. Thank you, Ruth, for not hating me. Please call me when you know he's home. This is Willie's phone. Here is my number."

Sarah gave Ruth the number of her private cell.

The patrons sat in silence as a very large man walked with his arm around the famous actress through the restaurant, out the door, and to a parked car. The German car retraced its path and headed south to New Orleans. At first, there was silence.

Sarah: "You know, he knew about the wager."

Willie: "You sound a little tipsy. Ms. Sarah, you know you're not supposed to drink in front of Matt."

Sarah: "All I had was the house wine of the South."

Willie: "You just need to sit there. I'll get you home soon."

Sarah: "You know, he doesn't have any money. I looked in his checkbook. You were eating banana pudding. Apparently, men don't have a right to privacy in the South when they are eating chocolate pie or banana pudding. We should have a law in this country that if you have that little money, you will be taken out and shot. . . . Sorry sir, you're two dollars short. Now, go wait outside for the gunman. Next!"

"He told me he bought that ugly mirror, gave away a truck load of furniture, and even paid to ship it to my store so he could spend a few hours with me. That is the nicest, sweetest thing a man has ever said to me. I started to jump him in the restaurant."

"Then just moments later, he is saying those terrible things to me, out of the same mouth. I don't understand how he can do that. I didn't mean anything bad when I said Haiti would be a snap. Why did he say those things to me?"

"And I prayed in public. We held hands, and I closed my eyes this time. I don't understand prayer, Willie. If my eyes are open, does that mean God doesn't hear me? If one eye is open and the other is closed, does that mean he only hears every other word?"

Sarah leaned over the consul, looking at Willie, and started winking both eyes so that one was open when the other was shut.

Sarah: "Does this just sound like static? Does the Angel Gabriel say, 'Don't worry about the static, Sir. It's just little Billy horsin' around again.' I don't believe in God. I have money. I have more money than a sailor at the grand opening of a whorehouse. But his prayers are so sweet. They are so simple. There are only two times in my life when I felt God might be real, and Matt was praying both times."

"He prays like that then, out of the same mouth, he says those terrible things to me. All I was trying to do is help."

"Then he comes over to my table and says he is sorry. He sounds like a ten year old little boy apologizing for eating the last slice of pie."

There was silence. Sarah sat with her eyes closed and head against the headrest.

Willie: "Now, you just sit there and rest, Ms. Sarah. I'll get you home."

Sarah jerked. Her arms grabbed her stomach as if she were sick. She leaned forward as far as she could. She swayed back and forth, sobbing.

Sarah: "Willie, I didn't do it. I didn't kill Andy. I didn't make Matt lay under that filthy blanket with Andy's body. I didn't make him carry Andy through that room full of men that wanted to mutilate poor Andy. I didn't make Matt strangle that man. I didn't make Matt carry Andy so long in the dark that he heard him say, 'Thank you Matt.' I didn't do it."

Willie was patting Sarah on the back with one hand and driving the car with the other.

Willie: "Now, Mrs. Sarah, you got to stop thinkin' about those things. War's terrible, but we don't need to think about that now. You got to help me get you home safe. You are an important person, and you need to help me get you home."

Sarah: "I wish I never met him so I wouldn't have to know these things. Willie, you don't know what he had to do. You don't know what terrible things he had to do for Andy."

———————

Willie came onto St. Charles from the levee end and turned right off St. Charles onto the side street. He double parked the car by the side door and went around to the passenger side to help Sarah out of the car.

Sarah: "Willie, look. We forgot to return Idella's clothes. She is going to think I'm a terrible person."

Willie: "I'll make sure Idella gets those clothes."

Sarah kissed Willie on the check.

Sarah: "Willie, you are a good friend to me."

Sarah's phone rang.

Sarah: "Hello. . . . Good. Thank you so much for calling me. . . . Yes, I will. Goodbye. Willie, he is home. I promised Ruth I'd pray for him, but I don't know how."

Willie: "Let me help you inside. Why don't you get some sleep first? There will be time to pray for Matt tomorrow."

Willie helped Sarah to the security guard and returned to the car.

Willie: "Thank you, Sweet Jesus."

To Sarah's relief, mention of the fight between her and her boyfriend in a public restaurant in Louisiana never appeared in print or social media in any form or version.

# Chapter Eleven

## Way Down Yonder In Connecticut

Sarah: "Hello, Mother."

Elizabeth: "Who is this?"

Sarah: "It's Sarah. I'm bringing a man with me next week for our visit."

Elizabeth: "Mark?"

Sarah: "Who?"

Elizabeth: "Mark."

Sarah: "Mark who, Mother?"

Elizabeth: "Apparently, this man must be a new boyfriend?"

Sarah: "He is new, but he is not my boyfriend. I need everyone to do me a favor."

Elizabeth: "Certainly, dear, anything for one of your gentlemen friends."

Sarah: "First, he is from Mississippi."

Elizabeth: "The state?"

Sarah: "No, Mother, the river. He is going to say things like yes ma'am and no ma'am, yes sir and no sir. Just let him. Don't try to tell him that it is not necessary. To him, it is very necessary. Mother are you still there?"

Elizabeth: "Yes, ma'am, dear."

Sarah: "Also, I know liquor will be served. That's fine. It's fine to offer him a drink. But no one should insist. Respect his no, thank you."

Elizabeth: "Is there anything else, dear?"

Sarah: "Yes, he and I will have separate rooms."

Elizabeth: "Let me be sure I have this straight so I can tell your father. You are bringing home a very polite, gay man from Mississippi who is an alcoholic."

"One more thing dear, will there be any dietary requirements?"

Sarah: "Yes, he is a vegetarian. He doesn't eat his chitlins boiled."

Elizabeth: "Yummy, more for us. We look forward to meeting your new gentleman friend."

Sarah: "Thank you, Mother. I knew I could count on you."

Elizabeth: "Always, dear."

---

Sarah made all the arrangements. They would fly first class out of New Orleans, and Matt would meet her at the gate. The restaurant incident had occurred two weeks earlier. They had very limited contact during this period, primarily due to Sarah's filming schedule.

She was unsure how the first few moments of this meeting would go. She wanted to get this behind them. Matt checked his duffel bag, went through screening, and made his way to the gate. The last time he flew, he was on active duty. He wore a white shirt, his best jeans, cowboy boots, and no baseball cap.

Sarah waited in a VIP lounge and, as was her habit, viewed the gate without being seen. She could tell Matt was nervous. He was looking around expectantly for someone. There were no Doodle, no Odell, no Ruth, and no Idella. She could do anything, but for once in her life, there was some doubt.

As she watched him, she thought he was the most capable man she had ever met. Yet he was not capable of a simple visit away from the farm. He could make her laugh and was kind, but he was also capable of great physical violence. She would do this for him. Give him a chance to experience something away from the farm. Then she could say goodbye.

She approached and was glad to see him smile. She was caught off guard by how much this meant to her.

Matt: "Hey, Sarah. I hope what I have on is all right. Bein' chickens, they voted for the white shirt."

Sarah: "What did Doodle say?"

Matt: "Doodle's not speaking to me right now. Odell brought me."

Sarah: "Who is looking after Doodle?"

Matt: "I left her the truck keys and a few dollars. She should be fine."

Sarah: "Doodle has a Mississippi Driver's License?"

Matt: "She has a commercial license, double trailer rated. But the real question is where does she carry the license."

Sarah: "Cowboy boots?"

Matt: "They are a peace offerin'. I knew you would call me a cowboy, and I didn't want your parents to think you're stupid, so I got some cowboy boots. Did you know you can buy them used?"

Sarah: "You are wearing someone else's clothes?"

Matt: "No, they're mine now."

Sarah: "I don't think it works that way. Whose socks do you have on?"

Matt: "Actually, they belong to Odell, but that doesn't change anything. The boots are mine."

Sarah: "You don't have a clue how this works, do you?"

This conversation continued until both were seated in first class.

Matt: "This is the first time I've flown first class."

Sarah: "Matt, there are many, many, many things I've done that you haven't."

Matt: "Sarah, there's one less now."

Sometimes Matt could say things that made her just want to jump him. She could do it right now. She could be discreet. No one would notice, but Matt would be hollering one less now, one less now. The thought made her smile.

Sarah lowered the service tray and produced some papers, a pen, and a highlighter.

Sarah: "I need to review some scripts. Stay in your seat and don't wonder off."

Matt: "I brought a book, biography of Dietrich Bonhoeffer."

Sarah: "Did you remember your colors?"

Matt did not open the book but watched as the other passengers boarded. After a few minutes, he leaned over to Sarah.

Matt: "All these men look at you when they walk by. I could pick their wallets, and they'd never know. We could get us some walkin' around money."

Sarah did not look up from her scripts and smiled.

Sarah: "We don't need the money. I have truckloads of the stuff. Give those men their wallets back."

The plane took off and gained altitude. The standard notices were issued: you could remove your seat belt, but don't; you could move about the cabin, but don't.

Matt: "When we get to your folks' house, are you gonna leave me and go see friends or somethin'?"

Sarah: "Don't be silly. I don't have friends."

Matt: "So you're goin' to be with me the whole time."

Sarah: "Matt, let's play a game."

Matt: "Like the picture game."

Sarah: "Yes, exactly like the picture game but completely different. The name of the game is diamond in the compost."

Matt: "Like diamond in the rough."

Sarah: "Diamond in the rough is an expression. I think we have established we are talking about a game. Think of what happened that night at Middendorf's as the compost. The game is to sift through that compost and find a diamond, something good."

Matt: "You first."

Sarah: "Okay, I'll go first. . . . Matt, when you bought that ugly mirror, gave away a truck load of furniture, and paid to ship that furniture to my store, just so you could spend some time with me, well, that was the sweetest thing any man had ever done for me. I was touched, and that doesn't happen to me very often. Your turn."

Matt: "I stopped that night in the middle of the room because Doodle told me I was wrong. I had it all backwards. You are rich; you do come from Connecticut; you do live in LA; and you are a wildly successful actress. So why do you care about an old broke down Marine?"

Sarah: "Answer, see above."

There was silence as they looked at each other. He grinned, flashing white teeth.

Matt: "Let's hold hands and pray."

Sarah: "Where's the stewardess? What's our altitude? I'm going to have you forcible thrown off this plane. Also, you are not a broke down Marine. You are a broke down cowboy. You have only one pair of cowboy boots, and they are not even yours."

Matt: "One more thing, we got in trouble that night because

somehow the truth got loose. Let's agree, goin' forward, it will be all lies, all the time."

Sarah: "Agreed."

They shook hands on the deal.

Sarah: "Remember now, my father's name is James. He's an investment banker on Wall Street. My mother's name is Elizabeth. I think you will like her. I'm the oldest of the three children. The older brother is named Peter, and he is married to Charlotte. They have two children. My younger brother is named Chris. Do you need to write this on your hand or something, or can you remember all of this?"

Matt: "Sarah, I got this. Your father's name is John, and he delivers pizzas. Your mother's name is Ellen—she has a drinkin' problem. You have two younger sisters, Pamela and Christina. One of 'em is a single mom, and I'm not to ask about the dad."

Sarah: "I should have brought Doodle and left you at home."

Matt: "Doodle said the same thing. She said you were makin' a big mistake, and you'd be sorry. You know, in a post-feminist society, hindsight is fifty-fifty."

Sarah: "Hindsight is twenty-twenty!"

Matt: "I shudder to think what they taught you at Yale."

Sarah: "Hindsight, sight, vision, twenty-twenty."

Matt: "Even with hindsight, you still get it wrong half the time, fifty-fifty."

Sarah: "I got it wrong this time. I mean, look at you. You don't speak English. You wear other peoples' clothes. You tease me constantly. You make me laugh when I don't want to. You talk about the silliest things. You are such a cowboy."

Matt: "What are you tryin' to say? Sounds like somebody's got themselves a little cowboy crush."

Sarah: "Don't flatter yourself."

Matt: "You know, denial ain't just a river in Egypt."

Sarah: "I need to pee. Please don't make me laugh. Is there anything else you want to say to me before I go to the bathroom?"

Matt: "Yes, Willie told me how much money you have."

Sarah: "Note to self, have Willie fired on return to New Orleans. We'll discuss this after I get back. Now let me out."

Matt rose and stepped into the aisle letting Sarah exit. When he sat down, Sarah turned to the male passenger sitting across the aisle from Matt.

Sarah: "Sir, don't talk to this man. You will regret it if you do."

She rubbed the top of Matt's head and proceeded to the first class bathroom.

Male Passenger: "Is that—"

Matt: "Yes."

As Sarah exited the restroom, she saw a stewardess, the male passenger, and Matt in an animated conversation. The stewardess walked toward Sarah, moved to one side to let her pass, and spoke as Sarah stepped by.

Stewardess: "Ms. DuMont, your brother is so cute. I love that accent. He tells the funniest stories. Is he married?"

Sarah: "He is precious. The family is so glad he has finally been released. I mean, honestly, the girl looked much older than fourteen."

Sarah continued down the aisle, leaving the stewardess with her thoughts. She tapped Matt on the shoulder. He rose letting her in. She sat down and buckled her seatbelt.

Sarah: "My brother! Why do you do things like that? My brothers don't have scares on their foreheads from bar fights, don't live alone on broke down farms, don't have in depth conversations with their dogs, and don't keep a Bible on their kitchen tables."

Matt: "There are several things your brothers and I don't have in common, and I'm glad for that."

She looked at Matt for a few moments in silence.

Sarah: "You're right. I'm sorry. For the remainder of this flight, you are my brother."

Matt: "They were askin' all kinds of questions. What was I gonna tell'em—I'm a broke down Marine and Sarah DuMont's charity project?"

Sarah: "Self-pity doesn't become you."

Matt: "I know. That's why I told'em I'm your brother. Gives me more options."

Sarah: "Brother actually gives you fewer options. There are things I can do with a broke down Marine that I won't do with a brother."

Sarah leaned over and softly blew into Matt's ear.

Matt: "Leave my ear alone. Woman, what are you talkin' about?"

She spoke into his ear with a breathy whisper.

Sarah: "You know . . . things."

She sat up straight with a smile on her face.

Sarah: "You are blushing. The cowboy blushes."

Matt: "I'm being taken to Connecticut by the Whore of Babylon."

Sarah: "Ah! I can't believe you said that, but I think I like it, yes, the Whore of Babylon."

She leaned over, blew in his ear again, and whispered.

Sarah: "When I'm finished with you, you'll stutter like Odell."

Matt: "I don't think my mama would approve of you."

Sarah: "Don't be silly. Your mother and I would be dear friends. She would want me to make a man out of her little boy, a man that stutters."

Matt: "This is no way to talk to your brother."

Sarah: "I know the game you play. You use this whole Southern shtick to manipulate me. You know I'm helpless against it. Well, I also have a shtick, big boy, and you know it. I know how to manipulate men. That is why you told these people you are my brother, isn't it? You think that gives you some kind of protection."

Sarah leaned over and whispered into his ear again.

Sarah: "Well, it doesn't, not from me."

Matt: "We need to change the subject before I faint. This reminds me, how much money does a sailor need at the grand openin' of a whorehouse?"

Sarah: "Willie is so fired. Depends on the sailor."

Matt: "I would think it depends on the whorehouse."

Sarah: "Don't be silly, and you a Marine. Marines are sailors, sailors that don't know how to sail, by the way. Why do they even let you on the boat?"

Matt: "You don't know anything about the Marines, do you?"

Sarah: "I know this, when they are in town the bars run out of liquor, things go missing, and young maidens become pregnant."

Matt: "You've insulted my Marines. You've left me no choice but to pout all the way to Connecticut."

Sarah: "Do you even know how to pout?"

Matt: "Yes. I've watched Doodle. She does it all the time."

Sarah: "Exactly how does Doodle pout?"

Matt: "She lays on her back with her legs in the air and ignores me. If you'll just help me get this seatbelt undone, I can get started."

Sarah: "Something tells me not to let this go any further. You win. I'm sorry. I should not have said that about your Marines. But they still should not have let you on the boat."

Matt: "What did you tell your family about me?"

Sarah: "I said you were a vet with PTSD, and for them not to make any sudden moves or shout Allahu Akbar around you."

There was silence as they exchanged a look.

Sarah: "Gotcha, I didn't tell my family that. I told them you were a friend."

Matt: "A temporary friend?"

Sarah: "All my friends are temporary, goes without saying."

Matt: "What about Lucy?"

Sarah: "You don't have a clue how this works, do you?"

With a layover in Atlanta, Sarah and Matt went to a VIP lounge and ordered a snack. The check was brought to the table. They were in a discussion about who should pay when Heidi Van Lutton walked up and picked the check from Sarah's hand. Nothing was said for a moment as the two women exchanged a look.

Heidi: "Please, let me treat the two of you."

Sarah: "Heidi Van Looney Tunes."

Heidi: "I haven't heard that name in years. I'm Heidi Smith now. Married to Dr. Norman Smith, a gynecologist."

Sarah: "What else would he be?"

Heidi: "I think you were out of the country when it happened, making one of your little movies. We are on our way now to the Caymans for a little r and r."

Sarah: "Heidi, this is Matt Shepherd."

Matt stood and extended his hand.

Matt: "Nice to meet you, Mrs. Smith."

The two shook hands, and there was an awkward moment as Heidi continued to hold Matt's hand after the greeting.

Heidi: "Oh, this is just too delicious."

Heidi pulled out a chair and sat down as Sarah groaned.

Heidi: "Matt, I detect a slight hint of an accent. I take it you are from . . . Georgia?"

Matt: "Miss'sippi."

Heidi: "Even better. And what is it you do? . . . I mean what do you do for a living? I know what you do for fun."

Heidi turned and looked at Sarah.

Matt: "I do some carpenter work and have a farm."

Heidi: "Wonderful! I know Sarah has a field that sorely needs plowing. Do you have a tractor, Matt? Oh, I bet you do."

Matt: "Yes, ma'am."

Heidi: "Well, there you are. Matt, Sarah is several years older than me, and I've always thought of her as the big sister I never had. Do you mind if I ask you a personal question?"

Sarah: "Heidi, you have no idea what you are doing."

Heidi: "Matt, considering your upbringing, do you think of yourself as a religious person?"

Matt: "Yes, ma'am."

Heidi: "This is just too delicious."

Heidi stood with the check in her hand.

Heidi: "Sarah, I'll have my mother call your mother. Matt, it has been a pleasure to meet you. Please, don't get up. Sarah, until next time."

Sarah looked at Matt as Heidi walked away.

Matt: "She's certainly a nice lady—bless her heart. You know, Sarah, when she was talkin' about plowin' a field and a tractor, I don't think she was talkin' about farmin' at all."

Sarah looked at Matt as a wry smile spread over her face.

Sarah: "No, Matt, I don't think she was."

Once on the connecting flight, Sarah did not review any script, and Matt did not open his book. A conversation continued uninterrupted through the rest of the flight, through baggage claim, through the ride in the waiting car, and down the long driveway of the DuMont estate. It finally ended as Matt was looking out the window at the home of James and Elizabeth DuMont.

Sarah: "And close your mouth. You are going to embarrass me."

Matt: "Your family lives in the country club?"

Sarah: "This is just one of those little bungalows in the suburb of Connecticut. Come to think of it, you should keep your mouth closed the whole time we are here. That may be the only chance my family has."

Sarah and Matt arrived after the nightly dinner. The family was waiting in the blue room for the travelers. The mansion had so many rooms, you could not use names like the parlor or the setting room; there were just so many rooms that qualified.

As Sarah and Matt approached, the family rose and moved to the center of the room. There was no physical contact between Sarah and Matt. If he were one of her old boyfriends, there might have been hand holding in this situation, or Sarah may have held an arm as they walked in. Sarah and her mother made eye contact.

Sarah: "Hello, everyone, this is a dear friend of mine, Matt Shepherd."

Sarah inched out of the way so she could view her family, one by one, as they introduced themselves to Matt. Sarah knew the stages. First, you had to come to grips with the fact that he was actually as he appeared. What you saw was what you got. Next was the accent. It would take a few meetings before you were able to pick out actual words. Then the final phase started, you knew the word just spoken, but why is he using that word in this situation? Does he not know what that word means? Does it have a meaning unknown to other speakers of English? Is it a Southern idiom? What, in all that is holy, is this man trying to say? Sarah was giddy with anticipation.

James: "Hello, Matt. I'm James DuMont, Sarah's father."

Matt: "Nice to meet you, sir. Appreciate y'all invitin' me."

And so the introductions and handshakes went around the room. Matt was standing on an antique, Oriental rug worth more than his gross annual income. None of this was lost on Sarah.

James: "By the tan lines, I assume you play golf."

Matt: "No, sir. I'm a farmer and carpenter. I don't have the maturity to play golf."

James chuckled at Matt's golf comment.

James: "Have you done that long?"

Matt: "A few years. Before that I was in the Marines."

James: "Sarah didn't tell us that. Were you involved in the Middle East?"

Matt: "Some."

The point of the trip was to help Matt, not enlighten her family. Besides, she wanted to watch them discover Matt all on their own, without her help.

Charlotte made eye contact with Sarah and mouthed the words "the scar," pointing to her own forehead, out of sight from Matt's view. Sarah responded with a knowing grin.

Elizabeth: "Matt, I'm Sarah's mother. I would like you to call me Elizabeth, but I understand from Sarah you won't do that."

Sarah: "Mother."

Matt: "No, ma'am, if you don't mind. I can only do that with my daddy's permission, and he's not here."

Elizabeth: "I understand. Then please call me Mrs. DuMont."

Sarah: "Matt and I are going to the kitchen for a snack. We haven't eaten since lunch. Matt likes to go to bed early. We'll feed him and get him to his room."

As they made their way to the kitchen, Sarah walked past her mother and leaned in toward her ear.

Sarah: "Don't worry, he's housebroken. But do tell the staff to keep an eye on the silverware."

Juanita waited for them in the kitchen. She lived in a servant's apartment in the DuMont home and was a widow with two grown children. James DuMont had been instrumental in helping her children establish careers in insurance and communication. Sarah would watch Juanita and Matt become fast friends during his visit.

Sarah: "Juanita, this is my friend Matt Shepherd. Could you make us a couple of sandwiches, no meat for me?"

Matt: "Since when?"

Sarah: "Juanita, don't listen to him. Listening to him will get you in trouble. I'm Exhibit A. And I told you, Matt, don't tease me about my eating. Now, what would you like?"

Matt: "Ms. Juanita, it is a pleasure to meet you. This looks like a wonderful kitchen. Why don't you show me around and show me where you keep the fixin' for sandwiches, and let's see what damage we can do. It is free, isn't it? If I fix me a big ol' sandwich, you not gonna charge me are you? Did you know Ms. Sarah, the vegetarian, ate a whole plate of pulled pork at my house? It was so good, she went around and licked everyone else's plate. Does she do that here?"

Juanita: "Oh, Mr. Matt, I like you."

What had Sarah done? At one point this had seemed like a good idea. Now Juanita and Matt had their heads stuck in the Sub Zero Refrigerator, and Matt was telling Juanita about the time Sarah jumped into the manure pile. Sometimes that man did things.

After the snack and with Juanita in tears from laughing, Sarah showed Matt to his room. His duffle bag was there, and the bed was partially turned down.

Sarah: "As you can see, you have a bed, a private bath, and a sitting area. Considering what you are accustomed, this should be adequate. But I have to admit, in all of this estate, we can't match your old barn at sunset."

Matt: "Sarah, I do appreciate this. I promise I won't—"

Sarah raised her hand for the international sign of shut-up.

Sarah: "Matt, I don't think you could burn this place down in your underwear and embarrass me. But let's not test that theory. I'll check back with you in a few minutes to see if you need anything."

Matt: "All the way here, you told me not to embarrass you. Now you are tellin' me, I can't embarrass you. I'm confused."

Sarah: "Oh, sweet irony, thy name is Matt. The great confuser is confused. As ol' Heidi would say, this is just too delicious."

She left him with a perplexed look on his face, went to her room, changed into her standard sleeping clothes, put on a housecoat, and returned. She knocked on the door, opening it halfway without going in.

Sarah: "Knock, knock."

Matt was wearing an old t-shirt with USMC across the front and a pair of men's long pajama bottoms. He was sitting in the bed, legs crossed at the ankle, and reading a Bible.

Sarah: "I've not seen that Bible."

Matt: "My old Bible from my Marine days."

Sarah: "Thought you read it in the morning."

Matt: "I met your family. I need some encouragement."

Sarah: "Good night, Matt. Tomorrow morning I'll give you a tour of the place."

She closed the door, stopped, and then opened the door part of the way.

Sarah: "Those pajama bottoms are new, aren't they?"

Matt: "How'd you know?"

Sarah: "Well first, it is hotter than three hells in Mississippi. No Southern male would add unnecessary clothing with long legs. Second, your saintly mother probably told you not to sleep in your underwear at someone else's house. And third, I can see the sales tag."

Matt: "Guilty. Doodle picked'em out. I'm not sure where she got'em."

Sarah smiled and closed the door, just his mama's little boy. Sometimes that man did things. She went back to her room, entered, and found her mother waiting in the sitting area. Sarah wondered why her mother had taken so long.

Sarah: "Hello, Mother. Is it time to play twenty questions already?"

Elizabeth: "I'm afraid twenty questions won't cover this one. First, let the record stipulate that you brought a man home this time instead of the usual little boy. Let me go out on a limb here, I don't think he is gay. Why don't I let you just start talking on the assumption that the truth will pop out, sooner or later?"

Sarah: "Fine. Let me ask you a question. What do you think of that Southern accent? I mean, where does that come from? People have an Irish accent in this country because they are from Ireland. People have a Polish accent because they are from Poland. People have a Southern accent because they are from where, Dollywood?"

"I can't decide if it is the silliest thing I ever heard or the most beautiful. It is like someone is playing Bach's 'Brandenburg Concertos' on a five string banjo."

"And this whole Southerner thing is a joke. You know you can't become one. Oscar Rogers has lived in Macon, Mississippi for forty years, and because he was born in Indiana, Indiana for heaven's sake, they still refer to him as the Yankee."

"And this obsession with religion, as Matt would say you can't sling a dead cat by the tail without hitting a church or a building that is about to be a church or a school that is used as a church on Sunday."

"I asked him once if I am born again in Mississippi, does that make me a Southerner?"

"You know what he told me. [Matt voice] 'The grace of God is a powerful thing, Sarah. All your sins would be forgiven, and you would have a new life in Christ. But you would still be a Yankee.'"

"I don't know, Mother. He has a farm, a dog, chickens, a barn, an old tractor, and a pick-up truck. He lives in a farmhouse that is as old as Canada. He can't speak English. He reads his Bible every day, quotes scripture to me, and makes me pray with him. You know, everything in a man that I want. And he has issues from his service."

"He told me on the plane that I was the Whore of Babylon bringing him to Connecticut."

Elizabeth began to laugh uncontrollably as Sarah gave her mother a doleful look.

Sarah: "I fail to see the humor in that. If it had been any other man, I would have kicked his butt. I passed it off as a joke. I didn't want him to know he got to me."

Elizabeth: "Were you acting like the Whore of Babylon?"

Sarah: "I blew in his ear and made a few suggestive comments. He uses that Southern charm against me. I thought I'd use my considerable talents against him, for a change."

She gave a long sigh and looked at her mother.

Sarah: "Did you talk to Heidi's mother?"

Elizabeth: "Yes. Is he a charity case?"

Sarah: "No, he's the whole wing of a charity hospital. I'm playing nurse."

Elizabeth: "And lover?"

Sarah: "An opportunity presented itself to help someone who, at great personal cost, has helped others. I admit there are occasional flashes of physical attraction."

Elizabeth: "Occasional. Flashes. Sarah, I see the way you look at him. And tell me you don't notice how he looks at you."

Sarah: "How do I look at him, Mother, like a child that has just seen her first orangutan? And as for him, you should see the way he looks at his dog. If he ever looked at me that way, I'd marry him on the spot and give him five babies."

Elizabeth: "I knew the truth would pop out eventually."

Sarah: "The truth, you want the truth? I won him in a bet. I can't get rid of him. I just want to leave him in better shape than I found him."

Elizabeth: "Since when have you ever cared about the condition you leave your victims? Just be sure you don't get too close to the fire. I can tell this man is dangerous. You need to decide, is it in a good way, in a bad way, or both? I hope you know what you are doing. Goodnight, dear."

Elizabeth rose and headed to the bedroom door.

Sarah: "Goodnight, Mother. And no, I don't know what I'm doing. I don't know whether to scratch my watch or wind my butt."

Elizabeth froze and turned, exchanging a look with her daughter.

Sarah: "What?"

Elizabeth turned and left the room.

Sarah set an early wake up alarm. She did not want the dangerous man roaming the halls unsupervised and doing something to embarrass her. Was that even possible, anymore? She did not know. She had plans for this weekend, but not tonight. There would be opportunities later in the week. If all went as planned, she would get him to New York and then to the apartment.

---

The great kitchen contained a dining table that was used by staff for meals. That morning, Sarah found Juanita sitting at the table listening to Matt, who was standing before the commercial grade, gas range top preparing breakfast. Matt winked at her as she came into the kitchen.

Matt: "I gotta get me one of these. Sarah, we had a sign from God this mornin'. Ms. Juanita and I were lookin' to see what y'all had for breakfast around here, and we found an unopened quart of buttermilk in the refrigerator. Now what are the chances that the home of James and Elizabeth DuMont would have a quart of buttermilk? This has to be a sign, right? So I'm makin' us some biscuits and scrambled eggs with bacon, no grits though. Ms. Juanita said she'd make some breakfast potatoes, whatever that is. But I told her no. Eating potatoes for breakfast makes you constipated. Without grits, we'll just have to put a wheel on it and call it a wheelbarrow. She's gonna get some grits today."

Juanita: "But not instant, Ms. Sarah, because they make you constipated, too. Right, Mr. Matt?"

Matt: "That's right, Ms. Juanita."

What was it about Southerners and telling a lie? They did it so effortlessly with such grace. How could people who went to church every Sunday, who prayed in public, who quoted scripture all day long, lie so much? Matt could weave a story together of truths, half-truths, and lies until the victim did not know whether to scratch his watch or wind his butt.

She had given this much thought at night on St. Charles Avenue. She would lie in bed, run some lines, look at her toes, and then contemplate this mystery. She had developed the General Theory of Southern Lying. It made her the Albert Einstein of Southern culture. She could not prove her theory, but it was consistent with all observable facts, which included Matt and certain well-known Southern politicians.

The theory was as follows: There was actually an Eleventh Commandment that only Southerners knew about. God could not tell Moses because his people were from Egypt and that disqualified him from ever being a Southerner. The commandment said if the lie makes a good story, it is not a lie. So their religion did not prohibit them from telling a lie, but only from telling a lie that did not make a good story. A corollary to this theory explained why they were such good storytellers. They did not want to go to hell for lying. This explained why Mississippi had produced so many great authors. They just did not want to go to hell.

Three men entered the kitchen.

Matt: "Hello, fellas. Breakfast will be ready directly."

Sarah had no clue who these men were.

Matt: "Sarah, did you know that *Hector* here told me that he, *Larry* and *Larry* have worked for your family, maintainin' the grounds, for a combined forty years. Can you believe that?"

Sarah: "Good morning, Hector, Larry, Larry."

Matt: "Look, Sarah, I know you are a busy, important person, and Hector, Larry, Larry, and I were talkin', and I know you wanted to show me around this mornin'."

Sarah: "You want to abandon me and visit with your new friends."

Matt: "I could see how it might look that way to someone not as carin' and understandin' as you."

At that moment Sarah's mother entered the room.

Elizabeth: "Sarah, don't just stand there. Help Juanita set the table. You know, Sarah, this . . . I'm not a morning person . . . routine gets a little tiresome. Matthew, now don't overcook those scrambled eggs. I like mine fluffy and shiny."

Matt: "Yes, ma'am."

In all her life she had never seen her mother eat at this table. Seats were taken, plates were served and, yes, grace was said. Prayer for Matt was as natural as talking to Doodle.

Matt: "I checked around, and y'all don't have the right kind of syrup to go on buttermilk biscuits. So you have two choices, jelly or maple syrup. Now jelly goes on toast, not biscuits. And I'm a little concerned about puttin' maple syrup on Southern biscuits. I heard about a man that did that once and fell out dead when he took his first bite."

Elizabeth: "Well, Matthew, what do you think we should do?"

Matt: "I think we should put a little of this maple syrup on a biscuit and let Sarah try it."

Elizabeth: "Excellent idea. Juanita, prepare her a biscuit."

Sarah: "You do know what he is doing? Tell me you are all not that stupid."

Elizabeth: "Hush, dear. Eat the biscuit."

Sarah took the biscuit from Juanita's hand and took a bite. Everyone watched her chew the biscuit. After an appropriate interval, Matt made a medical assessment.

Matt: "Bon appétit. That's French for hope y'all are hungry."

He then explained to everyone that the syrup you put on Southern biscuits is made from sugarcane and how the juices are squeezed out of the cane and cooked down to make the molasses. In the past, a mule would walk all day long in a circle turning the press. At the end of the day, the mule would be dumbfounded that he had done all that walking and not escaped. At that point, Sarah covered her mouth, which was full of biscuit, with one hand and pointed at Matt with the other.

Sarah: "Oh, oh, Matt, tell them about the rented mule."

Matt explained how stubborn and aggravating mules could be. His own grandfather was not allowed to be a deacon in the Baptist Church because of the way he had talked to his mules. However, they were very valuable, so a farmer didn't want to beat his own mule out of spite. If the mule were rented and belonged to someone else, then the calculus was different.

Once breakfast was finished, Juanita insisted that Matt go with his new friends. She would do her job and clean the kitchen.

Sarah ordered the staff to set up a beach umbrella, a beach chair, and a table and to prepare some lemonade so she could keep an eye on Matt, run some lines, and do it all in the utmost comfort.

After she was situated, she saw Matt and his friends moving in and out of one of the numerous rose beds on the estate. James DuMont loved roses. Eventually, Matt, on his hands and knees, crawled among the rose bushes.

He saw her and approached the throne. She was wearing a white tennis outfit and had on a pair of high-end sunglasses and a wide brim sun hat. Matt was wearing his work boots and heavy denim work pants. He apparently had anticipated a working vacation.

Sarah: "What are you children doing?"

Matt: "There is a broken sprinkler head in that bed, and they're gonna let me fix it."

Sarah: "So, you are . . . *fixin'* . . . to fix it. Do you know anything about . . . *fixin'* . . . an irrigation system?"

Matt: "I know there are water and pipes. What else do I need to know?"

Sarah: "Oh, I don't know. Maybe those rose beds are dear to my father, and we have enough money to buy the state of Mississippi, and we have an irrigation service on retainer. Gee, why wouldn't my father want you to take a look at it? Do the three stooges over there know you lie constantly?"

Matt: "Be quiet, Sarah. I told them I do this all the time at home. I even made up a great story of how me and Odell saved the day at the Ole Miss football game when a sprinkler head broke in the fourth quarter. Ole Miss won the game, and they put a plaque with our names on it in the Grove. It's a good story."

Sarah: "And what makes you think you can fix it?"

Matt: "Oh, I don't know. Maybe because me and Odell wired and plumbed that farmhouse. Or maybe because we overhauled my uncle's old saws that had setup for years with no one usin'em. We had to go as far away as Memphis to find parts. Or maybe because my John Deere tractor was wore out when I was born, and it's still runnin'. Or maybe because no one gave me a book that said make this furniture and get a date with a beautiful movie star."

Sarah: "You think I'm beautiful?"

Matt: "Yea."

Sarah: "Okay, you have my permission to destroy my father's rose bed."

Matt: "Thanks, Sarah."

Matt returned to his three new friends. Sarah, looking over the top of her sunglasses, watched him run away.

She grew nervous when the shovels and big hole appeared next to the rose bed. Then with Matt yelling, a large geyser of water erupted.

Matt: "Hector, turn it off! . . . No, the other way, the other way!"

In time, the geyser stopped, the hole was filled, and Matt came walking over to Sarah.

Matt: "Well, that's done. Can I have some of that lemonade?"

Sarah: "No, leave my lemonade alone. This is my house, and you can't have any. Did you fix it?"

Matt: "Sarah, please."

He drank the confiscated glass of lemonade. She was accustomed to being around men when they sweat. But somehow, sweating from racket ball or working out in a gym or playing tennis was different from the sweating Matt was doing. This was how a man sweats when he does physical labor. Sometimes that man did things.

Matt: "What are the plans for the rest of the day?"

Sarah: "Well, we have dinner tonight at seven. They are doing a lunch-brunch by the pool in about an hour, and everyone is going swimming this afternoon."

Matt: "Okay. Larry wants to show me one more thing. Then I'll get a quick shower and find my way to the brunch."

Sarah: "Matt, I think you are doing very well. I'm very proud of you."

Matt: "I just need to stay busy, Sarah. I just need to stay busy."

What Larry wanted to show Matt was a new, zero-turn riding mower with a 72 inch deck and 26 horse power, liquid-cooled, fuel injection engine. The tractor Matt used on his farm was a John Deere Series 1010 that were manufactured from 1961 to 1965. Around 44,000 were made, and one was still in use on the Shepherd farm.

Sarah heard the mower start from inside a maintenance building that she had never seen on the inside. Of course, the architecture of the building was consistent with the rest of the estate. She wondered where Matt was. Presently, she knew. Through the open double doors came her houseguest, sitting upright on the tractor.

He gave the tractor full throttle and began to make ninety-degree turns. As a young boy, his parents had taken him to the State Fair in Jackson each October. He was now sitting on the Scrambler from the days of his youth.

Sarah had no idea that such a machine existed, and, if one did exist, what was its purpose. Matt returned the machine to the front of the maintenance building. He turned the motor off, went inside the building, and returned with a toolbox and his three friends. The three amigos looked over Matt's shoulder as he did a little of this with this wrench and a little of that with that wrench.

Once finished with all the adjustments, the three amigos pointed to the back of the property. Matt returned to the seat, started the engine, and then headed to the indicated location. Sarah could see him go this way, then that way, this way, then that way.

Sarah: "For heaven's sake."

She walked over to the patio for brunch, leaving her throne to be gathered by the staff. Sitting next to her brother, Peter, she lunched on a salad and more lemonade.

Peter: "We've not had much of a chance to visit. How are things going in New Orleans?"

Sarah: "Fine."

Sarah continued to look toward the rear of the estate.

Peter: "I assume that is where you met Matt."

Sarah: "Yes."

Peter: "Was it at some kind of party, maybe at a restaurant, a livestock auction—"

Sarah: "I met him; okay, I met him. He's here; I met him."

Peter: "He seems to take most of your attention. Where is he, anyway?"

Sarah made a half-hearted motion toward the rear of the estate. Peter looked in that general direction.

Peter: "Is he playing tennis?"

Sarah: "No."

Peter: "Has he been down there hitting golf balls with Father?"

Sarah: "No."

Peter: "Okay, Sarah. I give up. What is he doing?"

Sarah pointed across the estate toward the zero-turn, liquid cooled, fuel injected mower.

Peter: "Sarah, all I see is Hector cutting the lawn."

Sarah: "That's not Hector."

Peter looked at Sarah intently.

Peter: "Is this the latest cause celeb, save the redneck? Is that what this is all about?"

Sarah: "No, that is not what this is all about. A little advice, he doesn't like it when I call him cowboy. Imagine what he might do if he hears you call him redneck. He didn't get that scar on his forehead at church; though, if you ask him, he will tell you he did."

Sarah paused.

Sarah: "I should not have said that. Matt is an incredible, kind, sweet person, who just has a few issues. I doubt you could say anything to him that would provoke him. But I strongly recommend you not test that theory. I, on the other hand, can provoke him. I don't know what that says about me."

Peter: "It says he has feelings for you. The people that make you the maddest are the ones you care most about."

Sarah: "Well, he got pretty mad at me, but there is more to it."

Peter: "I do like him. But, Sarah, you have to admit, he is not like any of your other boyfriends."

Sarah: "Is that a bad thing or a good thing?"

Peter: "Watch yourself, sis."

Sarah: "I will. Thanks."

With Matt still on the mower, Sarah returned to her room and took a short nap. She had learned this skill due to the long days required for her chosen profession. When she woke, she put on her two-piece bathing suit with a cover and stepped into the hall. Here came Matt.

He seemed so out of place in this house just now. She thought about the time when she was in the sixth grade, and the mansion had plumbing problems. It was the sixth grade because it was the last year before boarding school. The plumbers had fascinated her. In fact, she pretended to be ill so she could stay home and watch them. They were oblivious to the fine furnishings of the mansion. One had taken out a tape measure, measured the distance from a corner, marked the wall, took out a hammer, and began hitting the wall to remove the plaster. It was the coolest thing she had ever seen. She half expected Matt to begin removing plaster at any minute.

This was part of her fascination with him. He seemed oblivious to fine things, but he could turn reclaimed lumber into a fine thing.

Matt: "Where did you go? I wanted to show you what I could do on that thing. Larry said I could cut some more tomorrow. I may even be able to cut some of your neighbor's grass. I met two teenage girls that said I could."

Sarah: "We have plans for tomorrow."

Matt: "I need to talk to your father. Y'all are sittin' on a gold mine here. You know, Sarah, if my idea pans out, your family won't have to continue to live like this."

Sarah: "What, in the name of all that is holy, are you talking about?"

Matt: "First, take the cuttin' deck off that mower. You can use an old John Deere tractor to cut grass. I don't know what idiot decided to put a cuttin' deck on that fine piece of machinery. I can assure you, he wasn't from Miss'sippi. Then we sell time on the mower to adventure seekers. You call them rednecks, I think. I bet we could get twenty dollars for thirty minutes. Call it Adventure Seekers Park. The motto could be 'Hey, y'all—watch this.' We could add some bleachers and charge five dollars to cover parkin' and what not so folks could watch the adventure seekers. Ms. Juanita could sell hotdogs and cokes. Y'all are sittin' on a gold mine here. Your family doesn't have to continue to live like this."

Sarah: "First, back up a step or two. You smell like a field hand."

Matt: "How do you know what a field hand smells like?"

Sarah: "I don't. That's a line from a movie I did. I thought it was appropriate."

Matt took one huge step back.

Sarah: "Second, we are expected at the pool, and I'm guessing you didn't bring your bathing suit."

Matt: "I don't own a bathin' suit. You don't swim in a cow pond in a Ralph Lauren bathin' suit. I told Doodle I needed one to come up here, and she fell out laughin'."

Sarah: "A dog can laugh?"

Matt: "I wish they couldn't. It'd make my life more pleasant."

Sarah: "I swear Matt, what were we talking about? Oh yes, a bathing suit, I'll get one from Chris. He is more your size. Take a bath first and meet me at the pool. And no more talk about adventure seekers or laughing dogs. You are going to embarrass me."

Matt: "Only in Connecticut do you take a bath before you get wet. And I'm only lookin' out for your family, bless their hearts. There's no reason for'em to continue to live like this."

———————————

Sarah and Charlotte were in adjacent recliners, enjoying the sun and each other's company. Sarah had always liked Charlotte, who always treated Sarah like a sister-in-law and not a famous actress. Matt bathed and joined the family by the pool. He was in the pool along with Chris and Peter's two boys.

Sarah watched Matt in the pool for a while. He was teaching everyone a game similar to Marco Polo, but his version was called Rhett Butler. She could tell he was making up the rules as they went along.

Charlotte: "I have to say, Sarah, your boyfriend is different. I never pictured you with someone like him. But the more I see you together, the more I think it works."

Sarah: "No comment."

Charlotte: "What are those scars on his back? He even has scars on his left leg."

Sarah: "I have never seen those."

Charlotte: "You've never seen him without a shirt?"

Sarah: "Our relationship is complicated. If I could explain it, I would. He fought in Iraq and Afghanistan. Got some medals. So I suppose that is where those scars came from. I knew about the ones on his leg, but I can't discuss it. He has more scars than are visible on the outside."

Charlotte: "What about that scar on his forehead? Do you know where that came from?"

Sarah: "A bar fight. He beat the stuffing out of three very large men."

Charlotte: "Sarah, should I let the boys be around him?"

Sarah: "The safest place in the world for your boys is standing next to Matthew Shepherd."

Two young teenage girls had joined the pool party and were learning the rules to Rhett Butler along with everyone else.

Charlotte: "Who are those two young girls?"

Sarah: "I think they are from one of the adjacent homes."

Charlotte: "I didn't know your mother had invited anyone else."

Sarah observed the girls a moment.

Sarah: "Don't you see what's going on here? Watch the girls and then look at Matt."

Charlotte: "I see what you mean."

Sarah: "Those girls were minding their own business, just trying to score some beer for tonight when they heard it. They probably heard Matt when he was on the tractor hollering, 'Sarah watch this!' Not the fake ones you hear on TV. No, the real thing. That honey dripping, home wrecking, sin inducing Southern accent. The one that moves as slow as the Mississippi River in August. That hangs low on the live oak trees on St. Charles Avenue. That is as blue as a Louisiana swamp in the moonlight. That says come see my barn, ride in my truck, stay for dinner, try this pulled pork, come back and see us anytime."

Charlotte: "Sarah, are you all right?"

---

Dinner with guests at the DuMont house was a many faceted event. There were the food and the usual dinner conversation. But there was also discussion. The DuMonts were liberals in the classical sense. No intellectual or political position was forbidden, as long as those holding that position could make a coherent and reasoned argument. More important than the position taken was the ability to defend that position. Dinners at the DuMont home were what higher education in America once was.

Sarah had been a double agent. She had not prepared her family for Matt, but she had not prepared Matt for her family. Sarah's mother loved the exchange at dinnertime. Sarah had seen her cause Presidents of Ivy League Schools to stutter like she imagined Odell did. She wondered if her mother could make presidents of colleges stutter, could she make Odell speak fluently? Sarah believed her mother could.

Sarah reasoned that the dining room tonight was the Shenandoah Valley. Matt was Stonewall Jackson, and her family were the hapless Union Generals. They would underestimate him, and he would do the unexpected. The outcome would be similar to the historical one.

Matt knocked at Sarah's door.

Matt: "Sarah, are you in there? It's almost seven. I don't wanna be late."

Sarah spoke from inside the room.

Sarah: "Hold your horses, cowboy. You are the guest of honor. It won't start without you."

She opened the door to see him in his now trademark white shirt, his best jeans, and those cowboy boots. Juanita had his white shirt laundered, no starch. For a brief moment, nothing was said as they stood in the doorway.

Sarah: "What are you looking at?"

Matt: "I tell you Sarah, sometimes."

Sarah: "Sometimes what?"

Matt took a deep breath and slowly exhaled.

Matt: "If I had the paperwork—"

Sarah: "Paperwork? What foolishness are you talking about now? Let me look at you."

She gave him a once over. She smoothed his shirt over his shoulders, adjusted his collar, and used her hand to brush his hair.

Sarah: "Grin like this and let me see your teeth."

148

He grinned, showing his front teeth, which she inspected.

Sarah: "Okay, I guess you'll do. Not much to work with here. Tonight my family may ask you some questions. It is not an inquisition. There are no wrong answers. Just be yourself and answer honestly."

Matt: "This sounds a lot like eatin' barbecue outside Odell's shack on the picnic benches. A man better be able to defend his opinion."

Sometimes that man said things.

The menu for tonight consisted of sautéed ham steaks with fresh green peas and a border of mashed potatoes. Sarah would eat everything but the ham, in spite of Matt's influence. Wine would be served, but the wine glasses for Matt and Sarah would contain fruit juice.

To emphasize the sophistication of the DuMont clan, everyone held hands, and Matt said grace. Sarah sat directly across from him. She wanted to be able to see his facial expressions and run interference, if necessary. She would not leave her man behind.

James: "Matt, I understand you served with the Marines."

Matt: "Yes, sir, Third Battalion Fifth Regiment out of Camp Pendleton."

James: "In Iraq?"

Matt: "Iraq and Afghanistan."

Sarah wanted to jump up and scream he fought in the Second Battle of Fallujah. But this was Matt and not her. She had gotten in terrible trouble before when she injected herself into this part of Matt's life. She learned her lesson.

Elizabeth: "What do you think about the decision to go into Iraq?"

Sarah knew now that the game was afoot.

Matt: "Ma'am, Marines don't ask why; they ask how."

Sarah was seeing a side of Matt she had not seen before. This was the Marine that went looking for Andy.

Elizabeth: "War is such a waste and is so unnecessary."

Matt: "I agree that it is a terrible waste. But with all due respect, ma'am, sometimes, it is necessary. Where I come from, we believe that everyone should have the opportunity to hear the Gospel of Jesus Christ; however, we also believe there are some folks that just need killin'. You can't reason with them, and you can't make them stop hurtin' others. They just need killin'."

Peter: "Are you a killer, Matt?"

Matt: "Yes."

The startling thing was not only the answer, but also the calm, assured way in which it was delivered.

Matt: "Under the authority of the Constitution and the direction of the Commander-in-Chief, I will kill anyone they tell me to."

Peter: "What if they ask you to do something that might be considered immoral or wrong?"

Matt: "I'm not a trained lawyer. I'm not a trained theologian. I'm a trained killer. Those above me had better think long and hard about the orders they give me. As best I can, I kill the enemy and keep my Marines alive."

Peter: "Are things really that simple?"

Matt: "If they are not, then we are talkin' about diplomacy. If they are, then we are talkin' about the U.S. Marines."

Sarah began pumping her arm in the air.

Sarah: "Ooh-ra!"

James: "What about turning the other check?"

Matt: "Jesus said to turn the other cheek when it is my check bein' slapped. He didn't say for me to look away when someone else's cheek is slapped."

Sarah saw how her mother now looked at Matt. She was not sure that her mother had ever looked at her with such affection. What was it about DuMont women and cowboys?

James: "Well said. Some may not agree with all the content, but it was concise and well thought out. You have given us something to think about. I'd like to make a toast to Sarah's new friend, but first I think Sarah should lead us all in a cheer."

All the family: "Ooh-ra!"

After the toast, Sarah saw the familiar Matt appear. She knew that this Matt could be as dangerous as the Marine.

Matt: "Mr. DuMont, I don't know if you know it, but y'all are sittin' on a gold mine here."

Sarah tapped her glass with her fork.

Sarah: "I'd like to make an announcement before Matt goes any further. I have not been totally honest with you about him."

All the family turned and looked at Matt as if he had a highly infectious disease. He smiled as if he knew the game was over.

Sarah: "Matt will tell you stories that contain so many truths, half-truths, and out right lies, eventually, you will lose all contact with reality. During this whole process, you will think he is the biggest fool you have ever met, right up to the point that he convinces you his dog talks to him and sweet tea comes out your nose."

Elizabeth: "Don't be silly, dear. We are not having sweet tea tonight."

Charlotte: "Matt, let me ask you something. This yes ma'am and no ma'am business, I don't understand the rules. I thought it would apply to someone in authority over you or perhaps to someone older than you. But you seem to apply it to everyone."

Matt: "Well, the Apostle Paul told the Philippians to consider others better than themselves, so everyone is my superior."

Charlotte: "That's beautiful."

Sarah: "I'm warning you."

Matt: "Sarah's just upset. When Doodle dropped me off at the airport, she said Sarah was a little overrated as an actress."

A noise came from Charlotte's side of the table.

Sarah: "I thought you said Odell dropped you off?"

Matt: "Don't be silly. Odell stutters. You know he can't drive."

In a matter of moments, James was asking Elizabeth why someone who stutters couldn't drive. Elizabeth was asking Sarah who was this Odell. Peter was telling Chris that he thought Doodle was a dog, and Charlotte had wine coming out of her nose.

Matt looked at Sarah.

Matt: "This was too easy."

Sarah: "You are just Stonewall in the dining room."

Sometimes that man did things.

---

Weather permitting, and even occasionally when it did not, James Dumont would withdraw after supper and sit by the pool with a cigar and brandy. The affair was invitation only. This night, James asked Matt to join him.

James: "Matt, would you care for some brandy?"

Matt: "No, sir, thank you."

James: "Are you a teetotaler or do you have some demons in your past?"

Matt: "The latter."

James: "I have several friends in that situation. Do you belong to AA?"

Matt: "No, sir. I have close friends and family that help me. My uncle, the local sheriff, will put anybody in jail that gives me liquor."

James: "So, I could be breaking Mississippi law as we speak."

Matt: "It's a gray area, but yes."

James: "Would you like a cigar?"

Matt: "I doubt if I'd finish it. I'd hate to waste one of your cigars. They look expensive."

James: "Don Carlos, they might be, but I think we can spot you one cigar. Please."

James clipped the cigar, handed it to Matt, and lit it for him.

James: "How's that?"

Matt: "Sure beats the smell of a wet dog. Reminds me of the smell of the reclaimed lumber I use to make furniture. Especially after I've cut several pieces and the sawdust is in the air."

James: "Oh by the way, thank you for repairing the sprinkler head near my rose bed. Hector tells me I should give you credit for that."

Matt: "You're welcome, but Hector, Larry, and Larry did most of the work."

---

Elizabeth: "Sarah, this habit of yours of watching people unseen is very rude."

Sarah: "It's not a habit; it's a gift. Look at them. I know they are talking about me."

Elizabeth: "Not everything is about you, dear."

Sarah: "What an odd thing to say. Father has given him a cigar. I didn't know Matt smoked cigars. I'm worried about him out there."

Elizabeth: "Don't be silly. Matt can handle himself."

Sarah: "I meant Father."

---

James: "Do you hunt?"

Matt: "Not much. I mostly fish. My uncle is the hunter."

James: "What does he hunt?"

Matt: "Deer, squirrel, duck, turkey."

James: "I enjoy deer hunting. What methods does he use?"

Matt: "They mostly use a deer stand, usually attached to a tree. Seems like every year we get someone hurt fallin' out of a stand. Last year Ovid Sullivan fell thirty feet out of one of those stands."

James: "Did it hurt him?"

Matt: "No, sir. He landed on his head. You can't hurt a Sullivan by hittin' 'em in the head."

James: "Something tells me you have firsthand knowledge in that regard."

Matt: "Well, I'm ashamed to say, yes. I got in a bar fight with the three of 'em one night. That's how I got this scar. It was actually more like two-and-a-half. I hit the youngest one, Homer, with a bar stool while he wasn't lookin', and he wasn't much good after that."

---

Sarah: "Father is laughing and just blew a big puff of cigar smoke into the air."

Elizabeth: "That means he's enjoying himself. Please come away from that window."

Sarah: "I thought I made it very clear to everyone that Matt lies. He is a liar. If he is telling you something, even *and*, *but*, and *the* are suspect."

---

Matt: "When Ovid fell out of the deer stand, he did land on his head, but it was on top of a wild turkey. It killed the turkey. He came into deer camp carryin' that bird with a dazed look on his face, and blood streamin' down his forehead. There was a game warden in camp, and it wasn't turkey season. The warden confiscated his gun and his truck and took the turkey. Ovid is still mad about it."

James: "Ovid and Homer, aren't those unusual names for your part of the country?"

Matt: "Yes, sir. The third brother is named Virgil. They're named for classical poets, I think. Their daddy, at one time, taught the classics at Princeton. He got caught in an indiscretion with a young coed, who happened to be from Miss'sippi. Well, he ended up marryin' her, and they moved back to her home place. They had those three boys, and none of them were like their daddy. They never finished high school, and each one of'em is as rough as a corn cob. They haul pulpwood for a livin'. The mama left'em. She ran off with a fertilizer salesman when those boys were young. The daddy did the best he could. It is one sad tale."

James: "What happened to the father? Does he still live there?"

Matt: "No, sir. The last I heard, he was livin' in the French Quarter and recitin' poetry to tourists on Bourbon Street for tips. Those boys send him money. I giv'em this, they look after family."

---

Sarah: "I'm going out there. This has gone on long enough. I know Matt is telling him about the chicken manure. I'm sure everyone is having a big laugh at my expense."

Elizabeth: "You know your father. Do not go out there. . . . What about the chicken manure?"

---

James: "Matt, this has been most entertaining. No wonder my daughter likes you. You do know, she has been watching us?"

Matt: "Yes, sir, at the window just to the right of the side door."

James: "Yes, you are a Marine. Why don't you and I sit here a little longer and enjoy our cigars? Even though she knows better, I'm sure Sarah will be here shortly."

Matt: "I think she is on her way now."

James: "Then please excuse me. I don't want to be a third wheel. It has been a pleasure to talk to you. I'll leave you to the tender mercies of my daughter."

Matt: "You must have a daughter I haven't met yet."

James laughed.

James: "No, just the one. Good luck, Matt."

James rose and headed to the house, passing Sarah along a stone path outlined in the warm glow of landscape lighting.

James: "Sarah."

Sarah: "Father."

Sarah sat down in the abandoned chair.

Sarah: "What were you two talking about? Were you talking about me? What did my father say? I saw him laughing at one point. Did you tell him about the chicken manure?"

Matt: "Hush, woman. It's a beautiful night. I'm sittin' on the Dumont estate as an invited guest smokin' a Don Carlos cigar under a cloudless sky next to a beautiful swimming pool and fountain. Doodle's goin' to be so jealous. . . . We didn't talk about you at all."

Sarah: "What an odd thing to say. Matt—"

He put his fingers to his lips.

Matt: "Shhh!"

Sarah: "That cigar is going to get you in trouble, cowboy. I forbid you to smoke another one."

Matt: "Sarah, sometimes silence is a good thing."

Sarah: "Don't be silly!"

In a rare moment of their acquaintance, the two sat in total silence as Matt puffed on his cigar. The only sound was the splashing water of the fountain.

———

Elizabeth: "Well, James, what do you think?"

James: "I think I may have found another place to deer hunt."

Elizabeth: "Typical—that's a good man. Now you leave me no choice. I'll have to talk with him."

James: "I think Sarah may have met her match. Perhaps, you should stay out of it. "

Elizabeth: "Don't be silly!"

---

Sarah discretely observed Matt and imagined him sitting under a night sky in Iraq or Afghanistan. On nights like this, did he think about Andy? Middendorf's had shown that much was very near the surface and easily accessed. Did she really want to know what else might be near the surface?

With the fountain as the only source of any sound and cigar smoke hanging in the still night air, he startled her as he began a poem:

> I take to the riggings
> and search the sea
> into the night
> for the Sarah Morgan Leigh.
>
> Many a tale
> of fight and flee
> is told by those
> who seek her like me.
>
> Long of line,
> twin spars like trees,
> and sails of black
> are the Sarah Morgan Leigh.
>
> My only thought
> as I move even higher
> is to catch a glimpse
> of my heart's desire.
>
> I cling to the riggings

and search the sea
into the night
for the Sarah Morgan Leigh.

There! I see her
on the ocean's swell
just for a moment
as my shouts do tell.

But then she's gone;
was it her I did see
in the moonlight
the Sarah Morgan Leigh?

Sailors have searched
under sun and stars
for just one glimpse
of the famous twin spars.

I cling to the riggings
and search the sea
with cigar in hand
for the Sarah Morgan Leigh.

Sarah stood without saying a word and headed toward the house.

Matt: "Wait, Sarah—don't go off and leave me."

Matt rose and followed her.

Matt: "Did you not like the poem? . . . Are you mad? . . . You walk fast when you're mad. . . . I can't find my room at night."

She whirled around.

Sarah: "You are a liar! You lie to me all the time and I know it. If you can write poetry, serve in Iraq and Afghanistan, and beat up three men in a bar fight, you can find your room. And put out that cigar. My mother will not let you in the house with that thing."

Matt: "Don't leave me alone;/ I'm afraid to be/ without a smoke/ or my Sarah Morgan Leigh."

Sarah: "You know, I don't like you, and poetry is not going to change that. Did you write the poem or did Doodle?"

Matt: "Doodle. You should be mad at her not me. . . . The nights get long on the farm at times."

Sarah: "And poetry helps?"

Matt: "Thinking about you helps, especially the twin spars like trees."

Sarah: "You are an awful tacky man. Give me your arm. I'll take you to your room but don't say anything else to me."

Sarah took Matt's arm, and the two walked along the stone path.

Matt: "Liar's kinda harsh, don't you think? I'd like to get the charges reduced."

Sarah: "To what?"

Matt: "Talking under the influence."

Sarah: "What influence? You don't drink anymore."

Matt: "Not liquor, you."

Sarah: "I make you intoxicated?"

Matt: "Sarah, you are a double shot of Booker's Bourbon, straight-up."

Sarah: "Why can't you be a normal boyfriend?"

Matt: "You said boyfriend."

Sarah stopped and turned toward Matt.

Sarah: "I did not."

Matt: "You did."

Sarah turned toward the house and continued walking.

Sarah: "Did not."

Matt: "Did. I'll take the job as long as it's indoor work with no heavy lifting. What do I get?"

Sarah: "One free cigar. Now shhh—sometimes silence is a good thing."

Matt: "The non-cigar person can't shhh the cigar person."

Sarah: "This is my house."

Matt: "You have a familial relationship with the owners. I have the cigar."

Sarah: "That's sexist."

Matt: "In a post-feminist world, the concept of sexist is still in flux. Me and Odell haven't nailed it down yet."

Sarah: "Matt, do the poem thing again."

Matt: "Anything for Sarah Morgan Leigh."

He would recite the poem two more times for Sarah and once for her mother.

After depositing Matt in his room, Sarah lay awake in bed thinking about her houseguest, the Sarah Morgan Leigh, and other things. She realized what he meant earlier by paperwork. She had called it foolishness. Something about it was foolish, as foolish as the poem. But was it him for saying it, or her for not knowing what he meant? At any rate, Sarah Morgan Leigh had plans for tonight.

Matt was just before turning out the light when he heard a soft knock at the door.

Matt: "Yes."

Elizabeth opened the door.

Elizabeth: "Hello, Matt. May I come in?"

Matt: "If you are lookin' for Sarah, I suppose, she's in her room."

Elizabeth: "I'm not looking for Sarah. I'd like to talk to you . . . alone."

Elizabeth took a seat in the sitting area of the bedroom.

Elizabeth: "Come over here and join me. And you are dressed fine. A Marine t-shirt and pajama bottoms are the perfect attire for a late night conversation."

Matt: "Yes, ma'am."

Matt took a seat across from Elizabeth.

Elizabeth: "Sarah tells me that your mother passed away several years ago."

Matt: "Yes, ma'am. I was still in high school."

Elizabeth: "I like you, Matt. I don't think Sarah has ever met anyone quite like you. My daughter is a very complex, competitive person who treats men like an accessory. As a mother of two sons, I would be very concerned if one of them brought home a girl like Sarah."

Matt: "There are other girls like Sarah?"

Elizabeth: "You know what I mean."

Matt: "Yes, I do. I'd be concerned if she'd shown up in my platoon. How did she ever wind up in actin'? Seems to me, she should be in business, maybe Wall Street."

Elizabeth: "She was at Yale, being groomed for the family business on Wall Street. She had not done any acting. They tried to get her to participate in the theater productions at boarding school, but she told them she would rather walk around campus poking a stick in her eye. Then on Christmas break her sophomore year, she mentioned to me that one of her friends had been accepted to Juilliard School of Drama. She said she might like to do that. I made the mistake of telling her I didn't think she could get in. She did."

Matt: "I'm not surprised."

Elizabeth: "She has very few female friends. Lucy, her closest friend, worked in a coffee shop in New Haven. Lucy lived in our New York apartment while Sarah went to Juilliard. She has that store to scratch her business itch and to keep Lucy in her life."

There was a moment of silence.

Elizabeth: "I see the way Sarah looks at you. Her divorce hurt her more than she lets on. You are both over thirty and don't need the well wishes or opinion of an old woman. I don't want to see either of you get hurt."

Matt: "I'd never do anything to hurt your daughter."

Elizabeth: "I can see that, Matt. And you need to be aware, approach Sarah DuMont with caution. I'm sure a Marine knows how to proceed with caution."

Matt: "Yes, ma'am. I do."

Elizabeth: "Good, my conscience is clear. And I wouldn't mention this conversation to Sarah."

Matt: "Oh no, ma'am. This will be our little secret."

Elizabeth left the room, but not before checking the hallway to make sure Sarah was not around. Matt was reaching to turn off the light when he heard another knock at the door. This time, he went to the door. It was Chris who was nervously looking down the hall towards Sarah's room.

Chris: "Hi, Matt. Can I come in and talk with you just a minute?"

Matt: "Sure."

Chris stepped in the room and made a point of closing the door.

Chris: "I need to talk to you about Sarah."

Matt: "My favorite subject. Does she know you're here? Would you like me to go get her?"

Chris: "No, no and don't tell her. Only Peter knows I'm here. Let's go sit down."

This time Matt heard the cautionary tale about Sarah from the point of view of the brothers. Chris explained how growing up with Sarah followed a predictable pattern. First, she challenged one or both, usually both, of her brothers to some kind of contest. If they refused, she would then taunt them until they agreed to compete. If she won the competition, which usually happened, she would taunt them again. If she lost, she taunted them even more. Then the process would repeat itself based on some new competition.

The contests were varied: who could run the fastest, climb the highest, scream the loudest, hold their breath the longest, stay awake all night, eat the most, eat the least. Once the younger brothers matured physically, the competitions became more cerebral: who made the best grades; who could solve a puzzle first; or who got what awards.

Chris explained that he thought Sarah had found a home in acting because of the competition, not due to the love of acting. You either got the part or you did not, and if she did and you did not, well.

It took some time, but Chris would eventually finish his story and let Matt go to sleep, hours after his normal bedtime.

# Chapter Twelve

# Play Ball!

The next morning, following the defeat of all the Union forces in the dining room and the poem recital, Sarah found her mother sitting at the staff table in the kitchen, Juanita with flour up to her elbows, and Matt explaining how spring wheat makes the best biscuit flour. It has less protein content; somehow, that made a better biscuit. She wondered if any of that were true.

Elizabeth: "Matt is teaching Juanita how to make his biscuits. At our next dinner party, we are going to serve Southern buttermilk biscuits with beluga caviar and foie gras."

Matt looked at Sarah.

Sarah: "Fish eggs and goose liver."

Matt: "Well, that explains why you people won't eat boiled okra or collard greens."

Sarah: "I've been saving today for a surprise. My trainer is on me about a workout. After I finish, let's go into the city."

Matt: "What city?"

Sarah: "New York City, Matt—I see that smile. See, Mother, I tried to warn you about him. But no, Sarah is stupid and so is her boyfriend."

Elizabeth: "We never thought Matt was stupid, dear."

Sarah: "Anyway, a friend of mine is doing Othello, off Broadway.

We could go to a matinee and cough, laugh, and sneeze at the wrong times to throw the actors timing off. Then we could take a cab to Central Park. You could ask the driver, [Matt voice] 'Friend, where are your people from.' Of course, he wouldn't be able to understand you because of your accent. So you could just say it louder and louder."

"Then, I know of a restaurant near the park that specializes in Southern cuisine. We could order everything on the menu, and you could tell the waitress, [Matt voice] 'Ma'am, I need to speak to your chef.' And when he came out, you could get in an argument over collard greens. Then we could walk through Central Park and throw rocks at the squirrels. Our driver will meet us on the other side and bring us home. You would be back before your bedtime. How about it, Matt? It would be so much fun."

Matt: "I have to say, Sarah, those are the top items on my bucket list. But you're not bein' honest with me. A little bird told me your family has season tickets to the Yankees, and, since they are playin' Oakland today in a matinee, we could go to the game. And, since we could gorge on ballpark food, we could skip the restaurant, but still torment the squirrels in Central Park."

Sarah: "That little bird's name wouldn't be Chris, would it?"

Matt: "Now Sarah, you know Chris told me not to tell."

Sarah: "Oakland, Matt? The house staff has a bigger payroll. Please don't make me go?"

Matt: "How 'bout a wager? I win, ballgame; you win, Macbeth."

Sarah: "Othello. What's the wager?"

Matt: "I've conducted a reconnaissance at night while y'all were asleep. And I don't think there's a Bible in this house, and Ms. Juanita's Bible doesn't count. So here's the wager, produce a Bible in the next fifteen minutes, a family member's Bible, and I go to Macbeth. If not, then it's 'play ball.'"

Sarah: "That's absurd. Matt, there are thirty-two rooms in this house. Of course, there is a Bible somewhere. Thirty minutes."

Matt: "Twenty."

Sarah: "Done."

Matt: "Ms. Juanita, hand me that egg timer."

Sarah froze as if at the starting line. Matt adjusted the timer.

Matt: "Go!"

Elizabeth: "Don't be silly, dear. We have a family Bible."

Sarah: "Where is it, Mother?"

There was a telling silence.

Elizabeth: "James! James! Get up James! We have a family emergency!"

Sarah raced up the stairs to Chris' room to find he was still asleep in bed. She jerked the covers so hard that not even the top sheet remained to cover the informer.

Sarah: "You told that cowboy about the Yankee tickets. Get up! Get up! If I don't find a Bible in this house in twenty minutes, I have to go to a Yankees game."

Chris: "Sarah, have you lost your mind?"

Sarah: "No, but you're going to lose a kidney if you don't get up and help me."

Eventually, every descendant, by birth or marriage, of the French Huguenots who fled Europe due to religious persecution in the mansion of James and Elizabeth DuMont were in pursuit of the Holy Word of God.

At one point, Chris believed he had found one.

Chris: "Got it; got it."

Sarah: "You idiot, that's not a Bible. That's *The Prophet* by Kahlil Gibran."

Eventually, a Bible was located, but the egg timer had spoken.

Sarah completed her workout in the exercise room and was returning to her room for a shower, passing a window that over looked the side yard. Below were Matt, Chris, Peter's two boys, the two teenage girls from the pool, Hector, Larry, and Larry, all playing touch football. In less than two days, Chris had a bro-crush; two teenage girls were willing to give Matt children; Peter's boys were saying yes ma'am and no ma'am for the first time in their lives; James DuMont still believed people who stuttered couldn't drive; her mother was serving buttermilk biscuits with caviar at her next party; the entire household had spent the morning looking for a Bible; and Hector, Larry, and Larry were now Ole Miss football fans. How did the South ever lose the Civil War? They probably did it on purpose because they didn't want to hurt the North's feelings. That was the only logical answer.

Sarah rang the kitchen and told Juanita to tell Matt playtime was over. Time to go to the City.

---

Matt: "This is so cool! Yankee Stadium, we're so close to the players that we could help them spit and scratch. I think I will."

Sarah: "Do not embarrass me. You make me uncomfortable in public. I never know what you might do or say."

Matt: "I think what you're tryin' to say is there's never a dull moment."

Sarah: "I guess so, not even on a broke down farm in Mississippi."

Sarah smiled at him, removed his new Yankees baseball cap, and rubbed the top of his head.

Sarah: "You won the bet. Enjoy the game."

Sarah informed the beer vendors in their area that they could not sell Matt a beer. If they did, they would be spending tomorrow night in the Macon, Mississippi jail.

Vendor: "Yea, whatever you say lady."

Sarah was amused by how flippant they were. There was a hard reality, and that reality was Billy Pruitt. But for distance, they would be taking her warning very seriously.

In the middle of the third inning, the lady sitting in front of them turned to speak to Sarah.

Lady: "Where is your boyfriend from?"

Sarah: "He is not my boyfriend, but he is from Mississippi."

Lady: "I would pay good money just to listen to that man talk."

Sarah: "Oh, if you listen to him, you'll pay for it."

Sarah noticed that the home plate umpire would move closer and closer to where they were sitting between innings. In the bottom of the seventh, he actually spoke to them—Matt was staying until the last out. She had never seen an umpire do that before.

Umpire: "Say, where are you folks from?"

His accent was as thick as Matt's.

Matt: "I'm from Macon, Miss'sippi. You?"

Umpire: "Mobile. When I was a little boy, we went to family reunions on a river outside of Meridian, Miss'sippi."

Matt: "The Chunky River. So did we. My last name is Shepherd, but the reunions were on my mama's side. She was a Pruitt."

Umpire: "My mama was a Pruitt."

Matt: "Looks like we're family. How 'bout that?"

At that, Sarah stood up.

Sarah: "Do you think I believe any of this? [Matt voice] 'My mama was a Pruitt on my uncle's side, twice removed, until she remarried her first cousin.'"

Umpire: "Bless your heart."

Sarah: "I bet you are one of his old Marine buddies, and he put you up to this."

Sarah looked at Matt.

Sarah: "This is why you dragged me to this ballgame, isn't it?"

The umpire was walking away in the process of putting on his mask.

Umpire: "Enjoy the game. I was never in the military."

Sarah: "Well, my boyfriend was. And you better start calling them both ways, or he will kick your butt. And he can too. He's killed a man with his bare hands."

She could not believe she said that. She knew, the minute the words were formed in her mouth, it was wrong. Words just move so fast sometimes.

Sarah sat down very slowly next to Matt. Both of them were looking straight ahead. She had the palms of her hands resting on her upper legs. The woman, sitting in front of them, gave a quick glance over her shoulder at Matt.

Sarah: "Matt, I'm so sorry. Please don't be mad at me. Please don't fuss at me. I don't think I could take it if you fussed at me. I don't know how to be around someone like you. There is a gulf between us. I'm rich, and I live in a make-believe world without God. You're not wealthy, and you live in a very real world with God. Please don't be angry with me."

Matt reached out and put his hand on the back of Sarah's hand. It was one of the few times she could remember that he had reached out and touched her when they weren't praying.

Matt: "Don't worry about it, Sarah. I'm not angry with you."

As he concentrated on the late innings of a close ballgame, Sarah concentrated on Matt. She needed to make this up to him. Tonight she would slip into his room and seduce him. She intended to do it last night as a reward for his victory in the dining room or for his service to his country or whatever. It was her patriotic duty to a veteran. But she heard voices in his room. What could he and Chris talk about for so long? They must have been talking about her. She had dressed for seduction but woke up, before six a.m., drooling on her pillow, lying on top of the covers. She went to his room hoping to catch him, but he was gone. This was really not supposed to be this hard.

She would try again tonight. What man could refuse Sarah

DuMont? But what then? By morning, she would be the person that seduced him into betraying his religious beliefs and his honor. His beliefs were so outdated. Who needed the paperwork anymore? "The two shall become one." What did that mean anyway? And his honor, he was a guest in her father's house; that meant something to him. He would not even call her mother by her first name out of respect for his deceased father. He had told her no in so many ways. But could he tell her no with just the two of them alone in the New York apartment, no Willie, no Doodle, no family?

Damn his religious beliefs. Damn his honor. But without them he would not be Matt. Without them, he would not have turned his life around after the bar fight in Lester's. Without them, there would have been no cowboy in Mrs. Fontenot's store with furniture to sell. Her first husband had cheated on her. He had no meaningful beliefs, no honor. Did she really want Matt to compromise those things?

The cowboy would honor his marriage vows. She knew that with as much certainty as life affords. No doubt, if she got him alone in the New York apartment, she would win, but it would be a hollow victory. Did Sarah DuMont have the power to turn Matt into the same kind of man as her first husband? She did not want to know the answer to that question. But she knew what the first step would look like, her seducing him in the apartment.

It would be passionate. Perhaps that is where she got the image of Matt burning down the mansion in his underwear. She put her hand on his shoulder and gave him a pat as he watched the game. With a wry smile, she knew the cowboy would not be getting lucky tonight, a change of plans. There would be no sleeping with Matthew Shepherd tonight.

Perhaps there was another way she could make it up to him.

Matt: "What are you lookin' at?"

Sarah: "Do you really want me to answer that?"

Matt: "You should be lookin' at the ballgame and not me. You might learn somethin'. I really need to talk to the Yankees pitchin' coach."

Sarah: "A cowboy from Mississippi knows more than the Yankees pitching coach?"

Matt: "I'm as surprised by that as you are."

Sarah: "Let me make a call and see if we can do something about that."

After the game, Matt met several of the Yankee players and coaches and received an autographed baseball. The players and coaches had the opportunity to thank a veteran for his service and to take a selfie with Sarah DuMont. Sarah made it up to Matt without compromising anything.

True to Matt's prediction, no supper was needed at the faux Southern restaurant near Central Park. True to Sarah's prediction, the cab ride over to the park was a hoot. Matt meant no disrespect and only had a friendly curiosity about the family origins of the cab driver.

They exited the cab at the park. This was obviously not new territory for Sarah. She knew where to get the rocks, and she knew where the best squirrel hideouts were located.

As they made their way, a young man raced by, grabbing the purse of an older lady who was walking in front of them. The woman resisted, and the young man pushed her to the ground, taking the purse.

---

Sarah and Matt returned home shortly before midnight. She went with him to his room and helped him out of his clothes. His wounds, while not life threatening, were fresh, and assistance was appreciated.

Sarah: "Matt, I help raise two brothers and was once married. Nobody is going to burn in hell because I helped you get undressed tonight. Put on this Marine t-shirt and, for heaven's sake, just sleep in your underwear like you do at home. The doctor told you to take these pain pills. I know you don't want to. I'll leave them on the nightstand in case you change your mind. I'll get a glass of water and sit it next to the pills. Look, I'm right down the hall if you need anything."

Sarah helped Matt into the bed, retrieved a glass of water from the bathroom, walked to the door, turned out the light, and stood there for a few moments looking at him.

She returned to her room and found her mother waiting. This time, she was glad.

Elizabeth: "You know it has made it to cable news. They have a video shot by a bystander. I guess with one of those cell phones. Matt has the knife in one hand and is giving the purse back with the other. You can see his arm and side are bleeding, and you are in the video. I mean, Sarah, a decorated war veteran disarms a would-be attacker in Central Park, and by the way, he is the boyfriend of Sarah DuMont. I suspect your publicists is pleased."

Sarah: "We didn't wait for the police or an ambulance. We'd still be there if we had. They would have wanted statements and descriptions. I'm counting on Father to smooth that over."

Elizabeth: "There is blood on your clothes."

Sarah: "Yes, there is more in the car—even got on my cell phone when I called our driver. I've never seen a man bleed that much. We used his white shirt as a bandage to stop the bleeding until we could get him to the hospital. He held a part of the shirt on his arm, and I held part on his side."

"I fussed at him the whole way. He could have gotten himself killed over nothing. Nothing!"

"I asked him why I should even care. I told him he was just too much trouble. He needed to grow up and get over himself—he can't save the whole world."

Elizabeth: "Sarah, please, you didn't say that, did you?"

Sarah: "Yes, I did. And I meant it. . . . No, I didn't mean it. I apologized. See what he does to me."

Elizabeth: "What did he say?"

Sarah: "For once in his life, he kept his mouth shut. He looked at me while I was fussing at him and didn't say anything. I wish he had said something—insulted me, called me a name, teased me, called me the Whore of Babylon again, anything. He just looked at me. It was awful."

Elizabeth reached over, took her daughters hand, and gave it a squeeze.

Sarah: "Thank you for calling Dr. Sterling. He met us there, and they took us right in. He couldn't have been nicer. He said the wound in Matt's side is to the muscle and that Matt was very lucky. I almost lost it at one point while he was talking to Matt. He said the cut on Matt's forearm is deep and long but should heal without any problems. He asked Matt if he wanted a plastic surgeon to sew it up. Dr. Sterling said that he was just an old cutter, and the plastic surgeon could do it without leaving a scar. Matt told him he had scars all over his body, and one more wouldn't matter."

"I had to go out in the hall and sit down in a chair. The nurse came by and said not to worry; Matt would be just fine. I couldn't talk. She continued to look at me. I think somehow she knew. She sat down in the chair next to me and held my hand."

Elizabeth: "What happened?"

Sarah: "Well, we hadn't been in the park long when this mugger grabbed the women's purse in front of us. I wasn't touching Matt. But I could tell that he didn't flinch until the mugger pushed the woman down. If she had just let go of that purse, none of this would have happened."

"When the mugger pushed the women, you could just feel him tense. I knew what was about to happen. I grabbed him and said, 'Matt don't.' But I couldn't hold him."

"He was wearing those old cowboy boots, and the mugger had on a pair of running shoes. I have the same—funny how you notice something like that. I thought good. Matt will never be able to catch him, and we can laugh about it in the car."

"Matt ran that boy down wearing those cowboy boots. I was running at them, begging Matt to stop. The mugger realized Matt was about to catch him. He stopped and turned with a knife in his hand. Matt never slowed down or hesitated and went right into the mugger, full speed."

"That boy made a terrible mistake. He brought a knife to a Matt fight. What happened next was faster than any staged fight I'd seen in any of my movies. I could measure it in heartbeats. On the first heartbeat, Matt had disarmed him. On the second, he had him pinned on the ground. On the third, he began to beat that boy. The first heartbeat was about the lady. The second heartbeat was about the mugger. The third heartbeat was about Andy. I knew that boy was in for a world of hurt."

Elizabeth: "Who is Andy?"

Sarah: "I'll tell you sometime when Matt tells me I can. I didn't think I would ever get there. I'm sure it was just a matter of seconds, but it seemed like an eternity. Anyway, I grabbed his arm on the up swing. When he started down, it almost made my knees buckle. He stopped. He just stopped."

"I told him, 'Let's go back and give the lady her purse. It's over now.' He stood up, walked over, picked up the knife and purse, and then headed back. I looked at the young boy and told him that he better get out of there before Matt comes back. He had no idea how close he had just come. You should have seen his face, the look—the blood. His eyes told the whole story. I guess being an actor, you notice things like that. I followed Matt a little ways and turned around. The mugger was nowhere to be seen. You know the rest."

Elizabeth: "When you were a little girl, you brought home a stray dog. You named him Checkers. It turned out that his name was Mr. Rutherford, and he was a champion Airedale Terrier owned by Judge Williamson. You cried when you returned the dog. One of the few times I remember you crying as a child, and I'm not counting the fake tears you used on your father."

Sarah: "You knew about the fake tears?"

Elizabeth: "Yes, I was impressed. That's why I didn't say anything. The point, strays make you cry. What are you doing?"

Sarah: "I don't know. When I'm around him, I want to be somewhere else. When I'm not, all I can do is think about him. About the only time we even hold hands is to pray."

"I tell myself that I can help him, then I make him so mad at me. Even today at the ballgame, I said something I shouldn't have. I'm just a nurse that makes the patient worse."

At that moment, Chris knocked and opened Sarah's door in one motion.

Chris: "Sarah, I hear Matt calling for you in his room. You better go see what he wants."

Sarah jumped up, went to Matt's room, and opened the door. The room was dark. Her hand moved to the light switch, but she did not turn on the light. Her eyes scanned the darkened room, but Matt was not in the bed where she left him.

Sarah: "What are you doing over there?"

He was sitting against the wall with his knees drawn up toward his chest. She went over and lowered herself to one knee. Her eyes were growing accustomed to the low light. Oddly, he had a faint smile on his lips, but she could tell by his eyes he was hurting.

Sarah: "What do you need, Matt? Do you need Doodle? She's not here."

Sarah rose and retrieved a pillow and light blanket from the bed. She covered his legs with the blanket and lay down beside him with her head on the pillow. He began to stroke her hair.

Sarah: "Doodle is not here, but I am—I am."

———————

Sarah was awakened a few minutes before six a.m. by Juanita knocking at the door. Sarah sat upright in the bed. She had begun the night on the floor, she was now in Matt's bed, and he was not in the room. She went to the door, still wearing the blood stained shirt from the night before.

Sarah: "Juanita, what do you want? Have you seen Matt?"

Juanita: "Mr. Matt is gone. He left a note in the kitchen. I read the note, but it wasn't folded or anything. It was just lying there. I didn't touch it, Ms. Sarah. He left you his beautiful Bible."

175

By now Sarah had moved past Juanita and was on her way to the kitchen. Juanita followed continuing to explain.

Juanita: "Hector, Larry, and Larry are out looking for him. Mr. Matt doesn't know his way around."

Sarah entered the kitchen well ahead of the older, slower Juanita. As Juanita said, there was a note and Bible on the staff dining table at the place where Sarah had tested the maple syrup biscuit.

The note was in Matt's handwriting.

> Please thank your family for their wonderful hospitality. I hope my abrupt departure is not seen as a comment on their efforts to make me feel welcome.
>
> Due to the events of last night, I think it best that I go home. I'm sure you can understand.
>
> If the New York Police want to talk with me, please have them call Uncle Billy. He has experience with me in these situations, and I'll do whatever he says.
>
> Please accept the Bible I carried with me in combat as a gift. If a gift is measured by the value to the giver, then I have given you a treasure. (Matthew 13: 44)
>
> Goodbye,
>
> Matthew Ezra Shepherd

The Bible had a burgundy, worn leather cover. She ran her fingertips over the eagle and anchor imprinted on the cover and opened the Bible. She was astonished to see how it had been treated. She had assumed that, due to his reverence for Scripture, the Bible would be pristine. It was not. There were at least three shades of highlighter, underlining by pencil and pen, and notes written on any blank space not otherwise taken. Pages had been opened and handled by hands that were less than clean. There were obviously some pages that had once come in contact with blood.

Sarah was furious.

Sarah: "He can't even put my name on this letter, but he signs it Matthew Ezra Shepherd. Like we would confuse him with another houseguest named Matthew. [Matt voice] 'Hi, I know you slept with me last night in a shirt covered with my blood, so I'd like to introduce myself. I'm Matthew Ezra Shepherd.' What does he think we've been doing? Am I Matt, and this is my Olivia letter? I bet Olivia at least wrote Matt's name on the Dear John letter. Matt is a coward."

Juanita: "No, Mr. Matt is very brave. I saw on TV what he did. Mr. Matt is a very brave man."

Sarah: "Everyone says that. Matt is so brave. But he is a coward. He is afraid of me."

Juanita: "Ms. Sarah, everyone is afraid of you."

Sarah took the letter and the Bible, left the kitchen, and headed to her room. Once in the room she called her assistant.

Sarah: "I'm sorry for the hour, but I need to get to Macon, Mississippi as soon as possible. . . . I understand, but this is what I want you to do. First, check commercial flights into New Orleans, Baton Rouge, or Jackson. . . . That is in Mississippi. Next, see if you can get me a ride on any private jet leaving from this area and going to that area of the Gulf Coast today. If necessary, I can helicopter to whatever airport to meet them. Money is no object and use my name if that will help. . . . Yes, I know, but this is important to me. . . . Yes, it is related to last night. I'm going to run that cowboy down like he ran down that mugger. Call me when you have something."

Sarah took a quick shower. The events of the prior night had not allowed time. She was packing her luggage and dressing when her mother came into the room and sat down. Sarah did not look up.

Elizabeth: "I take it you are going after him."

Sarah: "You know he's gone?"

Elizabeth: "I talked with him this morning as he was leaving."

Sarah stopped and looked at her mother.

Sarah: "You didn't stop him or come get me? Why?"

Elizabeth: "He and I talked."

Sarah turned, walked to the end of the bed, and sat down.

Sarah: "Never let that man open his mouth. Other women complain because their men can't carry on a conversation. They know not what they ask."

Elizabeth: "Is he your man, Sarah?"

Sarah: "I did not intend this. How can a farmer from Mississippi do this to me? I was perfectly content and happy with my life. I fully expected to meet someone, fall in love again, and have a good life. Maybe even have some children."

Elizabeth: "Sarah—content, happy?"

Sarah: "I know. But still, he got me on that farm. He put me in that truck with his dog. We sat in that barn and talked about nothing. I ate pulled pork, for heaven's sake. I listened to a ghost story in the dark with my shoes off and ended up naked in his bathroom. I felt more like a woman alone in that bathroom than I did at anytime during my marriage. I rode home that night across Louisiana swamps in someone else's clothes, without any underwear, and all I could say to myself was thank you Matt."

"Then, he holds my hand, and I think, 'What am I doing?' His hands are big and rough. Holding his hand is like holding the business end of a shovel. What woman would find that desirable?"

Elizabeth: "I certainly can't think of one."

Sarah: "Please, don't patronize me, not now. I don't need him. I would be just fine if I had never met him. But I did, and that's the problem. So I'm going after him. I'm going to continue to find ways to be around him until it is no longer possible. . . . I can't let the things I said in the car on the way to the hospital be the last things I say to him. He deserves much better than that."

Elizabeth: "Why don't you let him go?"

Sarah: "Is that what he said to you? Did he say that? I'm going to make him pay for what he has done to me."

Elizabeth: "Exactly what is it he deserves—reward or punishment?"

Sarah: "I don't know right now. But I'm creative. I'll find a way to do both. It will give me something to think about while I make a fool out of myself chasing after him."

Elizabeth: "Is there anything I can do to help?"

# Chapter Thirteen

# Olivia

Sarah: "Hello, Ruth, Sarah. . . . Yes, I invite your brother up here for a little vacation, and he makes it to cable news. . . . His wounds will be fine. We had one of the best surgeons around sew him up. Your husband will need to check on Matt when he gets home, which brings me to the next thing. He had a flashback last night. . . . I stayed with him. But some time during the night he left. In a note he said he's going home. . . . I don't know. But I bet sometime today, Odell will get a call from Matt asking him to come get him. Could be Jackson, New Orleans, or even Baton Rouge. . . . That's what I'd do. I'm making arrangements now. I'm hoping to beat him to Macon. . . . Let's just say, he tried to pull an Olivia on me, and we have some unfinished business."

" . . . She's there! She is in Macon. Does anybody know what she wants? . . . Well, looks like the cowboy has got two women running him down. One's married and the other is mad. . . . As soon as I know my plans, I'll let you know. . . . Yes, call me as soon as Odell hears something. And, Ruth, if we can work it out, I'd like to talk to Olivia before she talks to Matt. . . . Ruth, I think they need to talk. . . . Let's keep in touch and see if we can run him to ground."

Sarah would fly to Atlanta on a private jet, commercial to Jackson, and then rent a car for the last leg to Macon. The private jet carried a group of Texas oilmen returning from Canada by way of Atlanta. She could tell they wanted to hear about what had happened. She agreed to tell them some of the story, if they agreed not to discuss any of it with reporters for the tabloids. Upon hearing that Matt was a Marine and former combat veteran, a gentleman's agreement was reached. At one point, the pilot requested that Sarah sit near the front of the plan so he could also hear the story.

With the story told, the private jet made the approach into Atlanta. Sarah looked out the window and let her mind wonder. What if she ran into Heidi Van Looney Tunes again in the Atlanta Airport? What were the chances? What would Heidi say? Heidi would look at her and know exactly what was happening. She would have no choice but to strangle Heidi in the VIP lounge.

She would get ten to fifteen years for manslaughter, a small price to pay. The judge would sentence her but would let everyone in the courtroom know where the real quilt lay—the cowboy from Mississippi and his dog. Everyone in the courtroom would turn and look at them in disgust. The judge would further order both Matt and Doodle to visit her every day. She would do her time in a Georgia prison for women. Matt would smuggle her cigarettes, and she would use them to barter for all kinds of neat stuff. She would wear a dreadful orange jump suit but would make it work with the right makeup and accessories.

Yes, that is what she would do—strangle Heidi, see Matt and Doodle every day, and smuggle cigarettes. All of this would be his fault, and he would know it. She would wear orange and look fabulous. He would say things like Sarah will you ever forgive me. Of course, she would say no. It would all be so much fun.

She held up her hand as if she were admiring a diamond ring and smiled. She would have "MATT" tattooed across the knuckles of one hand and "DAWG" tattooed across the other—the two people most responsible for the tragedy. Sarah collected herself as the wheels of the jet touched down in Atlanta.

In the Atlanta airport, she saw CNN news reports on the monitors about the events of the prior night. All of this because she wanted to help Matt, and he wanted to help a woman in Central Park. The opportunity to strangle Heidi would have to wait for another day.

Just south of Jackson, Sarah's phone rang.

Sarah: "Hello, Lucy."

Lucy: "I talked to your mother. Where are you?"

Sarah: "I've rented a car. I'm on the interstate headed to Macon."

Lucy: "Are you still angry?"

Sarah: "Yes, but not at him. I'm mad at myself. The stray ran away. I should just let him go. If I see him tomorrow, I'm telling him goodbye. I tried to help him, now time to move on."

Lucy: "I saw what happened last night on the news."

Sarah: "I've never seen anything like it. One minute he is this warrior. I had to tell him that he was wounded. He didn't even know. A few hours later, he is a little boy that needs his dog. Since the dog wasn't there, guess who he turned to? . . . I slept with him last night."

Lucy: "Sarah!"

Sarah: "But it is not what you think. I don't know how to describe it."

Lucy: "It sounds like my prediction is coming true. I'm a prophet."

Sarah: "What prediction?"

Lucy: "You, a cowboy, and love."

Sarah: "Don't be silly. People want to be in love. I don't want this. This is some kind of collard greens, come to Jesus, voodoo swamp spell. He wants to go to Haiti with some church thing. Well, that dog can't go. I'm not going to Haiti with him to take the place of the dog. I'm not doing it."

Lucy: "Has he asked you to do that?"

Sarah: "No, but I'm not doing it. He's damaged. His military service left him damaged. There are things I know I haven't told you, or anyone, for that matter. I don't want a needy, religious cowboy. I have rules about that sort of thing. And I'm not going to Haiti. I'm not doing it."

Lucy: "Does he make you laugh? . . . Sarah?"

Sarah: "Yes."

Lucy: "That's all I need to know."

Sarah: "But that doesn't mean I'm going to Haiti."

Lucy: "Lorraine sends her love. She also told me to tell you that your boyfriend looks good on TV. She's glad you found a nice rabbi."

Sarah: "Tell her that he is not a rabbi and is not my boyfriend."

Lucy: "That is not what it looks like. Give me a call if you want to talk some more."

Sarah: "Thank you, Lucy. I will."

On the drive south down Interstate 55, she passed an exit for Natchez. Was any of that story about Shade Shepherd true? Did Matt turn the lights out? At least Natchez is a real place, or is it? She didn't know anymore.

She booked a room at the Holiday Inn Express, the same hotel where Olivia was staying. Ruth talked to Olivia, and she agreed to meet with Sarah the next morning. The place chosen was Lester's bar.

Lester's did not open until the afternoon each day, so the bar would be empty and was neutral ground. Also, everyone knew email and texting had only slowed the transmission of information in Macon. Meeting in the lobby of the Holiday Inn Express was equivalent to meeting under the statue of the Confederate Soldier on the city square with voices amplified by Peavey equipment, a Mississippi company.

Odell and Doodle met Matt's plane in Baton Rouge just before midnight. Doodle went, apparently, to share the driving. The cowboy was home.

Sarah entered Lester's bar a few minutes before eleven the next morning. As was her custom, she wanted to be there before Olivia. Grand entrances were for people who had little else to say. Sarah always had plenty to say. Lester introduced himself and showed Sarah to a table in the back. She said no. She couldn't see the front door from that table. Lester returned to the bar, standing near his shotgun.

Sarah surveyed the bar. She knew enough about the cowboy to recognize his handiwork. No wonder the WMU liked meeting here. She tried to imagine what it must have looked like with the Sullivan boys laying on the floor and the bar in shambles. She had seen enough staged fights in her movies to imagine the mayhem. But this was real and not staged. And those very large men had been beaten unconscious by one man.

Presently, a tall woman with black hair, big dark eyes, and wearing a designer dress entered the bar. Sarah knew staged mayhem and designer dresses. This must be Olivia. The light was dim in the bar, and Sarah's eyes had long since adjusted from the bright Mississippi sun. Olivia entered the bar with the bright light behind her, making her appear as an aberration. As she crossed the floor and came more into focus, Sarah felt intimidated, one of the few times in her life. Maybe she should rethink this whole grand entrance thing.

Sarah: "Hello. You must be Olivia."

Olivia: "And you must be Sarah."

They shook hands and sat down. Most people on meeting Sarah for the first time in a social setting would say similar things: I'm a big fan. I saw you in whatever and loved it. How naked were you?

Olivia gave no sign, whatsoever, that the Sarah sitting in front of her was Sarah Morgan Leigh DuMont. Lester brought two sweet teas with lemons.

Lester: "Ladies, I'll be right over there behind the bar if y'all need anything else."

Sarah knew Lester meant behind the bar by the shotgun.

Olivia: "I understand you want to talk to me about Matt."

Sarah: "I've not known Matt very long, but I'm not sure you know what he has been going through since the engagement ended."

Olivia: "I know everything."

Sarah: "How?"

Olivia: "Odell. He sends me letters, one a week, like clockwork."

Sarah was dumbfounded. She had come to enlighten Olivia, not the other way around.

Olivia: "I'm actually here for the benefit of the three of us: you, me, and Matt. I saw in some tabloid at a checkout stand that Matt was your boyfriend."

Sarah: "He is not my boyfriend. I'm just—"

Olivia raised her hand. She knew Matt.

Olivia: "Sarah, I saw the cable news. You have just chased that man halfway across the United States and are meeting with me in Lester's to talk about him. I don't know how you define boyfriend where you come from, but down here that is exactly what it means."

Sarah: "Why are you in Macon?"

Olivia: "When I saw that Matt was ready to see another woman, I knew I had to give us closure. We left the door open so to speak. Odell told me it was time."

There was a moment of silence as the wounded were tended and reinforcements were brought up. To allow time for these military maneuvers, each woman took a sip of sweet tea, yet another function of the house wine of the South.

Olivia: "Matt believes that I was the one that left him. But Sarah, he left me. He loved his Marines more than me. I was second. They came first. Then I met someone that put me first. I still loved Matt, but no woman wants to be second. Judge me for that. It is what it is."

Sarah: "I can't blame you for that."

Olivia: "He would come home from his deployments and be so distant. I couldn't get him to commit to a wedding date. I realized the cost of being the wife of Matthew Shepherd might be too high. I know that says more about me than it does him."

Sarah: "Don't be so hard on yourself, Olivia. Those things are passed now. And I know what you mean about the cost being high. I'm just a temporary friend and look what it has cost me."

Olivia: "To be honest, another reason I've put this off is that I didn't want to get within a mile of that man. Those white teeth—"

Sarah: "I think he gargles with bleach."

Olivia: "That would explain it. My husband is a wonderful provider. He is attentive. He loves our children. He is everything a woman would want. But he can't lie like Matt, and I miss that sometimes. My daddy believed that Matt's dog, Sarah, talked to Matt."

Sarah: "My father believes if you stutter, you are not allowed to drive. What? Did you say the dog's name was Sarah?"

Olivia: "Yes, Sarah was the name of the dog he had back then. Best I can remember the name had something to do with post-feminism and the Choctaw Indians. I assumed you knew that. I just knew if I got around that man, I'd end up naked in his bathroom again."

There was a sound from Sarah's side of the table. Olivia pointed to her own nose.

Olivia: "Sarah, you have a little sweet tea coming out of your nose."

After wiping her upper lip and composing herself, Sarah continued the conversation.

Sarah: "Would you mind telling me how that happened?"

Olivia: "Not at all, it was very innocent. Matt couldn't have been more of a gentleman. I was visiting the farm. He was showing me the beehives and some of those honey bees attacked me. They got all down my blouse and everywhere. Matt took me to the—"

Sarah: "Hose. He had you strip down, as modesty would permit, then hosed you off."

Olivia: "Sarah, did this happen to you to?"

Sarah: "No, mine was completely different, nothing at all like yours. Mine was chicken manure. Then I ended up in the bathroom of that old farmhouse."

Olivia: "No one lived in that house back then."

Sarah: "Oh, you should see it now. Matt has done a great job with that house. The kitchen is very nice with marble counter tops and . . . wait a minute. Let's not change the subject. Olivia, I'm going to ask you a question. If the answer is yes, I'm going get Lester's shotgun and solve everybody's problem. If I can get just one woman on the jury, I would never be convicted. Did you go home without underwear wearing a gray sweatshirt—"

Olivia: "That said MACON PANTHERS BALLETTES. That is not something you forget."

Apparently the "P" was lost in subsequent use.

Lester: "You can't have my shotgun."

Sarah: "Shut-up, Lester, or I'll buy the mortgage on this place and have you fired."

Olivia: "Don't you see, Sarah? Odell saw you naked in Matt's bathroom as a sign from God. That is why he told me now is the time. Matt is ready. He and I can talk, and you are here to help him move on. All things work together for good for them that love the Lord."

"I'll go see him after lunch. When I leave, you can go and check on him. I won't let him know I'm coming. I don't want to give that man time to prepare. There are things that need to be said."

Sarah: "Sounds like a plan. Lester, how about two Scotch on the rocks?"

Olivia: "I'm sure it's after noon somewhere. Make mine a bourbon with a splash."

Both women tilted their heads slightly, similar to what Doodle might do, narrowed their eyes, and stared at the other.

Olivia: "You know, Sarah, when this over, I think you and I could become good friends."

Sarah: "I think we already are."

Olivia: "Hold my hand and let me say a short prayer. Hurry, before the liquor comes. I'm a Baptist."

Sarah at least now knew what was expected. Olivia voiced a short prayer. Lester delivered the drinks, having judicially paused for the Amen.

Olivia: "I know about the trip to Haiti. I know how important this is to Matt. Sarah, you should go with him."

Sarah: "I'm a heathen. Matt said so. Apparently, I'm a sinner."

Olivia: "We are all sinners, Sarah, even those that go on mission trips."

Olivia called Lester to the table, gave him money, and instructed him to go to the cafe for three lunches.

Olivia: "Lunch will be on me. Sarah, I bet you haven't had food like this before."

Sarah: "I had dinner at Matt's."

Olivia: "That man can cook."

Sarah: "And keep house. . . . What does it say about you and me that neither one of us wants his domestic butt?"

The two sophisticated, beautiful women from different cultures laughed until tears streamed down their faces, each finishing their respective drinks of Scotch and bourbon.

Lester returned with three Styrofoam plates similar to the ones used to bring home the pulled pork from Odell's. Sarah opened the lid and saw plastic utensils rolled up in a napkin and a square of cornbread, sitting on a sheet of wax paper covering the food. She removed the wax paper and found collard greens, black-eyed peas, macaroni and cheese, and fried okra.

Olivia: "Thanks so much, Lester."

Lester: "Ms. DuMont, I got you all vegetables because I understand you're a vegetarian."

Sarah: "How do you know that?"

Olivia: "It's Macon."

Sarah looked at the vegetarian plate, collard greens and black eyed peas cooked in fatback. The conversation between the ladies continued over lunch.

Sarah: "Olivia, do you know anything about a Marine who served with Matt named Andy? He was from Kansas."

Olivia: "No. I never heard Matt mention him. Why?"

Sarah: "Just curious."

After lunch, Sarah remained at Lester's. Olivia was to visit Matt then call Ruth when it was over. Sarah walked over to Lester sitting down at the bar.

Sarah: "Lester, you are about to spill your guts to me. You are going to start with the night righteous judgment was visited on the Sullivan brothers in this bar."

Lester: "Yes, ma'am."

Sarah: "Correct answer. Lester, you are a smart man."

He began his tale. After about an hour, Sarah's phone rang.

Sarah: "Ruth, hang on just a minute. Lester, what happened to Oscar Rogers' dog?"

Lester: "He was still in the fishin' boat. He had caught two five pound bass usin' that green worm lure."

Sarah: "Huh. Sorry, Ruth, did you hear from Olivia? . . . Good. Good. I'm glad. . . . I told her. I can't believe what he did with that kitchen. . . . She didn't say anything about the bathroom, did she? . . . Good. Never mind, I was just curious. Looks like I'm next. Yes, I will."

Sarah returned her phone to a pocket in her jacket, smiling at Lester.

Sarah: "It has been a pleasure. Love the sign by the way."

Sarah pointed to an official looking sign above the bar that read,

"Anyone conveying alcoholic beverages to Matthew Shepherd will be prosecuted to the fullest extent of the law."

Not state law, but Billy Pruitt law.

Sarah: "Lester, I think you're missing a business opportunity here. Stop selling the hard liquor. Do you know anything about making craft beer? I see families, a lunch crowd, hamburgers, barbecue, and some craft beer. Make one with lemon overtones and call it Sweet Tea. You could make some money and not have to keep a loaded shotgun behind the bar."

"Oh yea, once a year have a music festival here. Publicize it in New Orleans. Make them think they are getting down to hear some gospel and blues."

Lester: "Yes, ma'am, I'll give that some thought. And on that pound cake, add the eggs one at a time, beatin' after each egg."

Sarah: "Thanks, I will."

Lester drew Sarah a map to Matt's farm from the bar on a napkin. She had the GPS in her phone, but these rural roads were not easy to navigate. On her way she passed what she assumed was Matt's church. She knew it was a white church because the parking lot was paved. She had learned that much anyway. She noticed there were several cars parked near the building.

She turned off the blacktop on to Matt's farm and drove the single lane road down to the circular driveway. The old barn came into sight. She was still amazed at how large it was. She parked the car, took a breath, and went inside the house. For some reason, she did not knock or announce her presence.

She entered the parlor and walked toward the kitchen. She found Matt sitting in a kitchen chair next to the table. His right arm rested on the table. He was facing Sarah, but he was looking at the floor. His left arm with the bandage lay across his lap. He was barefoot, so she knew Olivia had caught him completely by surprise.

He did not hear her come in. Doodle was in her bed across the kitchen. Her head rested on her crossed paws. The only sound was the tic-tic-tic of the old mantel clock in the parlor.

Doodle immediately announced Sarah's presence by lifting only her eyes to focus on Sarah. Matt did not respond to Doodle's eye movement. The patterned repeated itself several times: Tic-tic-tic, Doodle's eyes move, tic-tic-tic, Doodle's eyes move—finally.

Matt: "Gee, Sarah! You scared me to death. You don't know how to knock?"

That was the wrong thing to say.

Sarah: "Do you? You couldn't knock on the door, wake me up, and tell me to my face you were leaving? I helped you last night, not Sarah Morgan Leigh DuMont but Sarah. You didn't need my money or my fame or my looks. You needed me, and I helped you."

"I go downstairs to the kitchen and find the sweetest note. I could read *War and Peace* in one sitting if you wrote it out by hand. You left that Bible. It was just so sweet. But you couldn't stop there, could you, not Matthew Ezra Shepherd? It made me furious when I saw how you signed your name. As soon as I saw that, I knew I was going to tract you down and kick your butt."

Sarah froze. Apparently, saying the obvious out loud made it even more obvious. The expression on her face changed from fury to stoic resolve.

Sarah: "You knew that didn't you? You knew that would make me mad, and I'd come looking for you. You just couldn't say Sarah I need you; please come find me. I have to say, I've never known a man that could manipulate me at all, much less, as much as you do. . . . And what does the name Sarah have to do with post-feminism and the Choctaw Indians? . . . You will never get the chance to see these twin spars. You disgust me!"

Sarah turned and left. She half expected to meet another woman, waiting her turn to see Matt. She threw the screen door open with all her might. It slammed shut just as she reached the first step off the porch. She hoped it was in splinters.

Sarah's driving skills were at best adequate since others had driven her so often. But her skills on gravel and Mississippi mud, while angry, were abysmal. Most of the weather in Mississippi comes through Texas, Louisiana, and Arkansas unless it is coming straight up from the Gulf, which means the contra-flow on Interstate 55 is in effect and all lanes go north. Mississippi gets its fair share of rain and sometimes other folks' share.

Sarah sat in the rented car and gunned the engine on the circular driveway, causing the back of the car to fishtail off the gravel. At this point, most drivers would know to gentle step on the gas and coax the car back onto the driveway. Not Sarah, she gunned the engine again. Once the thin layer of St. Augustine grass was breeched, the dye was cast. The back tires encountered primeval, saturated Mississippi mud.

Sarah retraced her steps to the house and stood on the front porch. The screen door was still intact.

Sarah: "I need you, Matt."

Matt: "Let me get my shoes on. Doodle, go get my shoes and my belt. And bring me Odell's socks instead of mine."

Sarah: "I can hear you! That dog doesn't know the difference between your socks and Odell's."

Sarah and Doodle stood together by the car watching the man fetch the tractor. Apparently, Doodle was as disgusted as Sarah and was going to let the man walk to the barn by himself.

Sarah: "Doodle, you should have left him in Baton Rouge. Made him walk home. Look at him. One of us has to look out for him. He's so pitiful. Since I have a job and a life, it will have to be you, sorry."

Sarah and Doodle exchanged a look. For all the world, Sarah believed Doodle's look said yes, I know, and yes, I will.

Matt arrived on the yellow and green tractor that had done many things during its lifetime, but pulling the car of a famous movie star out of the mud was not one of them. Chains were attached, instructions were given, and Sarah's car was eased onto the driveway. During the whole process, she saw he favored his left arm and his side. She felt sorry that she had made him rescue her car.

Sarah: "Don't you say a word about my driving."

Matt: "I didn't say anything."

Sarah: "Yes, but you thought it."

Matt: "I did think it, but I didn't say anything."

Sarah: "I want to go to Haiti with you."

Matt: "Why, so I can disgust you in a foreign country?"

Sarah: "Yes!"

Matt: "There is no way they're gonna let you go. You're a heathen. This is a mission trip."

Sarah: "This is a free country, and if Pastor Mark says I can go, I'm going. Besides, you don't think I can do it, do you?"

Sarah opened the door to the car, pausing to look at Matt.

Sarah: "And let John look at your arm and your side. I swear, Matthew Ezra Shepherd, if you let them get infected, I'll never speak to you again, which I may never do, anyway."

She sat in the car, stepped on the gas, and promptly put on the brakes looking at Matt through the open window.

Sarah: "Whose socks do you have on?"

Matt: "I think you know the answer to that."

Sarah: "You don't quit, do you? No wonder that dog is the only friend you have."

As Sarah drove away, she could hear Matt yelling at the car.

Matt: "I have a lot of friends, one or two anyway, at least one besides this—"

She watched the man and his dog in the rearview mirror as the car moved down the gravel drive trailing a cloud of red clay dust. At what point had she lost all control over her life? What was she doing in a rented car on a gravel road in Mississippi? What had a chocolate brownie with pecans wrought?

By the time she reached the blacktop, tears were running down her face. She wiped them away, no time for this. One option was to keep going. Don't stop until you reach New Orleans. Complete the final filming of the TV series and then off to South Africa. Yes, that is what she would do. Work, time, and this would be just a memory. Yes, that is what she would do. Confident in that course of action, she pulled into the church parking lot.

She had never been in an Evangelical church before. Her few occasions in church had been in grand structures of Catholic or mainline Protestant denominations. There was one car left in the parking lot, parked near a sidewalk that led to a side door.

The door was unlocked. Sarah opened the door and went in. There was a framed picture on a wall, which she assumed must be of Jesus, a bulletin board decorated by children about feeding five thousand with fishes and loaves, and an announcement of a WMU meeting at Lester's. Sarah took a few steps further in. On one side was a double-hung door with the top part open. She could see baby beds and infant toys and smell baby powder. These churches seem to have everything.

Sarah: "Hello, is anybody here?"

Someone stepped out of a door further down the hall.

Pastor Mark: "Thought I heard somebody. Can I help you?"

Sarah: "I'm looking for Pastor Mark."

Pastor Mark: "You've got him."

Sarah: "Good, I was hoping I could talk to you."

Pastor Mark: "Come on down here to my office. We can talk in here."

Sarah proceeded down the hall and entered the office. The first office was clearly for a secretary. They proceeded through to the back, which was Pastor Mark's study. He did not sit behind his desk but joined her in one of the visitor chairs. She was struck by the number of books that surrounded them on the walls. The smell of the office reminded her of a library.

Sarah: "I don't believe we've met."

Pastor Mark: "I know who you are. I have TV and this is a close-knit community. What can I do for you, Sarah? Is this about Matt?"

Sarah took a deep breath and began.

Sarah: "I'm not a Christian, but I want to go to Haiti with your group."

He looked at Sarah and smiled. He paused a moment as if to compose his response.

Pastor Mark: "When Jesus was in the garden praying before His crucifixion, at one point, he prayed for future believers. He asked the Father to make them one, to have a unity of the spirit. As Christians, we believe we are at war. Individually, we war against the flesh. As the church, what we call the body of Christ, we war against spiritual forces of evil. We can't do those things unless we are united, one with ourselves and Jesus."

"To us, this trip to Haiti is not just about humanitarian efforts, but eternal issues. It is on trips such as these that our unity of purpose is tested the most. Things always go wrong. Accommodations are third world. The days can be long and hard."

"Matt will tell you, when you lead men into battle, they need to have unity of purpose and selfless devotion; if not, the outcome is not good."

"Under normal circumstances, I would tell you no but invite you to church this Sunday. But Matt, by way of Odell, has argued your case. Odell came to see me last week and brought a letter from Matt. He knows more about leading people into war than I do. He said he'd rather have you in the fox hole with him than some of the men he fought with."

"The most important thing I've learned as a pastor is when to get out of the Lord's way. So Sarah, we'd love to have you join us."

Pastor Mark retrieved a large business envelope from his desk.

Pastor Mark: "On a hunch, I put this together for you after Odell's visit. It has all the information. You will work with the medical team, taking blood pressures and temperatures. The information covers what to bring, what to wear, needed vaccinations, and our flight schedules. We are leaving from New Orleans, so I suppose you could join us there. As is always the case, we need to talk about money. Those going, for the most part, pay much of their own way. We are booking tickets now. I would need $900 dollars from you now and $600 by the time we leave. The Lord's work is freeing, but it is not free."

Sarah could not process everything she had just heard. She had a mind that was as fast as a formula one race car, but currently it was stuck in Mississippi mud. She retrieved her cell phone and dialed her assistant while questioning her own actions?

Sarah: "Hey. .... Calvary Baptist Church, Macon, Mississippi. .... I need you to send a payment of $10,000 to, just a minute. What's the mailing address here?"

Pastor Mark: "The total is $1,500. I don't want anyone saying we let you go on this trip for the money. Here is the mailing address."

He handed Sarah the address.

Sarah: "Make that $1,500 and let me text you the address. .... Yes, I'm on my way to New Orleans after this. .... I've talked to the cowboy and he is fine. I'll text you in New Orleans. Bye."

Sarah returned her phone to her pocket.

Sarah: "Is it okay if I call him cowboy? I didn't know if there might be some kind of rule or something against that."

Sarah was glancing around the room at all the books. Pastor Mark laughed.

Pastor Mark: "I guess it does seem to you we have strange rules, but that is not one of them. If you like to call him cowboy, then please continue."

Sarah: "Good, he doesn't like it. That's why I do it."

Pastor Mark: "Well, we don't want to get in the middle of that. There is a white sealed envelope in the package of information. It is a letter from me to you. I ask that you not open it until your first night in Haiti."

Sarah: "I'll do what you ask. I have a recent history with letters in white envelopes."

He then went behind the desk and returned with a stack of medical green scrubs.

Pastor Mark: "Also, I have three sets of medical scrubs that you can use. They should fit you. They ended up in my luggage last year. You'll learn, on these trips, we eventually have all things in common. We pack for three or four days then let some of the women in the village wash our clothes. That gives us room in our luggage for supplies and gives them some income. They wash them in a river and return them dry and folded. The clothes are folded inside out to keep the outside protected from all the dust. These have been folded that way."

Sarah: "I guess these would be better than yoga pants."

Pastor Mark: "Ruth can give you updates about the trip. Also, we will attend a worship service at a church in Thoman. The Haitians typically put on their best clothes for church and dress modestly. The women in our group usually bring long cotton skirts to wear for that. If you have any questions about that, Ruth can help you."

"We are being prayed over, and I will especially pray for you. Let me warn you, Sarah. Sometimes these trips can be life changing experiences."

Pastor Mark extended his hand. Sarah moved past the hand and gave him a hug.

Sarah: "Thank you."

As she retraced her steps out of the building, she realized there was a ladies restroom on her left. She went into the restroom and changed into a pair of the scrubs only.

Sarah, the world's first heathen Christian missionary, reached Hammond on Interstate 55 about sunset. Again it was a clear night, and she was riding commando to New Orleans in someone else's clothes. This place and the culture were as far removed from her life as the East is from the West. But the swamp, bathed in the blue light, was beautiful. And beauty is beauty, no matter where you find it.

# Chapter Fourteen

# Haiti In Seven Days

Haiti occupies the western part of the island of Hispaniola that it shares with the Dominican Republic. About the size of Massachusetts, Haiti has over 10 million people, making it the third most populous country in the Caribbean.

Discovered by Christopher Columbus on his first voyage, the island will eventually become a French possession and the most lucrative colony in the world, due to the sugar cane plantations worked by slaves imported from Africa.

Haitian slaves used the disruptions set in motion by the French Revolution to gain their independence from France in 1804. Haiti is the only nation in the world established by a successful revolt of slaves. In 1809, ten thousand Haitians migrated to New Orleans, doubling the size of that city's population and adding to the mix of cultures and foods.

In the original language, Haiti is the name given to the entire island of Hispaniola and means "land of high mountains." Located on the eastern side of Haiti in some of those mountains is the community of Thoman, sitting near the Dominican Republic and overlooking Étang Saumâtre, the largest lake in Haiti and also saline.

A Hope Center was built in Thoman by But God Ministries and includes medical and dental clinics, a pharmacy, and dormitories for visiting teams to heal the bodies and souls of Haitians. This Hope Center is the destination of the medical missionary team from Calvary Baptist Church.

The Center is built on the side of a mountain in three levels. A wide walkway, with periodic steps, runs up the center and meets a large common area at the top forming a T. At the bottom on the left side is the waiting area and clinics. The waiting area is an open courtyard with makeshift canvas covers used to provide some shade. On the right is an open work area where a diesel generator also sits. At the next level, on the left is a covered pavilion for meals and meetings with a kitchen on the right side of the walkway. At the top of the walkway are the dorms, bathrooms, and showers. There are two dorm rooms for women and two dorm rooms for men, each sleeping about ten. Two sinks, two toilets, and two showers make up the bath facilities for each pair of dorms. The men's and women's housing is separated by the outdoor common area. The showers for the men are cold water only. There is additional housing around the common area for interns and a missionary couple who manage the Center. A wall with guards surrounds the whole thing.

Water is supplied by a cistern, which sits under the common area, and electricity by the diesel generator. The water is not potable. Water for cooking and drinking must come from a separate source. A well was attempted, but nature did not cooperate. The generator runs all night but for only part of the time during daylight hours.

---

Upon her return to New Orleans, Sarah's schedule was filled with the final filming of the TV series. If all went as planned, this would end two days before the departure to Haiti on a Sunday. The team will stay in Haiti until the following Saturday.

Sarah and Matt had not talked directly. Sarah got her news about Matt and any information about the trip to Haiti from Ruth, the same source of Matt's information about Sarah.

With two weeks to go before the trip, Matt could get a signal without going to the barn and called Sarah.

Matt: "Sarah."

Sarah: "Hello, Matt. It's ten o'clock. What are you doing up?"

Matt: "Doodle can't sleep and when Doodle can't sleep, nobody sleeps. If I have to play one more hand of Go Fish with that dog, I'm goin' to sleep in the barn. I told her you were mad at me. More precisely, that I disgust you. She said she completely understands."

Sarah: "I shouldn't have said that. You can make me so mad. How are your wounds?"

Matt: "There're on the mend. Are you still goin' to Haiti?"

Sarah: "Yes, I am. Who will take care of Doodle while you're gone?"

Matt: "She's goin' to Ruth's; her daughters love her. Lee Arthur and Doodle get crossways over her herdin' his cows."

Sarah: "I don't want anyone fussing at that sweet animal for doing something she was bred to do. Take her to Ruth's."

Matt: "We are takin' a bus to the New Orleans airport from Macon."

Sarah: "I'll meet you in New Orleans; filming here is scheduled to be over by then. Willie is taking me to the airport. The Saturday we leave Haiti, I'm flying to New York and hope to see my mother. Then Sunday afternoon, I'm leaving for South Africa."

"I say all that to say you and I will have a week together in Haiti."

Matt: "A week with Sarah DuMont, a man can't ask for much more than that."

Sarah: "Sometimes you say the sweetest things, and then other times. Well, you know."

Matt: "It's a gift. Be aware, the people on this team are goin' to be like me. They are not spiritual but religious. They believe in a God of grace with expectations."

Sarah: "Let's hope they are not all exactly like you. I tell you what, you help me navigate these strange people, and I'll be your Doodle and help you navigate Haiti."

Matt: "It's a deal. Lesson number one. On this trip, smile continuously, be patient always, and be thankful no matter what."

Sarah: "Smile, patient, thankful, got it."

Matt: "I think I can go to sleep now. Sarah, I'll see you soon."

Sarah: "Matt, one more thing, they are having a party at the end of filming. It will be here, at the house on St. Charles. There will be executives from New York and LA, also some of the cast and crew. Everyone wants to meet you. They've all seen the news reports. If you don't come, they will all be very mad at me."

Matt: "Are you sure you want me there? I really don't have the clothes for that."

Sarah: "Yes, I am. And wear your white shirt and jeans. It is Wednesday of next week. Be here about seven."

Mat: "I don't have a white shirt anymore. The mugger ruined it."

Sarah: "Get another one—you can do this for me."

Matt: "I'm not sure I fit in with those people."

Sarah: "You don't, not even close. And I'm glad. Just be yourself. . . . I can't believe I said that. I'll do my best to protect them from you. Please, leave them with some dignity."

Matt: "Okay, Sarah. We'll see you then."

Sarah: "We?"

Matt: "Yea, me and Doodle."

Sarah: "Why not?"

Sarah discretely prepared the ground for Matt's visit. She let the property manager know he would be bringing his service dog. She was now lying for a liar. She also let everyone know Matt did not consider *Christ*, *Jesus*, and *Jesus Christ* to be swear words. Everyone was free to speak as they like, but they had been warned.

---

Around ten o'clock, on the Wednesday night of the party, Matt and Doodle walked along St. Charles Avenue as Sarah fetched a bottle of wine from the kitchen. Even though the party was still in progress, she went to her room, dressed for bed, poured herself a glass of wine, and called Lucy.

Sarah: "Lucy, can you talk."

Lucy: "Sure."

Sarah: "The party was tonight."

Lucy: "That's right. How did it go?"

Sarah: "Fine, I guess. His sister gave me his jacket size, and I bought him a nice navy blazer. The security guard held it for him. He wore his new white shirt and best jeans with those second hand boots. I was standing across the room when he entered, wearing that navy blazer and flashing that smile. I almost dropped my wine glass. And you know me, I have never dropped a glass of liquor."

Lucy: "How did he do?"

Sarah: "Matt was Matt. He charmed the whole room. These women would laugh at whatever he said and make it a point to touch him, like I'm his great aunt who didn't know what was going on. The executives think he's done some acting, and that someone named Odell Lauder is his agent. It will take me several weeks to straighten all that out. Maybe I should just let them call Odell's gas station. Serves them right for being so gullible."

Lucy: "Will I ever get a chance to meet him?"

Sarah: "Oh, that's not all. Everyone down here is either related to one another or goes to church with one another. There was a girl, working for the caterer, who is married to a young minister at Matt's church. The minister is attending some seminary here in New Orleans. Anyway, Matt starts helping her with the trays and introducing her all around. Soon, he is back in the kitchen, helping with the food, and she's talking with network executives from New York. He would take a huge tray of hors d'oeuvres and go around the room offering them to everyone with Doodle following him. The first time I saw him come out of the kitchen carrying a tray, wine almost came out my nose. I caught myself this time. He's not going to do that to me again, ever."

Lucy: "Sounds like he had fun."

Sarah: "I'm not done. I knew he would want to leave before the party was over. I walked with him outside. We reached the bottom of the steps at the side street. I was standing one step above him. He turned to look at me. I grabbed the lapels of the blazer and kissed him. I mean I really kissed that man."

Lucy: "What did he do?"

Sarah: "He threw up his hands and said this happens every time he comes to New Orleans."

Lucy: "Must have been quite a navy blazer."

Sarah: "I told him he deserved someone that would do that everyday. Someone that would live on the farm with him, and I wasn't that someone. I said I wanted to give him a week in Haiti, and then I had to go."

Lucy: "What did he say?"

Sarah: "He told me he understood and thanked me for going with him to Haiti. He took off the blazer and handed it to me. I said it was a gift and to please keep it. He said without me, he didn't need a fine coat like that. Then he held me and kissed me. I couldn't see, or think, for a few moments after. I stood there dazed, like a schoolgirl. Once my senses returned, I saw him and the dog under a street light round the corner onto St. Charles."

"If he had not left me senseless for a moment, I would have taken him up to my room and made a man out of him. But I don't know what we'd have done with the dog. I couldn't make love to him with that dog looking at me. . . . Ah! He knows that! That's why he insisted on bringing that dog, for protection. He knew he could kiss me like that, and there would be nothing I could do about it."

Lucy: "Listen to yourself. Do you honestly think that's why he brought the dog?"

Sarah: "Oh, you don't know. He is the most deceitful, devious, manipulative man I've ever met."

Lucy: "Usually you say something like that about a man that's trying to get you into bed."

Sarah: "See how devious he is. This just proves my point. "

Lucy: "Let's see Sarah, you once told me no cowboy. A few days ago, you told me you were not going to Haiti. Is there anything else you are not going to do?"

Sarah: "Yes, I'm never giving a navy blazer to a cowboy again. Apparently, I can't handle it. Like the cowboy says hindsight is fifty-fifty."

Lucy: "What, fifty-fifty?"

Sarah: "It's something that idiot says. I think just to irritate me."

Lucy: "What are you going to do, now?"

Sarah: "Right now, I'm going to lie here in bed next to the offending navy blazer, holding a jar of honey, and drinking wine, until I go to sleep. Don't tell my mother any of this."

Lucy: "I don't have to. She already knows. And what's with the jar of honey?"

**Sunday**

The bus from Calvary Baptist Church arrived at the Louis Armstrong New Orleans International Airport shortly before five a.m. There were three doctors, three first-year medical students, four nurses, a dental hygienist, a college student, a minister, and a former Marine. The famous movie star had not yet arrived.

The group was congregating near the ticket counter when Matt saw Willie and Sarah approaching. The two stopped and were talking.

Willie: "Ms. Sarah, you take care of yourself down there and watch after Matt. What y'all are doin' is very special, and I'll be prayin' for y'all."

Sarah: "You have been a very special friend to me. I don't know if we'll meet again. Here is a card with a phone number on it. If you or your family ever needs anything, you call that number and ask for me. Put it in a safe place. And if I find out something happened to you, and I could have helped in some way, and you didn't call me, then I will make you pay. Do you understand me, Mr. Willie

Roberts? Now bend down."

Sarah gave Willie a kiss on the check. Willie waved at Matt and watched as Sarah walked away. The group was busy with suitcases as Sarah approached.

Pastor Mark: "Everyone, this is one of our team members, Sarah DuMont."

For once in recorded history, a secret had been kept in the community of Macon. Pastor Mark, John, Matt, and Ruth knew Sarah was going and precious few others. The faces on the remaining members told their own individual stories from, "Who is Sarah DuMont, and why is she going?" to "I can't believe this." Eventually, everyone put together the news stories about Matt and Sarah and her presence.

Betty: "Sweetie, my name is Betty Upton. We've had a little emergency. The doctors brought those three action packers with medical supplies, and we've learned Haiti won't let them into the country right now. So we're trying to get what we can in the luggage. Do you have any room in yours?"

See looked to where Betty pointed and saw three large plastic bins that had been secured with straps.

Sarah: "I think so."

Sarah handed Betty her luggage.

Betty: "Oh, Sweetie, you shouldn't have brought such nice luggage. Haiti can be rough."

Sarah: "I didn't think I did. I brought the worst I had."

Betty gave her a hug.

Betty: "Bless your heart. Let's see if you have any room."

There, before God and everyone, Betty opened Sarah's luggage, moved clothes and personal items around, making room for kits for new mothers. While Betty was violating Sarah's right to privacy, others of the group introduced themselves. Matt stood at a distance.

Jake, one of the first-year medical students, approached the group with news that he had found a store that would sell them luggage.

Pastor Mark: "A store open at five a.m. to sell us luggage. Thank you, Jesus."

Luggage was purchased, and items were transferred from the action packers. Thoman would get its medial supplies, and Sarah was reminded of what Pastor Mark had said, "all things in common." The group circled and held hands, and a prayer was said asking for God's provision. So began Sarah's first mission trip.

Matt was to sit next to Sarah on all the flights, due to her notoriety, and all tickets were coach.

Sarah: "I had no idea there was so little room in coach."

Matt: "Sarah, there are many, many, many things I've done that you haven't."

Sarah: "Matt, there is one less now."

Matt: "First, I want to show you somethin', then I want to give you somethin'."

Matt pulled out a smart phone and began to page through pictures.

Sarah: "When did you get a smart phone?"

Matt: "John upgraded his phone and let me have his old one. What do you see?"

Matt showed Sarah a picture on the phone.

Matt: "You call me cowboy, so I thought I should get a horse. Here's a picture of Doodle, me, and the new horse."

Sarah: "Oh, Matt, it's beautiful."

Matt: "She's a very special horse. She's only half horse."

Sarah: "What do you mean?"

Matt: "She's a mule, half horse and half jackass."

Sarah: "Please, Matt, tell me you didn't."

Matt: "Her name's Sarah. Every cowboy needs a horse. Now I have mine. Every time you call me cowboy, I'll think of Sarah. Here's a picture of her, by herself, wearing a straw hat. Any resemblance to the famous movie star is purely coincidental."

Sarah: "Send me a copy of that picture."

Matt: "I don't know how."

Sarah: "Give me that phone—I'll send it."

Sarah took the phone from Matt and began texting the picture to her phone.

Sarah: "You've been talking to my mother."

Matt: "We talk all the time. She likes me."

Sarah: "I don't like you two talking about me behind my back. I don't like you talking about me at all, for that matter."

Matt: "Sarah, everything's not about you. We don't talk about you . . . much. Besides, there's not much to say. Sarah did this; Sarah said that; then we laugh. Here, I got you a book to read on this trip."

Matt handed Sarah a copy of *Mere Christianity* by C. S. Lewis.

Matt: "I talk to all your family. Your father's bringing some judge down, and Uncle Billy's gonna take'em deer huntin'. Peter's oldest called. He and his brother want to stay with me on the farm for a week. I told him sure. I hope they do come. I'll tell them about Shade and Caroline while we sit in the dark. How Shade scared Aunt Sarah so bad, she ran and jumped in the manure pile."

Sarah: "Are you finished?"

Matt: "No. Juanita told me they gave you a little family party before you left for boarding school."

Sarah: "Yes, they did. It was sweet. I remember I was disappointed Juanita didn't make her chocolate cake. I loved that cake when I was growing up."

Matt: "Did you know, there was a second party the next day to celebrate after your departure, and Juanita served her chocolate cake? I love that story."

Sarah stared at Matt a moment.

Matt: "Sarah, is somethin' wrong?"

Sarah: "I'm a rich, famous, award winning actress. But I'm sitting in coach on my way to Haiti with an insane man, who has just shown me a picture of his new mule, named Sarah, and told me a story about how my family celebrated because I left for boarding school. Now, lean over here. I want to tell you something."

He leaned in, as if to hear a secret. She rubbed the top of his head then traced the scar on his forehead with her finger.

Sarah: "How would you like another one, on the other side? You know . . . I know people."

Matt: "You better know at least three of 'em cause that's how many it took to give me this one."

Sarah: "You are such a cowboy."

Matt: "I'm a cowboy with a very special horse named Sarah."

Sarah: "Just sit there and don't say anything else to me or show me anymore pictures. I'll read this book. Just please don't say anything else for a while."

———

In Haiti, a primary means of transportation are highly decorated vehicles, normally trucks, referred to as Tap Taps. They have fixed routes but do not depart until the vehicles are filled, usually well beyond capacity. A rider can tap the side of the vehicle to indicate a stop, which may be one possible explanation for the name. Many governments inform their citizens not to use Tap Taps because of mechanical and safety concerns. When asked how many riders a Tap Tap can carry, the answer is always the same, one more.

The team landed at Port-au-Prince and navigated the controlled chaos of the airport. Matt was instructed to bring up the rear. The heat and activity inside the terminal were only a taste of what awaited. In the uncontrolled chaos outside, every available piece of luggage had ten available porters, all certain of their claim on any tip.

The luggage and the team were ushered into the back of a large Tap Tap by Jerry, one-half of the husband and wife team managing the Hope Center. With Jerry were two Haitian translators employed at the Center.

The Tap Tap was decorated on every available surface with bright colors and words in Creole that appeared to reference Scripture. The passengers sat on boards, running on either side of the truck bed, under a metal cover with the sides open. One translator sat at the very back to discourage uninvited riders. The ride through Port-au-Prince to Thoman would take two hours if conditions were perfect. There would be hard seats, rough roads, dust, and heat. Jerry made sure everyone was on board with a bottle of water.

What Port-au-Prince lacks in infrastructure and wealth, it makes up for in human energy and activity. Matt and Sarah sat next to one another along one side of the Tap Tap. As the truckload of missionaries made its way, Matt reached over and took Sarah's hand. At first, she thought it was sweet, but then she realized he was squeezing harder and could tell by his body language, things may not be going well. She leaned over to speak. She had to be loud enough to be heard over the Tap Tap and noise of the city, but not heard by the group. She did the best she could.

Sarah: "Matt, you are hurting my hand. Are you all right?"

Matt: "Sorry. I'm just lookin' for IED's."

Sarah: "I don't think there are any in Haiti."

Matt: "A part of me knows that."

Sarah: "Okay, Matt, tell me what to look for."

Matt: "A ten year old Iraqi boy with a funky lookin' cell phone."

She laughed and patted him on the leg.

Sarah: "I just don't see any, cowboy. Bless your heart."

Matt: "Listen at you, Sarah. Thank you for bein' here, and bless your heart."

Sarah: "Matt, there is no place else I'd rather be right now than here with you. But before today is over, I'm sure you will do something to change my mind."

By appearance, all buildings in Haiti seem to have walls of cement blocks with reinforcing steal rods, rebar, of various lengths sticking out in all directions. Many reasons are given for not cutting the rebar from avoidance of taxes on finished buildings to possible future expansion. The urban landscape is of gray buildings with rebar tentacles covered by a patina of dust. The group saw all of this from the back of the Tap Tap, making its contribution to the noise and dust.

Once outside of Port-au-Prince, the frenzy of human activity declined as the dust increased. Desperate fields of banana trees, sorghum, and sugarcane came into view. Woman and children, with large bundles balanced on their heads, were seen walking on the side of the road. Motorcycles, with as many as four riders, passed the Tap Tap, having given the high pitch sound of a motorcycle horn. Periodically, transportation slowed to a crawl as lake-like potholes were navigated. Whether the road was two-lanes or four-lanes depended solely on the daring of the drivers and the current width of the road. Drivers were not burdened by any official markings.

After an hour, the Tap Tap turned off the main road, which leads to the Dominican Republic, and started the climb up the winding road to the village of Thoman. To Matt, the terrain resembled parts of Afghanistan, which did not help matters.

Matt: "Now I'm lookin' for ten year old Afghan boys with funky cell phones. I hope we get there soon."

Sarah: "We have another hour, Matt. You can make it. I know you can. Just hold my hand."

Matt: "I forgot how much I hate the dust. The place smells and tastes like Iraq."

Sarah: "Now, Matt, when you were in Iraq, you were not sitting next to Sarah DuMont."

Matt: "You're right. In Iraq, I held Louie Ludowski's hand. I do prefer yours."

Sarah: "I swear, Matt. I think I came all the way to Haiti just so you could make me laugh."

Matt: "You know what they say, Sarah, make her laugh; you gotta life."

She reminded herself to keep her guard up; goodbye was coming. As her mother said, this was a dangerous man. He did not let go of her hand for the rest of the trip. She was thankful it was her left hand.

Now the top speed of the Tap Tap was twenty miles an hour as they negotiated sharp turns on a lime stone road, overlooking deep ravines, which were home to a dry riverbed. Occasionally, they would see groups of woman below, standing in the riverbed around small pools of remaining water, with laundry spread in the sun on rocks.

Motorcycles with multiple passengers continued to pass. Along the road were make shift gas stations which consisted of dilapidated wooden stalls with displays of glass bottles partially filled with gasoline. In addition was the pungent smell of burning, as men made charcoal from any woody fibrous material that would suffice.

After another hour, covered in dust with sore posteriors, the smiling and laughing team pulled through the gate at the Hope Center.

Upon arrival, the team met Karen, the second half of the missionary team managing the Center, and Pastor Martin, a local Haitian pastor employed by the Center.

Pastor Martin: "My brothers and sisters in Christ, welcome to Thoman."

Karen: "We'll have supper ready around six. You have time to get settled and learn your way around. We are all so glad to have you here. The water in the bathrooms is not potable. It is fine for showering. You may want to use bottled water to brush your teeth.

Mosquitos have not been too bad, but you are aware of Chikungunya. We call it 'chicken gumbo.' You may want to use mosquito repellant, but it is up to you."

Karen laughed.

Karen: "You won't get any sympathy from the Haitians if you get it. You've met Jerry and Pastor Martin. Water is a premium right now. Please don't washout any of your clothes in a sink or in the shower. Let Pastor Martin know if you need something washed. Ladies from the village will do your laundry in the stream, which helps us save water."

"We have a bottled water dispenser in the kitchen. Be sure to fill your water bottles and remember to drink water. God bless all of you. We have been looking forward to your visit. Thank you for partnering with us to show the love of Christ to the people of Thoman, Haiti."

Luggage was distributed and bunks were claimed. The bunk beds were homemade out of 2x6 lumber. A magic marker hung by a string on each bunk. The practice was to sign your bunk on departure, leaving a message. Sarah picked a lower bunk and immediately realized there was no other types of furniture in the room. The floor around the bunk was the closet and dresser. With her and her luggage covered in dust, she sat on the bunk, looking around.

Sarah: "This is not quite as romantic as it first sounded."

The other ladies in the room laughed. Sarah made up her bunk with sheets brought from New Orleans, showered, and put on medical scrubs. Betty found her in the dorm room.

Betty: "Sweetie, I'm going to show you how to take blood pressure and temperature and show you an intake card. We did all this planning but ended up with only manual blood pressure monitors."

Betty spent the time before supper training the newest member of the health profession in Haiti. A laughing Matt approached Sarah and Betty sitting at a table in the dining area.

Matt: "Look at you, scrubs and a stethoscope."

Sarah: "Cowboy, after supper tonight, I'm going to practice on you. It is a new procedure, but we can't do it orally. It may not be so funny then."

Betty: "Something told me you two would be fun."

Matt: "Mrs. Upton, you have no idea. But watch her. She's been known to run and jump into manure piles and to sit naked for hours discussin' religion and actin' drunk. Bein' Sarah is a full time job."

Betty: "Sweetie, is this true?"

Sarah: "Yes."

Betty: "And I started not to come this year."

Supper was served: Haitian fried chicken, pureed beans over rice, *pikliz* (a slaw like dish), fruit, and fried plantains. By his expression, Sarah knew Matt thought he had died and gone to heaven. She ate in silent amusement, watching him. As promised, she practiced on Matt after supper.

As Matt sat across from her at the table, she took his left arm and ran her finger over the scar left by the mugger's knife.

Sarah: "You know they make creams that will help scars disappear."

Matt: "If that were only true."

Nothing was said for a few moments as Sarah continued to practice taking his blood pressure.

Matt: "Are my fingers really supposed to be this blue?"

Sarah: "I don't know, but what does it matter."

Matt: "It matters to me."

Sarah: "Well, you are the only one."

Matt: "Mrs. Upton, you better come over here."

The first day had started well before dawn in Macon and New Orleans and had ended on a mountaintop in Thoman, Haiti. As

Sarah lay in her bunk in the dark with the hum of an electric fan, she thought of what Matt's ol' daddy would say, "Never say never."

She remembered the envelope Pastor Mark had given her. She took out her flashlight and the envelope and read the letter.

> Dear Sarah:
>
> We are glad to have you join us. I want you to understand what we are about.
>
> We believe:
>
> We have all sinned, which means we have turned our backs on God. (Romans 3: 23)
>
> The punishment for our sin is death. (Roman 6: 23)
>
> But the gift of God is eternal life through Jesus, His Son. (Romans 6: 23)
>
> Forgiveness is given to anyone who would be a disciple of Jesus. (Romans 10: 9)
>
> For those who count the cost and follow Jesus, there is no longer any condemnation. (Romans 5: 1)
>
> The purpose of every Christian is to know Christ and make him known. This is why we are in Haiti. My prayer is that our group lives out these truths before you this week.
>
> Let me warn you, the Hound of Heaven, God's grace, has a way of pursuing people.
>
> Sincerely,
>
> Pastor Mark

She took Matt's Bible and read each one of the verses. He had highlighted, underlined, and made written notes around many of them, so, apparently, they were important. She was too tired to think about them now. She would think about them tomorrow.

## Monday

Each day for the team would begin officially at seven-thirty with a fifteen-minute devotion and prayer by Pastor Mark. For many of the Haitians, it would begin in the wee hours of the morning as they put on their best clothes and made their way to the gate of the Hope Center, many arriving at six, having walked miles in the dark.

Breakfast was not prepared for the team. Most Haitians eat only two meals a day; however, a large pot of Haitian coffee was ready for everyone and in time for the early risers, such as Matt.

For him, a man accustomed to a large breakfast of biscuits, eggs, and grits, breakfast bars would have to do. Sarah would join him around seven-fifteen.

Matt: "How did you sleep?"

Sarah: "Well, considering how loud you snore."

Matt: "I don't snore, and besides, you were in the women's dorm."

Sarah: "Several of us are going to carry your bunk outside the compound tonight to see if that helps. If that doesn't work, we are considering bribing one of the guards to shoot you."

Matt: "No one in my dorm has complained."

Sarah: "They don't want to hurt your feelings."

Matt: "Meanin'?"

Sarah: "I don't mind hurting your feelings."

Matt smiled.

Matt: "You know what they say, you only hurt the ones you love."

Sarah: "You are not going to make this easy are you, Matt?"

Matt: "I don't know what you are talkin' about, Sarah. Do you want more coffee?"

Sarah: "No, thank you."

Sarah sat through the devotion but did not understand any of it.

What were these people talking about? She understood them now about as well as she understood Matt the first time she met him.

By eight, she was at her table with a Haitian translator to begin intake for the clinic. Small groups of patients were allowed in to sit in the waiting area, to sit with Pastor Mark to hear the gospel and ask for prayer, and to sit with Sarah to have their vitals taken and symptoms registered. All this was done in the open courtyard with the makeshift tarps.

The doctors instructed Sarah to complete the intake cards. The translators were good, but not that good. Betty told her most of the complaints would be in the order of upset stomachs or headaches. The Haitians, in general, did not drink enough water each day. Sarah realized that the medical team would mostly dispense Tums, Tylenol, and love, what Betty called TT and L. Highly trained medical professionals, holding the hand of a Haitian and letting them know, through a translator, that someone loved them in the name of Jesus. This is not what she had expected.

She could hear, and occasionally see, Matt through the iron gate that separated the clinic courtyard from the maintenance courtyard, where he was working. The big differences were he had no shade, and the noise from the generator and power tools.

At one point, the noise subsided, and she could tell he was conducting an English lesson. He was, apparently, holding up tools, and the young Haitians would give the English name. Unfortunately for Sarah, Matt held up a clamp at the very moment she had taken a drink from her water bottle. When she heard the Haitians pronounce the word "clamp" in three syllables with a nasal drawl, water came out her nose. At least it wasn't sweet tea.

Work in both courtyards continued until noon. Lunch consisted of peanut butter and jelly sandwiches with fruit, mostly mangos and pineapples. Matt was dirty with a coating of sawdust.

Sarah: "I suppose you are accustomed to this heat."

Matt: "It's different. In Miss'sippi the heat comes from the ground up, by way of the humidity. Here, there's lower humidity and the heat comes from above. I'm accustomed to bein' marinated, not broiled."

Sarah: "Drink plenty of water. I've learned that much."

Matt: "How 'bout you?"

Sarah: "These people are so precious. They get all dressed up to come to the clinic. They wait patiently for their turn. Most of all, they just want someone to show them some compassion."

Matt: "Listen at you, Sarah. You're beginnin' to sound like Lottie Moon."

Sarah: "Who?"

Matt: "For someone who attended high end boarding schools, Yale, and Juilliard, there's sure a lot you don't know."

Sarah: "Apparently, if I only had a decent teacher. [Matt voice] 'Cleehamp.' Really, Matt?"

Matt: "Never said I was Shakespeare."

Sarah: "Just his younger brother, Billy Bob Shakespeare."

Matt: "So you have heard of me?"

Betty: "How long will this go on?"

Matt/Sarah: "All day."

Not all the medical team did involved only Tums and Tylenol.

Betty: "Sweetie, a young girl and her mother came directly into the clinic this morning without going through you. The girl had a compound fracture of her leg three years ago and the bone was still visible."

Sarah: "I thought something must have been going on in there. I could tell the med students were excited."

Betty: "Yes, they all wanted to see it. John didn't know how she's survived. They contacted a hospital in Port-au-Prince and found an orthopedic surgeon that can help her. The mother's to bring her back in the mornin' and Pastor Martin will take them to Port-au-Prince. You just never know, Sweetie, what you may find in Haiti."

As Matt returned to his woodworking and Betty returned to the clinic, Sarah sat alone a few minutes contemplating what she had already found in Haiti.

The heat in the afternoon was noticeable. Around four, Matt and his Haitian helpers called it a day. He showered, took a short nap, and went down the steps to the dining tables, looking for Sarah.

———————

They sat across from each other for the nightly meal. Others joined them as if they were the cool kids in school. As usual, Matt's eating fascinated Sarah. He did it with such joy and without any self-awareness.

Matt: "Not real sure what this is, but it's good. I went in the kitchen, but I don't think the Haitian cooks wanted me in there. Juanita liked me, but these don't want me around. Must be a cultural thing."

Sarah: "Juanita loves you. Why? When I look at you, I see a man whose hair is too short and is balding. You have one eyebrow, not two. One ear is much bigger than the other. I don't know why you don't drift to one side when you walk."

Matt continued to eat as if he heard nothing.

Sarah: "I never know which eye to look at when I'm talking to you. You have chicken lips. You do have beautiful teeth, but I know you have another pair in your room. And your clothes come from the Salvation Army spring collection."

Matt's unabated consumption of food continued.

Sarah: "That's what I see when I look at you."

Matt sat his fork down, looking at Sarah.

Matt: "Do you want to know what I see when I look at you?"

Sarah: "Yes. . . . Maybe, I reserve the right to end the conversation."

Matt: "The mainline for the Illinois Central Railroad is not far from my farm. A freight train comes down that line very early, most mornin's. On a cool mornin', you can hear it. When conditions are just right, Doodle and I will go down to the lake in the dark and sit on the dock. I'll take a thermos of coffee and some bacon for Doodle."

"We'll sit there, waitin' for the train and the sunrise. If we're lucky and everything falls into place, the first lights of the sun will hit the lake just as you hear the sound of the passin' train. That's what I experience when I look at you."

There was an awkward silence at the table. Others near them put their heads down and ate, as if they heard nothing.

Matt: "Are you goin' to eat that?"

Sarah: "No. You can have it."

Sarah slid her plate over to Matt.

Matt: "Thanks."

Sarah wondered if she would ever learn, never get in a verbal contest with Matthew Shepherd. She had no idea if any of that was true. But what if it was?

After supper, a guitar found its way into the correct hands. First the songs were secular and then came "What a Friend We Have In Jesus." It was done in English. Then the Haitian staff sang a verse in Creole, then everyone in English again. Even Sarah found herself singing, and she did not know the words.

One hymn led to another, some with special meaning to individual members of the group and all with unique origins. For example, in June of 1872, Annie Hawks was deeply involved in domestic duties, as a wife and mother of three in Brooklyn, New York, when she was "filled by the sense of nearness to the Master." From that experience she penned the words, "I need thee every hour." She would compose over four hundred hymns in her lifetime, but only one would continue to be sung over a century later and on a mountainside in Thoman, Haiti.

Jake, the medical student, took the guitar and sang "I Need Thee Every Hour." During the song, Sarah watched the faces of the team members, some mouthing the words during the chorus:

I need thee, oh, I need thee;
  Ev'ry hour I need thee!
  Oh, bless me now, my Savior;
  I come to thee!

Sarah sat quietly with her thoughts during the song. Most days, she did not understand Matt. This morning, she did not understand Pastor Mark's devotion. Today, she did not understand the point of the Gospel story repeated so many times to the Haitians. But she understood this. These people knew something—knew experiences, knew someone—she did not know.

The singing of various hymns continued and finally ended when some began to drift off to the dorms and showers.

Matt: "Well, how was your first day?"

Sarah smiled.

Sarah: "Good, but tiring. I heard the gospel presented about fifty times today, sitting there near Pastor Mark."

Matt: "I love to tell the story, the old, old story."

Sarah: "What?"

Matt: "That's another hymn you don't know. We don't want you to feel left out. Tomorrow night, we could sing one of the great hymns to atheism."

Sarah: "I don't think there are any. Apparently, your side has something to sing about. I give you that much."

"Anyway, I did what they told me. I took the temperature and blood pressure and wrote down the complaints. I could see you at times through the gate. It looked hot over there this afternoon. I was at least in the shade."

Sarah was visibly moved.

Sarah: "There was a woman today with two small children. The children looked fine, but it was clear what was going on. The mother was giving her food to them. This afternoon, I sat with those children while the mother went in the kitchen. They would smile at me and touch my hair. I don't think they've seen blonde hair before. The mother came out of the kitchen with a large bag of beans, and the three left. She was carrying the bag on her head and holding the hand of each child. Jerry gave her the food."

"He said the Hope Center did not have the means to be a food distribution center. The goal is for them to be self-sustaining. I guess Jerry gave her a bag of hope this afternoon."

Matt: "How 'bout you, Sarah? Did you give anyone hope today?"

Sarah: "I did what they told me to do. I hope I did it right. I'm not a nurse. These people deserve better than me."

Matt: "You are the best nurse I've ever had. You're doin' fine. They're docs. Trust me. If you weren't doin' it right, they'd let you know. Sarah, I'm tired, and I'm goin' to bed."

Sarah: "Me to, walk me back to the dorm. . . . I feel like I'm in college."

Matt: "I don't think Yale looks like the Hope Center in Thoman."

Sarah: "No, it doesn't, but I'm learning more here than I did there."

## Tuesday

Tuesday morning began without the appearance of the young girl with the leg wound and her mother. The consensus was that the mother was afraid of Port-au-Prince and what lay ahead for her daughter. Pastor Martin walked higher into the mountains, finally returning just before noon with the girl and the mother. With a few belongings packed, they loaded into Pastor Martin's truck and headed out of the Hope Center.

Matt was somewhat isolated from the clinic and asked Sarah to let him know if the young girl and mother returned. She walked into the courtyard to see Matt and his three helpers huddled around some lumber on a table, with one of the helpers making a mark with a pencil. She tapped Matt on the back.

Sarah: "The young girl and mother have left for Port-au-Prince. Looks like she will get the help she needs."

Sarah addressed Matt's helpers.

Sarah: "You young men learning how to make furniture?"

Matt: "Sarah, they don't speak English."

Sarah: "Neither do you."

Matt: "Sarah, this is Stevenson, Junior, and Junior."

Sarah shook the hand of each. Matt walked behind her, placing his hands on her shoulders, and looked at his helpers.

Matt: "We have something we want to show you. Men, this is . . . Sarah. Now, what do we say to . . . Sarah? Stevenson."

One by one, beginning with Stevenson, each of his helpers repeated a short sentence in English that they had learned from Matt. In a youthful, Creole accent, each one said, "Sarah is trouble."

Matt: "Great. Now let's try the next one all together."

Helpers and Matt: "But . . . we . . . love . . . Sarah."

Sarah turned around, put her hands on the brim of Matt's floppy hat, and pulled it down around his ears. With her hands still on the hat, she pulled his head down close to her face.

Sarah: "I really, really, really do not like you. I now know what a field hand smells like."

She stepped around him and headed to the waiting area for the clinic.

Matt: "Does this mean we ain't doin' lunch?"

She gave him a backward wave, reminding herself of the wave he had given her on his way to meet Willie in the parked car. Now they were even. She could hear him and his helpers giggling and slapping hands. She looked back just before going into the clinic courtyard. He was still standing there with his hat pulled down around his ears, laughing with his young Haitian charges. He was not making this easy. Haiti would not be a snap for her.

Except for the extraordinary young girl, Tuesday was mostly a repeat of Monday. In addition, Karen made the rounds with a smile and a "Hello my Christian sister." Again Sarah took the names, listed the symptoms, and looked into the faces of people who could smile in spite of the harshness of daily existence. To these people, she was not Sarah Morgan Leigh DuMont but Sarah. She thought about something Matt had once said, "The ground is level at the foot of the cross." Perhaps, this is what he meant.

In the middle of the morning, an expectant mother arrived, riding on the back of a motorcycle with another woman and the driver, making a total of three on the bike. The baby was delivered, and before the nightly meal was served, four left on the motorcycle. Sarah was impressed.

She ate with Matt and a group of nurses. He headed to his bunk early, and only Betty and Sarah remained at the table.

Betty: "Sweetie, you are not a Christian, are you?"

Sarah: "Is it that obvious?"

Betty: "You and I have more in common than you may realize. When I was your age, I wasn't a Christian either. Unlike most on this trip, I wasn't raised in a Christian home. My parents didn't take any of us children to church, not even on Christmas or Easter. I married a man who wasn't a Christian. It was fine for other people but not for me. In Mississippi, you learn to go with the flow on religion. Leave them alone, and, for the most part, they'll leave you alone."

Sarah: "What happened?"

Betty: "Cancer. Goin' through treatment, I became good friends with another woman goin' through the same thing. She was the sweetest person. I went into remission—she didn't. I watched that woman die. She clearly had somethin' I didn't have. I wanted what she had."

Sarah: "What did she have?"

Betty: "What a friend we have in Jesus. That's what she had. So Jesus and I made friends. You know the name Christian actually means 'little Christ' and was first used in derision. He said that would always be the case. Sweetie, that woman was Matt's mother."

"I often wonder why God took that saintly woman and left an old sinner like me. But I'm not in administration; I'm in sales. I am convinced that I will see Mary Shepherd again someday. And when I do, I will tell her thank you. And I'll tell her about you, and how you have looked after her baby boy."

"Well, I'm going to bed. Goodnight, Sweetie."

Sarah: "Goodnight, Betty."

Sarah sat alone at the table. This is not what she expected. Nothing was as it appeared to be from the moment she entered Mrs. Fontenot's shop. Betty was convinced, one day, Mary Shepherd would know about Sarah DuMont. How could that be true? How could it not?

## Wednesday

After the morning devotion, the medical team, including Sarah, packed a lunch, medical supplies, and extra water. They made the long hike further up into the mountains to the village of Mathias. There they set up a make shift clinic with Sarah doing intake in the shade of a tree. The level of poverty was even more severe than what she had seen in Thoman. She had not thought that was possible. But the smiles on the children's faces were real and more than adequate payment for the long hike over unwelcoming terrain under a Haitian sun.

Matt did not make the hike but remained at his makeshift workshop. He usually quit for the day around four o'clock, took a shower, and a short nap. He was very dirty by the end of the day and needed the shower before supper. At that time of day, he had the area to himself. To get from the dorm room to the shower required a walk outside onto a porch. Sarah noticed. On Tuesday, she was in the women's dorm and saw Matt walk to the shower with a towel wrapped around him.

On Wednesday, as Matt and his towel stepped onto the porch, Sarah and several of the nurses were seated on the women's porch across the way. She had assured some of the nurses that a special treat awaited after the long hike home from Mathias. On cue, they made catcalls and waved one-dollar bills as Matt made his journey to the shower. He was clearly embarrassed, and Sarah was clearly delighted.

Sarah: "Someone please make note of this moment. Matt Shepherd is embarrassed and speechless."

There were high fives all around. A discussion followed later that night.

Matt: "You know, I also had my underwear on. It wasn't just a towel."

Sarah: "That means I would have to pay two dollars. I'm not paying two dollars. I'll pay a dollar, but not two. How much would you pay for me?"

Matt: "I'm not goin' to discuss this on a mission trip."

Sarah: "Why, Matt Shepherd, you are blushing. Come on, Matt, how much would you pay?"

Matt: "More than any man you've ever known."

There was silence as she rubbed the top of his head.

Sarah: "I know, Matt. I know. . . . You know, that night after your big victory in the dining room, I came to your room to seduce you."

Matt: "Really, what happened? I think I'd remember if you had."

Sarah: "Every time I went down there, Chris was in your room. I finally fell asleep, waiting on him to leave. Were y'all talking about me? I said y'all."

Matt: "I like it when you say y'all. Yes, we were talkin' about you."

Sarah: "I guess we missed our chance. We are at the end of a love affair that never happened."

Matt: "I guess so. Trust me, memories can be overrated. Like everything else, there is a right way and a wrong way. Slipping around in your father's house, under his roof, would not have been the right way for me."

Sarah: "I knew it. I knew you would feel that way. Instead of a night with Sarah DuMont you got an autographed baseball from the Yankees. I'm not sure many men would knowingly make that deal."

Matt: "But we did stay together the next night. You fell asleep, and I carried you to the bed. It wasn't easy with my wounds. I thought I woke you. You looked at me and said somethin'. But then you went back to sleep."

Sarah: "I don't remember any of that. What did I say?"

Matt: "You know, Sarah, sleepin' Sarah told me not to tell. I pulled up a chair and watched you sleep for a while. That's when I knew I had to leave. I had embarrassed your family, like you said I would, and I couldn't be around you anymore."

Sarah: "Matt, you didn't embarrass anyone. I'm afraid to ask why you couldn't be around me anymore."

Matt: "I can't handle you, Sarah. You'll never give me the chance to do the right thing, and I won't do the wrong thing by you, if I can help it."

Sarah: "Are you my Shade?"

Matt: "Yes, and you are my Caroline."

Sarah put her finger across his lips.

Sarah: "Let's not talk about this anymore. It makes me sad. Please, make me laugh or go to bed. Those are your only two options."

Matt: "I'll go to bed then. I'll make you laugh tomorrow. I can't right now."

Sarah watched him walk away. So, she was his Caroline; someone he loved but would never have. She wondered what his ol' daddy would say about all this never business.

———————————

There comes a point in trips like this when any walls among team members have completely disappeared. Living, eating, and working together for the Lord tends to do that.

Several of the nurses, along with Sarah, were the last ones still up and sitting at the dining tables. The nurses were Betty, Ginger, and Kathy. They soon began telling stories about Matt.

Ginger: "How did you two meet?"

Sarah: "I made a wager with a woman in New Orleans and won him."

Ginger: "No, seriously, how did y'all meet."

Sarah: "Seriously, I won him in a bet."

Kathy: "That's too funny not to be true."

Ginger: "I'm two years younger than him and had a crush on him in high school. He was a senior, and I missed my ride home from school. He saw me standin' alone and took me home in his old truck. I couldn't even talk or look at him. I know he must've thought I was crazy."

"I'll tell you where he got that truck. Ruth had dated a boy all through high school. Just days before the senior prom, they had a big fight and broke up."

Kathy: "I remember that."

Ginger: "It was close to the prom, and Ruth didn't have anybody to go with. The family was still dealin' with Mary's death. Well, Matt took her. My brother was in Ruth's class. He was a starter on the football team and had a scholarship to play in college. He was a big man on campus. But he was also drinkin' and givin' my parents all kind of trouble. Well, he said somethin' bad about Ruth in the parkin' lot, and Matt heard him. Matt was two years younger and was third string on the football team. He gave my brother one ever more whoopin that night."

"At first, my daddy was real upset. But, when he learned it was a third string sophomore defendin' the honor of his sister, he drove the pick-up he used for fishin' over to Matt's house and gave it to him. Told Matt it was thanks for not killin' his son."

"My parents didn't have anymore trouble from my brother. I've heard my brother say it was one of the best things that ever happened to him. Helpin' my brother is what got me interested in nursin'."

"They almost suspended Matt, but because of everything the family had been through and my daddy, they didn't. Matt just went back to bein' Matt. He never was a starter on the football team."

Sarah: "Did he date anyone in high school?"

Kathy: "I don't think so. I don't think he was ever serious about anyone until Olivia came along. She was a looker."

Sarah: "I met her in Lester's."

Betty: "We all know; it's Macon. I was there the night they brought the Sullivan brothers into the emergency room. We didn't think we'd ever get those big ol' boys put back together. It was serious, but your first response was to laugh. There was John barkin' orders. In between orders, he'd say, 'I told you boys to leave Odell alone. I've been tellin' you.' Then a nurse would be workin' like crazy standin' next to a nurse that was laughin'. We had Sullivan brother from one end of the emergency room to the other. They're big men."

The nurses were laughing. Sarah assumed it was medical humor.

Sarah: "I saw it in Central Park in New York. I'm not sure what he would have done to that mugger if I hadn't been there. There are things going on with Matt I can't talk about."

Kathy: "From his military service?"

Sarah: "Yes."

Ginger: "Well, what's next, Sarah?"

Sarah's tone changed. She looked at the table as she talked.

Sarah: "I don't know. What can I do? He can't leave that farm. I have a career, demands, obligations. I can't live on that farm. I don't know what else to do but tell him goodbye when this is over. I've done all I can for him. I don't know what else to do."

Sarah looked up.

Ginger: "I meant, what's next for your actin' career. I wasn't askin' about Matt."

They all sat in silence.

## Thursday

Thursday began very early in the morning for Sarah.

Betty: "Sweetie, Matt's at the door. He needs to see you."

Sarah: "What time is it?"

Betty: "Almost one o'clock."

Sarah: "This is never good."

Sarah made her way outside and found Matt sitting on the steps, leaning forward with his elbows on his knees. Sarah sat down, put her arm around him, and began rubbing his head.

Sarah: "What's up, cowboy?"

Matt: "I woke up in a panic. Went lookin' for my weapon and couldn't find it. John woke up and turned his flashlight on me. He doesn't know how close he came. I had to get out of there."

Sarah saw Pastor Mark and John standing outside the men's dorm in the dim security light. She waved them back inside and started laughing.

Matt: "Are you laughin' at me? I really don't think you are supposed to laugh at a vet with PTSD. Doodle doesn't laugh at me."

Sarah: "She does all the time."

Matt: "How do you know?"

Sarah: "You know Doodle told me not to tell. Picture this, Matt, you and John are standing in front of Ruth. John has two black eyes and cotton stuffed up his broken nose. You say to Ruth [Matt voice], 'I couldn't find my weapon, so I beat up your husband.' That's funny."

Matt looked at Sarah.

Matt: "That's my t-shirt. How did you get my t-shirt? I knew I couldn't find that shirt. I thought maybe Doodle had it. . . . Stealin' the clothes of a disabled vet. What kind of person does a thing like that?"

Sarah: "This is payment for bringing in your laundry. I put this t-shirt and a pair of your Calvin Klein underwear in those plastic bags Willie carried to the car. I got them out of the clothes basket. You didn't think the Sarah Morgan Leigh DuMont laundry service was free, did you?"

Matt: "That underwear cost me twenty bucks."

Sarah: "Just think how much it's worth now on eBay. One pair of Calvin Klein boxer briefs worn by Sarah DuMont. How much do you think I could get?"

Matt: "As much as I make in a year."

Sarah: "Oh, I think I could do much better than that. What you make in a year wouldn't cover shipping and handling."

The two exchanged a look as Sarah rubbed the top of his head.

Matt: "I know some people so poor, all they have is money."

Sarah: "Ha! Come on, cowboy, let me put you back in your bed."

Matt reached and put his hand on her forearm.

Matt: "Wait. My . . . disorder . . . has done some things to me. But it hasn't made me a fool, yet. I'm sittin' next to Sarah DuMont in the dark under a Haitian sky, and I understand from reliable sources that my days are numbered. I'm goin' to kiss you, and then we are goin' to sit in silence for a few moments. This will be our goodbye kiss."

Sarah: "Matt—"

Matt put a finger across her lips.

Matt: "The silence starts now."

He moved his finger, kissed her, and held her hand. As requested, they sat in silence. The only sound was the mechanical whine of the diesel generator at the other end of the Hope Center. Finally, he rose and stroked her hair as he might do with Doodle.

Matt: "Long of line, twin spars like trees, and sails of black—"

Sarah: "Why black? . . . Never mind—please don't say it."

Matt: "I'm better now. I can't thank you enough for helpin' me. I won't bother you any more tonight. I'll see you in the mornin' and make you laugh. I promise—goodnight, Sarah Morgan Leigh."

For the second time that night, she watched him walk away, sitting there until he disappeared in the darkness. She stood and found Betty waiting at the door.

Betty: "I waited because I didn't know exactly what the problem might be. I thought you might need help. Sweetie, you are so good with him."

Sarah: "Yes, and Saturday we say goodbye."

Betty: "Sweetie, are you all right?"

Sarah: "No."

Tears began to stream down Sarah's face.

Sarah: "I hate him. I hate him so much. I hate the way he makes me feel and makes me laugh. I hate his honor. I hate the way he needs me. I hate it when he holds my hand. I hate his smile. I hate it when he kisses me. My brain goes blah, blah, blah, and I can't see. I hate that poem. I hate that farmhouse. I hate that mule. Most of all, most of all, I hate his dog!"

By now, Betty was holding Sarah's hand with one hand while brushing away tears with the other.

Betty: "I hate him too, Sweetie. Come on. Let's go inside. I didn't know he had a mule."

Sarah's tone changed.

Sarah: "He has a mule named Sarah, same as me."

Betty: "I see."

Sarah: "Betty, I know you don't hate him. Please, don't hate him."

Betty: "I won't, Sweetie. I won't."

Sarah: "Let me do that. I know how to do it better than anybody."

---

Sarah and Matt met for breakfast. Matt had no more problems, thanked Sarah again, and as promised, made her laugh.

As usual, everyone gathered for the devotion. She had not understood any of them until now. This one was about the Rich Young Ruler. She understood this time and didn't like it.

Again a pregnant woman arrived at the clinic by means of a motorcycle. The delivery was going so well, the doctors let the nurses and medical students handle the birth. They, of course, enlisted Sarah.

The nurses let her hold the baby while they tended to the mother. Sarah's time was up, and the baby needed to be returned to the mother. But Sarah was not following the script. After much kind insistence, she did as told.

---

After the evening meal, everyone dressed for the service at Pastor Martin's church. As instructed, Sarah wore a mid-calf cotton skirt in deference to the Haitian sensibilities. The service started at six p.m., but that was Haitian time, which meant anytime from six to six-thirty would be fine.

The current church building was new and located several yards from the Hope Center. The walls were cement block; the floor was finished concrete; the ceiling was vaulted using steel prefabricated rafters; and all was covered by galvanized tin. Each side window contained a metal grid, which gave the impression of a stained glass window with a cross in the center, but the windows contained no glass of any kind. The pews were made on site from two by six rough lumber and were surprisingly comfortable. Sarah was struck by the dignity of the simple building.

Moving from left to right, the platform contained a decorated

Christmas tree (no explanation was given), a baptistry, a podium, and musicians. An outside generator was started, and the lights, including those on the Christmas tree, an organ, and an electric guitar came to life.

Pastor Martin welcomed the visitors from Calvary Baptist Church, and each rose in turn to give their first name. The music began for the first song, the now familiar "What a Friend We Have in Jesus," sung in Creole. As the worshipers rose to sing, the guests outnumbered the members, and Matt and Sarah sat alone on their pew. As the song ended and everyone sat down, members now outnumbered the guests, and Matt and Sarah were surrounded by children. Two had worked their way between them, and one little girl sat on the other side of Sarah with her elbows resting in Sarah's lap and her eyes fixed on Sarah.

More singing was followed by a presentation of the now familiar gospel story by Pastor Mark, translated into Creole by Pastor Martin. This was followed by Scripture readings from two Haitian teenagers and a short sermon by Pastor Martin, all in Creole. Sarah thought of his first words to them as they arrived, "Welcome my brothers and sisters in Christ"—brothers and sisters in Christ, in deed.

A final hymn was sung in Creole and all stood holding hands as Pastor Martin prayed. The hands of the Haitian children seemed so warm to Sarah. During the prayer, she stole glances at Matt and could see some of the children looking at her. She winked and they smiled.

After the service, the generator was turned off, leaving everyone in darkness, which the Haitians seemed to navigate without a problem. Matt held Sarah's hand, and she used her cell phone as a flashlight as they made their way back to the Hope Center. Perhaps holding his hand was not exactly like holding the business end of a shovel. Nothing was said as the two made the walk back.

---

Matt and Sarah were sitting alone at the dining tables after the church service. He was sitting across from her with his back to the rest of the group. Since Sarah's unforced error Wednesday night, revealing her plans to say goodbye to him, the group had given them more space.

They were arguing about prayer.

Matt: "I don't know, Sarah. If you keep talkin' like that on a mission trip, I'm afraid God is gonna zap you. There'd be nothin' but a little pile of stinky charcoal. How'd I explain that to your mother?"

Sarah: "Stop talking to my mother. I forbid it."

Matt: "What are you doin'?"

Sarah had placed both her hands on the table, straightened her back, and closed her eyes. She would open one eye for a moment and then repeat the process.

Sarah: "I'm closing my eyes, praying that you disappear, then checking to see if my prayer has been answered."

She opened one eye.

Sarah: "Matt, Matt, where are you?"

At that moment Sarah screamed. Everyone in the group turned to see Sarah sitting alone. She smiled and waved a hand.

Sarah: "Sorry, sorry, everything is fine."

She leaned to the side and looked under the table.

Sarah: "Leave my leg alone."

Matt: "You may need to do a little hair maintenance."

Sarah: "My legs are fine. Now get out from under the table."

Matt: "I can't. You prayed me under here. You have to pray me out."

She closed her eyes and prayed in an audible voice.

Sarah: "Dear God, please get that fool out from under the table. Amen."

When she opened her eyes, Matt was sitting across the table.

Sarah: "You are psychotic!"

Matt: "Sarah, you know you love me."

They sat in silence a moment.

Sarah: "Something happened to me today. After the delivery, they let me hold the baby. An overwhelming sense came over me that someone wanted to give me something. It was surprising and wonderful. In your own words, Matt, tell me about Jesus."

Matt: "Well, C. S. Lewis says—"

Sarah: "I don't want to hear what Saint Paul says or what Saint Peter says or what C. S. Lewis says. I want to hear what you say."

Matt: "Okay, Sarah, fair enough. I was on my last deployment in Afghanistan and near exhaustion. The three things that kept me goin' were God, my Marines, and Olivia. Then I got the letter from her. It was like a dam broke. I got so angry. I'd lay awake at night plannin' on how I could take a bullet and just be done with it all. But my Marines needed me."

"Then after my discharge, the Corps didn't need me anymore. And the anger just intensified. I was livin' on the farm and hated it. Livin' in the farmhouse was like livin' deployed. I had to set up an outside shower and dig a latrine. But I hated bein' around people more, so I stayed there. Most people know about the prodigal son. Well, he had a brother, one that did everything asked of him and was mad at his father. That was me. I was just angry but, most of all, angry with God. I saw a pattern. Everyone left me: my mother, my father, Olivia, the Corps and, it seemed, even God."

"Drinkin' and fightin' made the anger go away so that's what I did. That night in Lester's bar, Lester pulled that gun on me to make me stop beatin' the Sullivan brothers, but that didn't mean anything. If he shot me, he would have been doin' me a favor."

Sarah: "Why did you stop?"

Matt: "Odell. He said, 'Matt, please stop.' It was the first time in my life, I ever heard him speak a complete sentence without a pause or hesitation. If it hadn't been for Odell, I might have killed those men that night."

"Odell took me home. I was sittin' in that farmhouse, and all I could think was how much I was like Andy, dead on the inside and without hope. I remember thinkin', 'Sweet Jesus, please help me.' I was reminded that Christ purchased my pardon on the cross, once for all time. I was refighting battles that had already been won. It is a powerful thing to be forgiven: past, present, and future. God's grace is a stubborn thing."

Sarah: "You mean the Hound of Heaven?"

Matt: "I've heard it called that. Every day I rely on His grace. I was just a couple minutes away from killin' someone, and now I live totally dependent on God's forgiveness and grace. 'God has placed upon Him the sins of us all' and 'by His wounds we are healed.'"

"You need to also know, I'm goin' to be all right. What God does for us, he does in us. Jesus gives us His Spirit to live inside of us. I like to think that Doodle is the dog version of that."

"You said someone wanted to give you somethin'. From where I sit, I'd say Jesus wants to give you the only thing He can, Himself, and, with Him, the abundant life. You need to do what's right for you."

Sarah: "Matt, I don't know what to say. I can't process all of this. It is so foreign to me and anything I've known. I should have never come on this trip. I don't want to hear or talk about these things. You need to go to bed now and leave me alone."

Matt rose, took a step toward the dorm, and stopped, turning to look at Sarah.

Matt: "If I have a flashback tonight, will you help me?"

Sarah: "Why don't you ask God's grace to help you?"

Matt: "That night in Fallujah, Jesus needed me to go get Andy. Not for Andy, but for the people that Andy loved. That night in the farmhouse, after the fight in Lester's, Jesus promised me He doesn't leave his Marines behind. He would send someone to get me. When I walked into Mrs. Fontenot's store and saw you, I said a short prayer, 'Please God, not her.' Yet, here we are. . . . Sarah, maybe you are God's grace for me."

Sarah: "I'll help you if you need me. Now go away."

Sarah sat at the table alone until well past the time everyone else had gone to bed. Eventually, a night security guard walked up and smiled. He did not speak English.

Sarah: "I'm fine. I'll go to bed now. Goodnight."

As she walked to the dorm, she hoped sleep would come soon. She did not want to think about these things.

## Friday

Friday was to be a half-day. Most of the group had not left the Hope Center during the week, spending their time in the clinic, or in Matt's case, making benches, desks, and bookshelves for the Center and Pastor Martin's school.

Sarah had found a window in the clinic pharmacy behind a row of shelves that allowed her to watch Matt and not be noticed by him or anyone busy in the clinic. During the week, she had gone to the window whenever the opportunity presented itself. She did so on Friday morning.

Betty: "Sweetie, what you lookin' at out that window? . . . Never mind. I wondered where you been goin'. I knew there were times when I had no idea where you were."

Sarah: "Betty, what am I going to do?"

Betty: "If I were in your shoes and knew what I know now, I'd never let that man get away. But if you tell him goodbye, make it quick and clean. He's a Marine. They know how to take a punch."

Sarah: "The Marine is bad enough. The little boy breaks my heart."

After lunch, several of the group piled onto the back of a four-wheel-drive, diesel pick-up truck, including Matt and Sarah, and were driven by Jerry through the village. They then hiked up a mountain to have a scenic view of Étang Saumâtre.

Children, who were everywhere, began to shout "blanco, blanco, blanco," under the Spanish influence of the nearby Dominican Republic. Laughing, curious children followed them up the mountain and enveloped the group. At the top, informal group pictures were made with as many Haitian children included as group members.

The mountain was crisscrossed with goat trails. Sarah passed a Haitian man herding four goats with coloring almost identical to Doodle's. The goats seemed as curious of the strangers as the children.

As Matt and Sarah started down, a translator said something to a young boy. The boy obeyed without saying a word. He positioned himself in front of Matt and acted as the guide down the mountain. Sarah watched from a short distance away as the pair descended. She stood there for as long as possible, not wanting to be left behind.

They were again alone after the evening meal and sitting next to one another at the very back of the dining area

Matt: "I haven't tried to beat up anyone. You were gonna give my underwear back."

Sarah: "I lied. I don't have your underwear. Matt, hold my hand. I need to talk to you."

Matt took Sarah's hand.

Matt: "I know what's comin'."

Sarah: "Please don't say anything."

Sarah took a breath and began.

Sarah: "As you know, I'm leaving for South Africa Sunday. What you may not know, Mississippi has not signed some communication treaty with South Africa, so we won't be able to communicate while I'm there."

"I've sent money to the veterinarian in Macon for Doodle. She is paid-up for the rest of her life. You make sure that vet looks after her. Also, take her to the lake and let her fetch that toy. She loves it so."

"I've talked to John, and he can give you annual check-ups. You need to take care of yourself. Let John look after you. You should also go back to the VA. They can help you."

"Lucy says your furniture is in high demand now with all the publicity. Take advantage of this to make you some money. Maybe even hire someone to help you."

"There should be a new pair of cowboy boots waiting for you when you get home. I don't want you wearing someone else's boots anymore. You deserve your own pair. I intended the navy blazer as a gift. It will also be waiting for you."

"I've also taken care of Mrs. Fontenot. You don't have to pay her anymore."

Matt: "Sarah—"

Sarah: "Please, I'm not going to let you talk. I was born on a Tuesday, but it wasn't last Tuesday. Make some more furniture, go down to Mrs. Fontenot's store, and pick out a young girl. You can strip down to your Calvin Klein's and chase her all around that farmhouse. Marry her first. I know how you people are about living in sin."

"Matt, this is our goodbye. Tomorrow will be busy. So let this be our goodbye. I won't have breakfast with you in the morning or sit next to you on the bus, and I don't want you sitting behind me, either. If you have a flashback tomorrow, I won't help you. I need to move on. I'm leaving you better than I found you. That is new for me."

Sarah put her arm around Matt and rubbed his head.

Sarah: "I need to ask a favor of you. In the months and years to come, if you ever think about me, please don't hate me. Jesus doesn't want you to hate me, Matt. You need to forgive me, like you did at the baseball game. I couldn't bare it if I knew you hated me."

Matt: "Sarah—"

She put her finger across his lips.

Sarah: "Please don't say anything now. You are not a broke down cowboy anymore. Just a cowboy, and I have too much to do. I don't have time for a cowboy. We both need to move on. Goodbye, Matt."

Matt retrieved a small, wrapped present and set it on the table.

Sarah: "What's that?"

Matt: "Thank you for helpin' me this week."

She took the present, stood, leaned over, kissed the scar on his forehead, rubbed the top of his head one last time, and walked away.

On the walk to the dorm, she realized the present was wrapped in notebook paper with the words to Matt's poem, "The Sarah Morgan Leigh," written on it. She carefully unwrapped the present and found a bottle of her favorite perfume, the expensive one that Doodle liked. The perfume they had discussed in the pasture after seeing the nursing calf. Feelings of nausea began immediately. Was it something she ate? Was it Matt? Was it the perfume? Was it the poem? Betty was sitting on the dorm steps.

Sarah: "I'm sick. I'm about to throw-up."

Betty: "Sweetie, go to the bathroom. I'll be right on."

Sarah went into the stall, bent over with her hands on her knees, and waited for the inevitable. Betty came in with a damp washcloth and held Sarah's hair away from her face.

Betty: "That's the way. Just let it out. Was it something you ate?"

Sarah straightened. Betty wiped her face with the cool washcloth.

Sarah: "It was Matt. I ate the same things everyone else did. Nobody else is sick."

Betty: "How did Matt do this?"

Sarah: "I dumped the cowboy. I did what you said, quick and clean. I go through men like cans of hairspray. When one's gone, I have another by the next day. This has never happened before."

Sarah bent over again.

Betty: "Sweetie, what do you have in your hand?"

Sarah: "Perfume."

Betty: "Why don't you let me hold—"

Sarah: "No! . . . No, I can hold it."

Betty: "Bless your heart. Just let the bad out."

She rose, and Betty wiped her face, continuing to hold back her hair.

Betty: "You sound a little drunk. This isn't from drinking, is it?"

Sarah: "No, I've sat with Matt all evening. I wish I had a drink. I should have started drinking the minute I met him and not stopped."

Sarah bent over for the third time.

Betty: "Sweetie, I'm here."

She remained bent over.

Sarah: "Why would God do this? Bring two people together who can't be together?"

Betty: "Gee, I don't know why God would bring two people together who love each other?"

Sarah: "I didn't say I love him. Did I say I love him? Nobody said anything about love. He clearly makes me sick. But I know what he thinks. He thinks I'm like everyone else, and I'm leaving him. I never told him I could stay. I never promised him that."

"And these Haitians, if God wanted me to help them, just tell me. I can write them a check, a big check. I could give every male over the age of fifteen in Thoman a Cadillac. Wouldn't that be better than what I'm doing?"

Betty: "First, you need to talk to Jesus. If you have problems with the Father, you have to go through the Son. Second, the Lord didn't bring you here to help the Haitians. He brought you here so the Haitians can help you."

Sarah: "What can the Haitians do for me?"

Betty: "Sweetie, they can teach you what's important and what just doesn't matter. I assure you, they have more to teach you than you realize. God doesn't want some of your money or some of your time. He wants you, all of you."

She straightened and Betty wiped her face.

Sarah: "I can take all this up with Jesus?"

Betty: "He's on call twenty-four seven. Sweetie, how do you feel? I don't think you have a fever."

Sarah: "I think the Matt Black Death has passed. Betty, you can't tell him this happened."

Betty: "He'll never hear it from me. You go lie down."

Sarah: "I'll shower first. I feel dirty. I'm going to wash the Matt right off of me. Then I'll lie down."

Sarah showered, used her perfume, put on a cleaner pair of scrubs, and got in her bunk. She fell in and out of sleep until after midnight. She rose, took Matt's Marine Bible and her flashlight, and left the dorm room.

Around four o'clock, Betty checked on Sarah. She found the bed empty, and Sarah sitting on the floor of the stall in the bathroom, leaning against the toilet, sound asleep.

Betty: "Sweetie, are you ok? You need to wake-up. Let me help you back into bed."

Betty roused Sarah and helped her up.

Sarah: "Betty, Jesus and I just had it out."

Betty: "Did you get all your questions answered?"

Sarah: "Not a one, but we're not done yet."

Betty: "I doubt very seriously if He is done with you, Sweetie."

**Saturday**

The journey to Port-au-Prince would begin at eight in the morning in a used yellow school bus from Neshoba County, Mississippi; the bus could get you down the mountain but not up the mountain. A picture was taken of everyone in the front of the Hope Center and another seated on the bus. Everyone was grateful for the big yellow bus.

Before leaving the dorm room, Sarah took the magic marker and signed her bunk leaving a message, "You never know what you may find in Haiti. Sarah DuMont."

On Saturday morning, Matt honored Sarah's request, kept his distance, and did not speak. He helped load Sarah's bag onto the back of the bus. She was watching him, saw him put something in a side pocket of her luggage, and smiled. Technically, she had not said anything about a note. In addition, he sat near the front of the bus, and she could watch him without being seen by him.

The bus arrived at ten in Port-au-Prince, and everyone made it into the terminal without incident. Sarah was the only one flying a different airline to Atlanta, not New Orleans. Everyone hugged and said goodbye to her except Matt, who stood at a respectful distance and watched. Sarah glanced at him, turned, and made the long walk to the other side of the terminal, one of the most self-conscious walks she had ever made.

Before checking her bag, she checked the side pocket, finding a note.

> Dear Sarah:
>
> That is not my mule. I don't have a mule named Sarah.
>
> I turned the lights off that night so I could tell you and Willie about Uncle Shade and Caroline. There really is a headstone in the old cemetery with his name on it, and he is not buried there. As a little boy, my grandfather saw Caroline make that daily walk, dressed all in black, to Shade's grave.
>
> Thank you for helping me this week. You and I both know I could not have done this without

you.

Sleepin' Sarah said, 'I love you, Matt.'

You have important things to do. Go do them. Thank you for helping me.

I pray that you, being rooted and firmly established in love, may be able to comprehend with all the saints what is the length and width, height and depth of God's love, and to know Christ's love that surpasses knowledge so you may be filled with all the fullness of God.

Ephesians 3: 17-19

Matt

She now wished he did own a mule named Sarah. But perhaps, it was best he did not.

She flew first class and only threw-up twice. For the first time in several months, she had no plans to see Matt again. She read through a proposed script for her upcoming project, sent a text to Lucy at every opportunity, and held the note without reading it again. A car met her in New York. She received a text from her mother who was waiting in the DuMont apartment. Sarah replied, "Long shower first—then talk—Matt gone."

———————

Sarah came into the den, drying her hair with a towel, and wearing a pair of scrubs.

Elizabeth: "Where did you get those? Why are you wearing scrubs?"

Sarah: "I didn't realize I was. Pastor Mark gave them to me. This is what I wore in Haiti. I guess it will take me a little while to adjust."

Sarah continued to dry her hair.

Sarah: "You can't imagine how much you miss a long shower. I've never taken a shower with so little water as I did in Haiti."

Elizabeth: "How did Matt do?"

Sarah: "He made it, but honestly, I don't think he could have if I weren't there. He loved working with those Haitian boys: Stevenson, Junior, and Junior. He taught them some carpenter skills and how to tease me. He was in his element, but sometimes the surroundings got a little too close to his deployments."

Elizabeth: "What about you, dear? How did you do?"

Sarah: "I did what they told me and took Matt's advice: smile continuously, be patient always, and be thankful no matter what."

Elizabeth: "Please tell me you didn't fake sincerity?"

Sarah: "The people on the team could not have been nicer to me. There was a nurse named Betty, about your age. She took me under her wing, taught me how to do blood pressure, and take temperatures. I did the intake for the clinic."

"The Haitian people are very impressive. I'd seen poverty like that in third world countries, but only from the inside of a Range Rover. This time I saw it one person at a time, taking each one of their names and listing their medical complaints. The faces, the eyes, and the smiles of those people will stay with me the rest of my life."

"My translator was a young man who taught himself English. His English was better than Matt's."

"Every morning at seven-thirty, we'd have a fifteen minute devotion by Pastor Mark. I didn't understand them. I'd have no idea what they were talking about. They would nod their heads, make comments, and it would be lost on me."

"As you say, I faked sincerity until Thursday. Early that morning, Matt had a panic attack. He couldn't find his weapon and almost beat up John, Ruth's husband. Then the devotion that morning was about the Rich Young Ruler. This young guy, who is rich, comes to Jesus and asks him how to inherit eternal life. Everyone agrees this is a good guy. He had kept every one of the Ten Commandments. But instead of telling him way to go, Jesus tells him he is lacking something. He needs to sell everything he has, give the money to the poor, and come follow Jesus. Well, the guy is very rich and doesn't do it. That made me so mad. I started to say something."

Elizabeth: "Why did that make you mad?"

Sarah: "I'm rich! But let me go on. Thursday afternoon, this precious Haitian woman gives birth. The delivery goes well, so they let me hold the child. While I'm holding the baby, I'm overwhelmed by this sense that someone wants to give me something. Something that my money, looks, and fame can't give me."

Elizabeth: "What would that something be?"

Sarah: "Matt said the someone and the something were the same thing, Jesus. That sense of someone, not of this world, was so strong the nurses had to make me let go of the baby."

"Thursday night I asked Matt to tell me about Jesus. I wanted to know exactly what he thought. You know, he never lets you know everything he is thinking. But this time he did. I could not process it. I told him to go to bed and leave me alone."

"We took Friday afternoon off, even Matt, and we hiked up a mountain overlooking the largest lake in Haiti. Some of the children from the village followed. There were goat trails everywhere. I saw four of the most beautiful goats. Anyway, when we started down, the translator said something in Creole to a little boy. He must have been about ten years old. That little boy didn't say a word. He made his way in front of Matt, who understood the boy was guiding us down the mountain. The boy would get a few feet ahead but always check to see that Matt was following. That's when I knew."

Elizabeth: "Knew what, dear?"

Sarah: "That God is real. That little boy had no idea who was following him. That man behind him has been through so much but would give his life in a heartbeat, without hesitation, to protect him. And Matt didn't know a thing about the boy. Chaos, Darwinism, chance, whatever cannot explain that. That's when I knew, 'no greater love than this,' and all. If I close my eyes, I still see that picture of Matt following the Haitian boy down the mountain."

Elizabeth: "What about Matt?"

Sarah: "I'm getting to that. Matt can't live any place but the farm. He does fine there with his PTSD. He has all that family and friends around him. I've always known, sooner or later, I would have to end it."

Elizabeth: "Did you ever start it, dear?"

Sarah: "I know you talk with him."

Elizabeth: "Not just me, the whole family talks to him. We all know about the mule."

Sarah: "You know Matt told me about the family party the day after I left for boarding school. I've never known a man that felt so comfortable around me, he could tell me that story. But that doesn't change anything. I told him I had to move on. He gave me a bottle of my perfume as a thank you present. I dump the guy, and he gives me an expensive gift, which he can't afford. I was nauseated as soon as I opened it and realized what it was. I threw-up three times. Betty looked after me. We decided it was the Matt Black Death."

"I asked her why God would do this to Matt and me. She told me if I had issues with God, to take them up with Jesus. That's how it's done, 'the only way to the Father is through the Son.'"

"Late that night, Jesus and I had it out. I learned you don't need a cathedral to talk to Him. You can do it in the bathroom while sitting on the floor next to the toilet. Did you know that the words of Jesus are written in red in a Bible, at least they were in Matt's Bible? I guess I knew it, but forgot. I've news for Jesus and his little friend, Matt. I'm not giving my money and career away so I can live a hard scrapple life on a farm in Mississippi. I'm not doing it. I may have won life's lottery, but I did win it. And I earned some of that money myself."

Elizabeth: "Did Matt ask you to do that?"

Sarah: "Heavens no. He told me in a note, I had important things to do—go do them."

Elizabeth: "I know you, your career, and your money will be very happy. Too bad the three of you can't have a child together. What would he look like? I know, the little man on the Monopoly Board. Did Jesus know He was talking to life's lottery winner?"

Sarah: "Yes, and I don't think He cared. He said I was playing the wrong lottery game. 'Narrow is the way that leads to life and few find it.'"

"You know, he was like Matt in some ways. Both are dangerous but good. You know how dangerous listening to Matt can be. Well, the words of Jesus, those words in red, are the same way, only more so. Also, I couldn't understand Matt at first. I read those words in red and think surely that's not what he meant. Then you realize, he was saying even more than you thought. I'm getting the feeling that Matt was only the warm-up act for the real thing to follow."

Elizabeth: "What are you going to do?"

Sarah: "As you know, I'm going to South Africa tomorrow for a couple of months. Pastor Mark says that you can be chased by the Hound of Heaven. We'll see if He can find me in South Africa. I'll take Matt's Bible and a book he gave me. I'm going to bed now and sleep for twelve hours. Or, I'm going to bed and be chased by the Hound of Heaven. We'll just have to see."

"I'm sure, in time, all of these feelings and thoughts will pass. Once I go back to work, my life will return to normal—I'm certain of that."

By now, Sarah was sitting on the opposite end of the coach from her mother. She sat there in silence, not moving with a vacant expression on her face.

Elizabeth: "I thought you were going to bed?"

Sarah became angry.

Sarah: "The mother died. The mother of those two precious children died."

Elizabeth: "Who are you talking about, dear?"

Sarah: "I've agreed to sponsor them in Pastor Martin's school. If I did that, then family members would be able to take in the children.

248

Matt said I was God's grace for them. Pastor Martin brought them to see me just before we left Saturday morning. Those two children hugged my neck. . . . God's grace, I don't want to be God's grace, not for those children, not for Matt, not for anybody! I want my life back. I feel like I've been evicted from my life. As of Friday morning, I didn't even believe in God. Well, all this ends now. I have things to do. I have plans."

Elizabeth: "Matt told me once, if you want to make God laugh, tell Him your plans."

Sarah: "I should have never gone to Haiti with him. I should have never gone to that farm in the first place. He's always saying something to me that hurts my feelings. He calls me the Whore of Babylon. He writes a poem to tell me I have a black heart. He tells me that some people are so poor all they have is money. What did he mean by that? . . . Don't answer; I know what he meant. He talks to me sometimes like I'm one of his Marines."

Elizabeth: "Well, Sarah, you know how he feels about them. He would do anything for his Marines."

Sarah: "Whose side are you on?"

Elizabeth: "This is not a competition."

Sarah: "And this whole religion nonsense—okay, there is a God. Big deal! I'm a good person. I'm not needy. Why doesn't He spend His valuable time harassing the evil and helping the poor? God, if you are listening, leave me alone! All of this because of Matt, I hate that man."

Elizabeth: "I'm quite fond of him. He makes me laugh."

Sarah: "Then you can have him. Rub his head, scratch his belly, feed him, and he'll follow you anywhere."

Elizabeth: "Who has the black heart now?"

Sarah: "The night he had the flashback, and I stayed with him, I told him, in my sleep, that I love him. If you do it in your sleep that doesn't count, does it?"

Elizabeth: "Well, you are awake now. Do you love him or hate him?"

Sarah: "Yes."

Elizabeth: "When did you first know?"

Sarah laid down on the couch with her head in her mother's lap.

Sarah: "When I first met him in the store in New Orleans. He was offering me a brownie. He leaned over and held the brownie to my lips. I was looking into his face. Those eyes were so full of mischief, like a little boy. The scar on his forehead said he was a dangerous man. The smile with those white teeth said pay no attention to the scar. Then he told me how pretty my eyes were. That's when I knew. And I do."

There was a moment of silence as her mother stroked her hair.

Sarah: "I went to Haiti so I could help Matt. I went as an atheist. I've come home without Matt, without my atheism, and with a favorite hymn which I don't even understand."

Sarah's voice began to fade.

Sarah: "I need thee; oh I need thee. Every hour —"

Elizabeth pulled back Sarah's hair and realized she was asleep. Elizabeth sat still for a few minutes. It had been a long time since Sarah DuMont fell asleep in the lap of Elizabeth DuMont. Eventually, the mother carefully stood, retrieved a pillow and blanket for the daughter, and left her oldest child to spend the first night home from Haiti on the couch in a luxury apartment in New York City.

Sunday, Sarah flew to South Africa, confident she was turning the page and moving on. During weak moments, she would contemplate the question of would she ever see Matt again? Strength would return, and she would think about other things. But what would that meeting look like? Would she meet Mrs. Matt Shepherd? Would they exchange a knowing glance? Would the Hound of Heaven finally have decided to leave her alone? Certainly, she could find answers in South Africa where work, career, and importance would overshadow surprising and wonderful.

---

Ruth found Matt sitting at the kitchen table. Doodle had her head in his lap. He was petting her head and staring at the table. A brand new pair of cowboy boots were on the floor at his feet, and a navy blazer was lying across the chair next to him.

Ruth: "Knock, knock."

Matt: "I thought I heard somebody. Come on in."

Ruth: "I brought you a chocolate pie. Thought you might like one after a week in Haiti."

Matt: "Thanks. I was hopin' you'd do that."

Ruth: "Looks like you've been shoppin'—new boots and a navy blazer."

Matt: "I don't shop. I have someone that does it for me."

Ruth: "All the reports on Haiti have been so good. Sarah was apparently a hit with everyone. And look at you, a week in Haiti without Doodle and Odell."

There was an awkward silence.

Ruth: "Matt, can we talk about Sarah?"

Matt: "No. Why would a sane man wanna do that?"

Ruth: "Look, I just want to help. You know that. It's been just the two of us lookin' out for each other for a long time. It's just me, Doodle, and you in this house. What was it about Sarah? Don't get me wrong, I like her. I just never understood what you saw in her? I would have never put you two together?"

Matt looked away and talked as if not addressing Ruth.

Matt: "Oh, I don't know. Her attitude is one thing. She was standin' in Mrs. Fontenot's, thinkin' she was in complete control, and was clueless about what was goin' on. No matter what I threw at her, she just kept comin' back. In hindsight, I should've hit her in the head with a cast iron skillet. Even then, I think she'd get up and say, 'How about it Matt, just one little date?'"

"Her looks are another. She may be the prettiest woman I ever saw. She was wearin' Idella's old gym clothes with lime green flip flops and was well worth the price of admission."

"I was walkin' down the hall to my room at her parents' house. She steps out wearin' this little bikini. Most of my wash clothes have more material. She has a little jacket over it. But it's not buttoned up so just enough real estate showin' to make you mortgage the family farm. If Pastor Mark had been there, we'd have done the paperwork, and I'd have taken her into one of those bedrooms. We'd have stayed until someone needed medical attention. Juanita would have to bring us sandwiches and sweet tea."

Ruth: "Who is Juanita?"

Matt: "It doesn't matter."

Ruth: "What did you do?"

Matt: "I started talkin'. I made up a story about adventure seekers or somethin'. The whole time I was up there, I had to just stay busy. I was hopin' she would go visit some of her friends and leave me alone some. But no, she doesn't have any friends."

"And she is so odd. She pulled her shoes and socks off in my truck and put her feet up on my dash, tryin' to get a compliment out of me. What kind of woman does that? Do you know if you say just the right things to her, you can make her drunk? I've seen it more than once. Who does that? . . . It's really fun to do that to her."

"I wish some of my Marines had her attitude, but she's afraid of squirrels. If I had Marines like her, they would have charged Fallujah armed only with pistols and then runaway when the insurgents released the squirrels."

"In Haiti, I was havin' a flashback, and she laughed at me. I'm a vet with PTSD, and she thinks it's funny. But there is no one I trust more to help me than her."

"They say don't talk about religion. She is the biggest heathen I know, and we can argue religion for hours. But she listens. She thinks about what you tell her."

Ruth: "Do you love her?"

Matt: "I see what you are doin' here. You are playin' bad cop to get me to talk about her."

Ruth: "Why don't you talk to Sarah?"

Matt: "Do the math, Ruth. How many people look out for me around here? Let's see, you, Uncle Billy, Odell, Lee Arthur, Idella, Pastor Mark. Even Lester, out of his own pocket, had that sign made for his bar about what happens if you give me a drink. Most of the folks in this county think it's a state law."

"Now, how many folks will be lookin' out for me in LA? There would be Sarah and that's it. How long before she gets tired of that job?"

"In New York, it took me about six hours to find someone that needed a righteous whoopin. In LA, it will take me about six minutes. I know; I was out there. Here people know. They know there are just some things I won't tolerate. Even the Sullivan brothers know they have to leave Odell alone. I'm supposed to go fishin' with them next week."

"Sarah looks at most people like she doesn't see them. She looks at me like she sees me. But what happens when she's had enough. Olivia had enough when she had only two options, me and Tex. How many options does Sarah DuMont have? If one day Sarah looked at me and didn't see me, I don't know what I'd do. This is best for Sarah."

Ruth: "Excuse me, but exactly when did the Lord give you the right to decide for Sarah. Maybe she doesn't need you to protect her from you."

Matt: "In the ride to the hospital in New York, she told me I was too much trouble. Sarah knows. She has decided."

Ruth: "I'm not so sure."

Matt: "She made it pretty clear. She told me I needed to move on. I guess I don't have any choice but to do just that. Move on. . . . I cling to the ropes/ and search the sea,/ but she is not here/ the Sarah Morgan Leigh."

Ruth: "What does that mean?"

Matt: "It means I move on."

Ruth walked over, put her hands on his head, kissed his forehead, and said a short prayer.

# Chapter Fifteen

## Ale Lakay

Filming was completed and Sarah was in a five star hotel in Johannesburg. She was alone and scheduled to return to the States the next day. It was around ten o'clock at night, and she was wearing her standard sleeping clothes, a pair of the scrubs she wore in Haiti. She had spent most of the early evening sitting on the balcony, watching an orange sky fade away to darkness. To her, the orange was the identical color of the orange she had seen from Matt's kitchen window. For a moment, she had smelled warm biscuits.

Earlier in the day, she sent Ruth a text asking if they could talk around two p.m. Macon time. Ruth agreed. This was the first communication she had with anyone in Macon since she left Haiti two months earlier.

Sarah: "Ruth, it's Sarah. How are you?"

Ruth: "Oh, I'm fine. Good to hear your voice. So you are in South Africa?"

Sarah: "Yes, I leave tomorrow."

Ruth: "My goodness, you really do live an interestin' life."

Sarah: "I know what you are saying, Ruth. An interesting life may not be a good life."

Ruth: "Sarah, I didn't mean—"

Sarah: "I know you didn't. How's Matt?"

Ruth: "Thanks to you, he's doin' real well. He's makin' furniture, sendin' it to New Orleans and to your store. He may hire a vet to help, someone the VA recommended. Sarah, he is also seein' someone. He met her at that store in New Orleans."

Sarah: "May I ask her name?"

Ruth: "Jennifer Turner, she has the most beautiful red hair, the same color as Doodle's. How 'bout that?"

Sarah: "I guess he tried a brunette, a blonde, and now a redhead. Hope it works. He's running out of hair colors."

Ruth: "You always did have a quick wit. I'm very sorry that things didn't work out between you two. I guess the gulf was just too great. But, Sarah, you helped my brother more than you will ever know. We will always be in debt to the kindness you showed him. He is still talkin' about Haiti. He wants to go back again next year. I know he couldn't have made it in Haiti without you. I know what you did for him."

Sarah: "Does he ever mention me?"

Ruth: " . . . No. The first day back from Haiti, we talked about you, since then, no."

Sarah: "I would tell you to tell him hello from me, but maybe not now."

Ruth: "Maybe not now. When I think the time is right, I'll tell him you did call and check on him. I'm sure it will mean a lot to him. I continue to pray for you, Sarah. I pray that you remain safe with all that travelin' you do, and that God uses you again to help someone, like you did my brother."

Sarah: "Thank you, Ruth. I'm so glad we talked. Tell John and the girls hello for me. Also, the next time you see Pastor Mark, please tell him thank you. He'll understand. Goodbye."

She now sat in the dim light of the hotel room in a chair next to the bed. On the nightstand were Matt's Bible and the jar of honey from his farm. She reached for the jar and gently touched the label with the tips of her fingers. There was not enough light to read the label, but she knew it by heart, "Honey From the Shepherd Family

Farm, Macon, Mississippi." She had researched beekeeping and had met with some local beekeepers in South Africa.

Did Jennifer know anything about bees? Could she toss the toy to Doodle? Could she hear the sounds in the old lumber? Had she sat in the parlor in the dark and heard about Shade and Caroline? Did Matt make her laugh? Could she help him if he had a flashback? Did she understand about Andy and Fallujah?

Her cell phone rang.

Sarah: "Hello, Sam, what's up?"

Sam: "Sarah, I just heard! They want you for the role of Francis. This is big, Sarah, big. Do you know how many copies of that book sold? The budget on this thing is huge. And they want you. Every actress with a pulse wanted this role."

Sarah: "Perfect timing, Sam. What's next?"

Sam: "I'll wait for you to get to LA. We'll go over everything together. They understand you are out of the country and need a few days. Just think, Sarah, you are the woman that gets everything she wants, and as your agent, I get a percentage. It doesn't get any better than this."

Sarah: "Sam, this is just what I needed. I'll give you a call when I get home. Thanks."

Sam: "I'll wait to hear from you."

She stood, retrieved the Marine Bible, and made her way in the faint light to the bathroom. Using her flashlight from Haiti, she sat on the floor next to the toilet and found what was apparently some of Matt's favorite verses. She knew they were a favorite due to all the underlining and highlighting. The verses were from the eighth chapter of Romans: "For I am persuaded that not even death or life, angels or rulers, things present or things to come, hostile powers, height or depth, or any other created thing will have the power to separate us from the love of God that is in Christ Jesus our Lord!"

She surveyed her situation and took in thoughts of Matt moving on, of God approaching and of Christ reconciling—all mixed together and intensified by a manifest love. She made a promise to never do this again.

---

The next day Sarah flew by a commercial flight to Atlanta and by a private jet to LA. She had spent the day chasing the sun and arrived at her home on Malibu Beach well after dark, having lost the race. She went to Lorraine's room and found her waiting up.

Lorraine: "Sarah, it is so good to finally see you again. You haven't been home in almost six months."

Sarah: "It seems like much longer."

Lorraine: "Would you like something to eat?"

Sarah: "No, I'll just get a glass of wine. We had plenty to eat on the plane. I'm exhausted. We can talk tomorrow."

Lorraine: "You look like you've lost some weight."

Sarah: "Between Haiti and South Africa, I think I have. I'll need to add a couple of pounds for my next role."

Lorraine: "I heard about that, congratulations. Heard anything from your rabbi?"

Sarah: "Lorraine, he was not a rabbi, and that's over. . . . What are you sitting in?"

Lorraine: "A rocker, I got it at your store. I know it doesn't match the decor of the house, but it's so comfortable. . . . Underneath the seat is a name of a church. Apparently, all the wood came from this old church. . . . What do you think? . . . Doesn't really fit in this house. . . . Looks to me like it should go in an old farm house. . . . Do you want to sit in it? . . . I just love it though. . . . Sarah, are you all right."

---

The commercial airliner made a banking turn as it began the approach into the New Orleans airport. Sarah could see the swamps below and was sure she saw where Interstate 55 joined with Interstate 10. She imagined riding with Matt and Doodle in the truck. Of course, she would be sitting in the middle, and Doodle would have her head out the window. They would go to New Orleans, buy something from Mrs. Fontenot for the farmhouse, eat beignets from Cafe Du Monde, and stop at Middendorf's on the way home. They would talk about nothing, and he would make her laugh. That night, it would rain, and he would hold her in the dark in the old farmhouse. Or none of that would happen, and she really would have to move on.

Willie met Sarah's plane in New Orleans. As a joke, he held a sign that said, "Sarah DuMont." Sarah greeted him with a big smile.

Sarah: "I could never forget you, Willie."

Willie: "I just wanted all these other people to know that I'm drivin' Sarah DuMont."

Sarah and Willie hugged.

Sarah: "Willie, I want you to take me to see the cowboy."

Willie: "Ms. Sarah, I prayed that you'd say that to me. Let's go. Oh, by the way, my wife's biscuits have gotten so much better. That Matt was really on to somethin' with his biscuit recipe. I tell you what."

Sarah: "Willie, why don't told you tell me all about in the car. I want to hear everything."

---

They were again headed west on Interstate 10, crossing the Bonnet Carré Spillway, when Sarah called her mother.

Sarah: "Hello, Mother. I'm in LA, just not the one you think. Here, talk to Willie."

Sarah handed her cell phone to Willie.

Willie: "Hello, hello . . . yes, ma'am. . . . Willie Roberts, Ms. Sarah's driver. . . . I'm taking your daughter to Matt's farm. . . . That's what I always thought. . . . I told my wife it was just a matter of time. Any fool could see that. . . . Yes, ma'am, I was. . . . All over her, even in her hair and ears. . . . He laughed. He found her some clothes but wouldn't get her any underwear. . . . She slept most of the way home. I think she enjoyed herself."

Willie glanced over at Sarah.

Willie: "Those tight, stretchy black paints. . . . Your mother said she doesn't—"

Sarah: "I don't care. Matt likes them. He told me he likes the packaging."

Willie: "Did you hear that? . . . Yes, ma'am, this kinda pale blue top with a white t-shirt underneath."

Sarah: "Tell her this is new. She's not seen it before."

Willie: "It's new; you haven't seen it before. . . . I like that one, too. Yea, the one with the black sleeves and the rest blue with the little white stripes. Your mother wants to know why you—"

Sarah: "Matt's already seen it."

Willie: "Matt's already seen it. . . . Your mother said men don't remember—I did! . . . Wavy but not curly. . . . Just below her ears. . . . I agree. Your mother said—"

Sarah: "Tell her I had to get it cut for my last part. I'm letting it grow out."

Willie: "She's lettin' it grow out. . . . Let me see your fingernails. Clear. . . . Your mother said good. Her toenails are clear too. . . . She's taken off her shoes and put her feet on the dash. . . . Your mother said to put your shoes on, sit up straight, and behave yourself."

Sarah: "No."

Willie: "Yes, he did, and they were good. . . . He gave my wife the recipe. . . . I've never tried'em with that."

Willie looked at Sarah.

Sarah: "Fish eggs and goose liver."

Willie: "Uh-huh. . . . No, ma'am, I don't think you're supposed to put maple syrup on'em.  . . . I don't know anything about a mule. . . . Well, it sounds like somethin' he'd do."

Sarah: "Tell her he doesn't have a mule named Sarah. He told me he didn't. I know he lies, but I believe him this time."

Willie: "Ms. Sarah says he doesn't have a mule named Sarah. She believes him even though he lies to her all the time.  . . . No, ma'am, her bare feet are still up on the dash."

Sarah: "Willie, hand me that phone. Mother, just thinking about Matt makes we want to take off some of my clothes. . . . Willie, she just called me the Whore of Babylon, my future husband and now my own mother. I think I'm detecting a theme. Mother, I'm going to tell him to marry me. . . . Don't be silly; he'll do what I tell him. . . . My mother's laughing. . . . She's still laughing. . . . Mother, he said I was God's grace for him. How can any man turn down God's grace? Oh, by the way, I've had a religious experience. In the future, when we talk, I'll be quoting liberal amounts of scripture, just as soon as I memorize some. . . . I don't care what other people think. . . . Then tell the brothers that if they annoy me after today, my Marine husband will beat the tar out of them. . . . She said Christians don't do that sort of thing. Pity, perhaps we should. I'll see if I can have that changed. Mother, the brothers don't know that, so threatened them anyway. I have to go now. Mr. Willie Roberts needs help with his driving. . . . I love you, too, Mother. Don't worry about me. You once asked me if I knew what I was doing. This time, I know. I'll talk to you soon. Bye."

Sarah: "Willie, you are not driving fast enough."

Willie: "I'm going five miles an hour over the speed limit now."

Sarah: "Speed limits are for the little people."

Willie: "Well, to the Louisiana Highway Patrol, we're all the little people."

Sarah: "Soon and very soon, I will be Sarah Morgan Leigh Shepherd, wife, mother, friend, vice-president of the WMU, children's Sunday School teacher, missionary, member in good standing of the Mississippi Beekeepers Association, gardener, housekeeper, dog owner, and child of the King. I have never been nor will I ever be one of the little people."

Willie: "Ms. Sarah, I don't think I have ever seen anyone this happy before."

Sarah wiggled her toes.

Sarah: "The Bible calls it joy."

Willie: "I don't know much, Ms. Sarah, but I know the Lord has his hand on you."

Sarah: "Then stop worrying about the Louisiana Highway Patrol and drive faster."

Willie: "Ms. Sarah, you just won't do. I tell you what."

---

Sarah left Willie sitting on the front porch, eating banana pudding, and drinking sweet tea with lemon. She passed the chicken coop and remembered the first time she saw it. How do you explain this to someone? She had tried and failed miserably. She saw Doodle standing at the door of the barn. As she approached, Doodle sprinted toward her as if she were headed off the end of the dock. Sarah kneeled and received a thorough face licking.

Sarah: "Doodle, I've missed you, too. Is the cowboy in the barn? I bet he is. Do you think he wants to see me? We'll see, won't we? Doodle, you need a bath."

She entered the barn, and Doodle waited in the doorway, watching the whole affair from a safe distance. The size and the smells flooded her with memories from that day. Matt was working on the tractor as she approached. He gave no indication that he saw her. She stood silently.

Matt: "Will you hand me that wrench by you?"

Sarah: "No."

Matt: "Same ol' Sarah. Maybe you should learn to say yes more often like a normal person."

Sarah: "Well, let's see. Come visit my farm—yes. Ride in my truck

—yes. Watch my dog jump into the water—yes. Sit in my barn—yes. Stay for supper—yes. Bring in my laundry—yes. Listen to my ghost story—yes. Meet my friend Idella—yes. Meet my sister—yes. Meet me at Middendorf's—yes. Invite me to Connecticut—yes. Listen to my poem—yes. Lay beside me in the dark—yes. Chase me across the country—yes. Go with me to Haiti—yes. Kiss me under a Haitian sky—yes. Miss me terribly—yes. Hand me a wrench—no."

Matt: "Same ol' Sarah. Well, if you didn't come here to help me work on the tractor, why did you come?"

Sarah: "As I said, the whole time I was in South Africa, I missed you terribly. At the end of each day, I wanted to tell you what happened. I wanted to see you and laugh."

"Reading your Bible helped me feel close to you. So that's what I did. I would find a private place at night and read the Marine Bible—the notes you made, the places you underlined. We spent several days in the bush filming. I would find a place away from everyone else. They told us not to do that, but I did it anyway."

"I decided my last night in South Africa was going to be the last night I felt that way. I would miss you one last time, read your Bible, and that would be it. I would be done with you. Then when I got back to LA, I saw a rocker you made."

"In Haiti, I heard Pastor Mark say over and over again that Jesus died, was buried, then rose from the dead. If that's not true, then your life is nonsense. If it is true, then my life is nonsense, and I'm a sinner in need of a savior. When I saw that rocker, I knew it was true."

"From the moment I walked in to Mrs. Fontenot's store, I've been pursued. Every time I tried to walk away, I would be drawn in. First, it was the wager, then a chocolate brownie with pecans, then chicken manure, then your sister, then Andy, then a meal at Middendorf's, then a mugger, then a navy blazer, then a trip to Haiti, and now a simple wooden rocker."

"Jesus told me He is preparing a room for me in a mansion. I told Him I already have a room in a mansion. He said how about a room in an old farmhouse? How about it, Matt? Can I have a room in an old farmhouse?"

Matt: "I'm seein' someone. I did what you said, but I've not chased anyone around the farmhouse in my underwear, yet."

Sarah threw a box at Matt, which he ignored.

Sarah: "It's Lady Clairol, Reddish Brown, the same color as Doodle's hair. Your refrigerator was filled with banana pudding. Let me guess, Jennifer made all that pudding. By the way, Willie is helping himself."

Matt: "Oh, is this a little projection here? You assume, just because you hid bacon in a bracelet, Jennifer must have colored her hair to match Doodle and made me tons of banana puddin'. Willie is not eatin' all her puddin', is he?"

Sarah: "You're right, Matt. I'm sure she is a fine person, but do you love her?"

Matt did not respond.

Sarah: "You cowboy, do you think it has been easy for me? I spent the last night in Haiti either throwing-up or sitting on the bathroom floor arguing with Jesus. I spent two months in South Africa determined to be over you. I have an offer, right now, to star in the biggest movie of my career. Instead of being in LA, drinking champagne with my agent, and signing a contract, I'm arguing with a broke down cowboy, in a broke down barn, on a broke down farm in Mississippi."

"You once told me Jesus healed the eyes of a blind man with mud. I found that story in your Bible. When they asked the man questions about how he had been healed, he said he didn't know. One thing he did know, once he was blind—now he sees. I don't know how this will work. But one thing I do know, I want to live with you on this farm by God's grace."

"I asked you how much you were willing to pay for me. You said more than any man I'd ever known. Matt, I'm willing to pay more than any woman you've ever known."

Sarah dialed her cell phone.

Sarah: "Sam, this is Sarah. . . . No, I'm not in LA. I'm in a barn in Mississippi. . . . That is not important, Sam. I'm not going to take the role of Francis. Tell them thank you, but no. . . . Calm down, Sam. This is not the end of the world. . . . I have more important things to do. I'm doing one right now, so I need to go. Bye, Sam."

"Your turn, cowboy."

Matt said nothing.

Sarah: "Oh, this is rich. I've spent the time I've known you asking, begging you to please hush. Now I want you to talk, and you won't. Wait, I know what this is. This is just one of those games you play, talk when I want you to shut-up, shut-up when I want you to talk."

Matt: "Shut-up hurts my feelin's."

Sarah: "Matt, there is not a person that could say something to you that could hurt your feelings. I don't think it is possible."

Matt: "Only you."

Tears came in Sarah's eyes.

Sarah: "This is not fair. You are the only man I have ever known that could be reading the contents of a ketchup bottle to me and then say something that—"

Matt: "Makes you drunk."

Sarah: "Yes, makes me drunk."

Matt: "Well how about this, I know you have my underwear. I counted them. You have one."

Sarah: "You bet I have one, and I'm not giving them back until you explain to my family that you don't own a mule named Sarah. My brothers ask me about Sarah every time we talk. My mother showed the picture to her entire bridge club. My father has that picture in his office on Wall Street."

Matt: "Well, about that—"

Matt looked over his shoulder to the back of the barn.

Sarah: "What's back there? . . . There's an animal back there. . . . Ah! It's a mule! You do own a mule named Sarah."

Matt: "Yea."

Sarah: "You know, denial ain't just a river in Egypt. Does Jennifer know?"

Matt: "No."

Sarah: "You haven't moved on, have you?"

Matt: "No, that's not possible."

A smile came across Sarah's lips, as tears streamed down her face, time for the public profession.

Sarah: "I'm sure Jennifer Turner is a fine person, and I wish her all the best in the world. But I love you, and you are mine. I've measured the cost. I want surprising and wonderful. I have been freed so that I can love you freely. I'm not going anywhere. This is my home. I will not be Caroline McKnight. I will not marry the wrong man, live the wrong life, or spend my time doing what doesn't matter in the end."

Sarah now startled Matt as she began reciting a poem:

> I took to his Bible
> alone, seeking joy,
> and thought of him
> my insane cowboy.
>
> He speaks no English,
> knows so little,
> and uses my heart
> for a mental hospital.
>
> A scar on his forehead
> and lies on his lips,
> he tries to convince me
> I am like a ship.
>
> A ship with black sails
> alone on the sea

with no love or joy
skippered only by me.

But that is not true
for the Author of joy
has given me a gift
an insane cowboy.

Matt: "I love you, Sarah Morgan Leigh. If we do this, you can't leave me."

Sarah: "I won't sail away. I'm in this for the duration. Doesn't the paperwork say something about until death do us part? As someone once said, 'I will never leave you nor forsake you.'"

Matt: "Sarah, you are just too much trouble."

Sarah: "Oh, my sweet Mattie, I am so worth it."

Matt: "You know, marriage is a serious business. What if we're not compatible?"

Sarah: "We're not compatible."

Matt: "What if you have some little habit or quirk that drives me crazy—like the way you put your feet all up on everything?"

Sarah: "You'll just have to get over it."

Matt: "What if I have some habit or quirk you don't like?"

Sarah: "You'll just have to stop it."

Matt: "You don't read the Wall Street Journal when you're naked, do you? You know, you're not supposed to read the Journal when you're naked."

Sarah: "Can you get the Journal delivered out here?"

There was a moment of silence as the two exchanged a look, and Matt smiled.

Matt: "Okay, Sarah Morgan Leigh Dumont, I'll marry you. Matthew Ezra Dumont, I kinda like the sound of that."

Sarah: "I kinda like the sound of Sarah Morgan Leigh Shepherd."

Matt: "What if I come over there and kiss you right now?"

Sarah: "No, you are all dirty and greasy, and there is a whiff of Mississippi field hand in the air. A little behind in our laundry, are we?"

Matt: "We weren't expecting company. Besides, it's not just me—Doodle needs a bath."

Sarah: "I know. She and I have spoken. I see I have my work cut out for me."

Matt leaned over and put his hands in a pan of oil drained from the tractor. His hands were black to his wrists.

Matt: "Is that better?"

Sarah: "Don't you dare. You can't catch me anyway."

Matt: "I caught that mugger. I can catch you, missy. Besides, I have a mule I can ride."

Sarah: "Don't call me missy, and you can't ride the mule unless I say so."

Matt: "Sinner is fine, but you draw the line at missy. You don't like it when I call you missy, so missy it is. And after the paperwork is done, I can ride the mule whenever I want."

Sarah: "After the paperwork is done, riding the mule will not be a problem."

Willie looked up when he heard laughing and saw Sarah running from the barn. He walked to the end of the porch for a better view. Matt was in pursuit with black hands. Like the mugger, Sarah learned it was hard to outrun Matt. It was almost as if he were the Hound of Heaven, and she was about to be baptized with used motor oil. Of course, Doodle, the third person of the family, was not far behind.

The end, for now.

# Chapter Sixteen

# My Favorite Thing

The final book of the Bible is about what is, what was, and what will be.

Sarah will join Calvary Baptist Church, Rural Route 1, Macon, Mississippi, as a new believer in Christ. She will be baptized in the lake on the farm so Doodle can attend the ceremony.

The couple will be married in that same church with Pastor Mark doing the honors. The ushers will be four Marines in dress blues. The only flowers will be a vase of Zinnias at the front. Odell will be best man since it does not require him to say anything. Lucy will be the maid of honor.

Dressed in their new robes, the New Jerusalem A.M.E. Church choir will provide the music. The first song will be "My Jesus, I Love Thee." The bride will enter to the music of "Come Thou Fount of Every Blessing," and the happy couple will exit to "What a Friend We Have in Jesus," which will go on for some time.

The reception will be at Lester's bar, decorated by the WMU, catered by Odell's Barbecue, with music provided by Willie's second cousin and his band. Ever true to his word, Uncle Billy will allow no liquor to be served.

The happy couple will honeymoon at the farm. Uncle Billy and the Sullivan brothers will provide security for the now famous couple.

Uncle Billy will explain to the reporters that Lee Arthur's bull now hates reporters. The Sullivan brothers will explain in great detail, including a display of scars, what Matt had done to them for simply disturbing him in a bar. Imagine what he might do to someone who disturbed him on his honeymoon. Of course, the reporters will have great difficulty understanding the Sullivan brothers, especially Ovid Sullivan who will recite long passages of *Metamorphoses* from memory in the original Latin.

All the DuMonts, along with Lorraine, Juanita, Lucy, and Ralph, will be invited to the farm to spend a day before they leave. Matt and Juanita will cook together in the kitchen, and the great hall will be used for the dining room. In the evening, all will go down to the lake to watch Sarah and Doodle demonstrate their talents on the dock.

Lucy will get her chance to finally meet Matt. The two will sit on the front porch, drinking sweet tea, and sharing Sarah stories.

A few months later, Ruth will bake a chocolate pie and take it to the farm. She will find Doodle on the front porch and the door locked.

Ruth: "Matt, are you in there?"

Matt: "Go away, Ruth."

Ruth: "What? Sarah, are you there?"

Sarah: "Go away, Ruth. I'm hiding."

Ruth: "What? Oh, Oh! But I brought a chocolate pie."

Matt: "Please go away, Ruth."

Ruth will walk over to Doodle, bend down, and give her a pat on the head.

Ruth: "Doodle, mission accomplished. Thanks for your help. I guess he's found something he likes better than chocolate pie."

Sarah and Matt will be told that they cannot have children. Since all members of the Shepherd's family are adopted, they will adopt a baby girl from the Mary Shepherd Orphanage in the Philippines.

They will name her Mary Andrew Shepherd and call her Andy.

As often happens in life, once Andy is settled into her new home, Sarah will become pregnant with fraternal twin boys, Samuel DuMont Shepherd and Timothy Leigh Shepherd. Elizabeth will tell her that this is payback for the way Sarah treated her brothers. A new wing will be added to the farmhouse to accommodate all. Unlike the Sullivan brothers, the apple will not fall far from this tree, and Sarah will see mischief in their eyes from the very beginning.

Almost everyone in Macon will know how to find Sarah on the first Saturday of the month for much of the year. She will be wearing a large sun hat and designer sunglasses and riding her zero-turn, 26 horse power, liquid-cooled, fuel injection riding mower on the grounds of Calvary Baptist Church located on Rural Route 1. While she may appear to be alone, there will always be someone nearby, either a former Marine or one of his many close friends.

She will help the Sullivan brothers obtain their GED's, and Ovid Sullivan will teach the Shepherd children to love the classics. She will help Odell develop and market his barbecue sauce, hot and sweet. She will learn of a potential merger of two grocery store chains being handled by a well-known investment banker on Wall Street. She will convince all parties that Odell's Original Barbecue Sauce must be included on the shelves as part of the merger.

Each member of the Shepherd family will have a favorite thing they like to do. Andy's favorite thing will be when her grandparents from Rural, Kansas come to visit every Christmas. They will sleep in her bedroom, and she will sleep in the great hall next to the Christmas tree. Her daddy will explain that Uncle Shade loves her and will watch over her as she sleeps in the great hall.

Her brothers' favorite thing will be to ride the mule that has the same name as their mother. It will never occur to them to ask why.

Her daddy's favorite thing will be to tell her and her brothers stories, as they and D2 ride around in the truck with him. Their favorite story will be about the crazy woman who jumped into the manure pile. Andy will say that a person will never do that. Her daddy will tell her to never say never.

Her mama's favorite thing will be to sit in the barn that special time of the year in one of Matt's rockers. While Andy, the brothers, and D2 play, mama and daddy will look up, see the light, and hear the music in her daddy's old lumber.

Sarah: "Thank you, Matt."

Matt: "For what?"

Sarah will wave her hand toward the children and the cavernous insides of the barn.

Sarah: "For all of this—all of this is due to you."

Matt: "Sarah, it's not all about me."

Sarah: "What an odd thing to say."

Andy's mama, with the help of Odell, will do important things for the rest of her life. Things determined in advance for her to do.

The Never Ending.

# Chapter Seventeen

# Suggested Playlist

The suggested play list of songs represents a complete retelling of the story. The songs were carefully selected and closely follow the story, and in some instances, tell more than is actually revealed. The reader is encouraged to add or subtract from the list as deemed appropriate.

**Rock Bottom**

Way Down We Go, Kaleo

**Sarah**

Drinkin', Holly Williams

Gotta Serve Somebody, Bob Dylan

**The Farm**

Mississippi You're On My Mind, Jesse Winchester

**The Wager**

New Orleans Wins the War, Randy Newman

Shed a Little Light, Foy Vance

Jesus Just Left Chicago, ZZ Top

**A Day In The Country**

Riptide, Vance Joy

First of July, Foy Vance

**Going Commando**

Old Old Fashioned, Frightened Rabbit

Lovin' You Against My Will, Jamie O'Hara

**Poultry**

Tara's Theme, John Williams and the Boston Pops Orchestra

**Ruth**

Nearer Blessed Lord, Nina Simone

**Fallujah**

Come Thou Fount of Every Blessing, Sufjan Stevens

**Beautiful Lake Maurepas**

Storm, Jose Gonzalez

No Angel, Birdy

**Way Down Yonder in Connecticut**

We Don't Eat, James Vincent McMorrow

**Play Ball!**

When the Man Comes Around, Johnny Cash

Arms of a Woman, Amos Lee

Come Back, Pearl Jam

**Olivia**

Waiting On an Angel, Ben Harper

Poison & Wine, The Civil Wars

Anywhere With Jesus, Amy Grant

**Haiti in Seven Days**

All My Days, Alexi Murdoch

Freedom Hangs Like Heaven, Iron & Wine

The Rest, Webb Wilder

What a Friend We Have in Jesus; Aretha Franklin, Live at New Temple Missionary Baptist Church, Los Angeles

Jesus (Live); Amos Lee, Live at Red Rocks with the Colorado Symphony

Skipping Stones, Amos Lee

**Ale Lakay**

Let It Be Me, Ray LaMontagne

I Need Thee Every Hour, Sarah Sample

Guiding Light, Foy Vance

One Hundred Million Years, M. Ward

**My Favorite Thing**

My Jesus, I Love Thee; Amy Grant

Amazing Grace, LeAnn Rimes

# Chapter Eighteen

# Shepherd Family Recipes

Food plays a major role in the story. The following recipes are presented with love from the Shepherd family to your family.

**Ruth's Chocolate Pie**

1 cup sugar

4 tablespoons of Hershey's Cocoa

4 tablespoons of flour

3 egg yolks

1 3/4 cup whole milk

2 tablespoons of butter

1 tablespoon of instant coffee (optional)

1 teaspoon vanilla

Sift and mix sugar, cocoa, and flour. Add egg yolks and mix. Add milk and cook on medium heat, stirring until thick and bubbles appear. Remove from heat and add butter and vanilla. Add cream of tartar and sugar to eggs whites, and beat for meringue. Use cooked pie shell and brown meringue. Use egg wash when cooking pie shell. Include coffee with dry ingredient.

## Lester's Pound Cake

1 cup of butter

3 cups of sugar

5 eggs

1 cup buttermilk

3 1/4 all purpose flour

1/4 teaspoon soda

1 tablespoon of water

1 teaspoon vanilla

Cream butter until fluffy. Add sugar, 1 cup at a time, beating well. Add eggs, 1 at a time, beating after each egg. Dissolve soda in water and add to mixture. Alternate buttermilk and flour. Add Vanilla. Pour into pan. Bake at 325 degrees for 1 hour and 15 minutes.

## Matt's Buttermilk Biscuits

Makes 4 to 6 biscuits.

1 1/8 cup of White Lilly Self Rising Flour (1 cup plus 2 tablespoons)

4 tablespoons unsalted butter

1/2 cup of buttermilk

Preheat oven to 500 degrees. Cut cold butter into flour with pastry cutter. Add buttermilk and stir with spoon, combining all the flour. Use butter to grease bottom of flat, cast iron skillet. Use liberal amount of flour to cover dough, hands, and sides of bowl. Pinch off individual biscuits and place on cast iron skillet. Coat tops of biscuits with milk for browning. Cook for ten minutes at 500 degrees.

Alternative Ingredients

1 cup White Lilly Self Rising Flour

3 tablespoons unsalted butter

3/8 cup buttermilk

1/8 cup heavy whipping cream

Cup butter into flour, add buttermilk and whipping cream. Prepare as above.

For syrup, Sarah recommends ALAGA Yellow Label Syrup. She gets it at the Piggly Wiggly.

Made in the USA
Lexington, KY
13 May 2018